Superstition

by

Veronica Blake

The Blood Clan Series
Book One

Superstition

Contact Information: info@thewildrosepress.com

Cover Art by *Debbie Taylor*

The Wild Rose Press, Inc.
PO Box 708
Adams Basin, NY 14410-0708

Visit us at www.thewilderroses.com

Publishing History
First Scarlet Rose Edition, 2017
Print ISBN 978-1-5092-1549-2
Digital ISBN 978-1-5092-1550-8

Published in the United States of America

Forever is not long enough...

Dawn sat back down on Mateo's lap, wanting him to feel how hot he made her. His cock was hard and pressing against the material of his black jeans. The ridge of it swelled into the area between her legs, making everything below her waist contract and quiver.

She released the tight hold she had on his hair and grabbed his loosely knotted tie. Her eyelashes narrowed as she smirked.

"I've wanted to do this all evening," she said in a suggestive tone as she leaned back slightly.

Her nimble fingers slipped the loose knot in his tie apart. The tip of his tongue dampened his parted lips. A soft moan escaped from her own mouth as her desire for him raged out of control.

"What else have you wanted to do to me?" A slight tremor in his voice hinted at his anticipation as he looked up at her with eyes hooded in growing desire.

She stopped short of letting the tie slide completely away from his neck as she grasped it close to his throat and used it to pull herself up to him roughly. Her lips hovered just over his, brushing lightly for an instant as she answered, "Everything."

Dedication

For Cecil Bettger:
My amazing dad…my bigger-than-life hero.

For Heather Blake:
My beautiful daughter-in-law. She was my writing
mentor and never failed to tell me if she loved
something I wrote or if she thought it was really awful.

For Michelle McGruder:
We packed a lifetime of amazing experiences into the
twenty years of our friendship.

All angels now. Fly free beautiful souls.

A very special thank you to the following ladies for
their help, encouragement, and constant support—
Tiffany Blake McGuire, Amanda DeNeice, Cathi Yost,
Crystal Corcoran, Charlotte Wuestewald, Kelly Grey,
Staci Chastain, Lynn Vickers, Debbie Teague, Kathryn
Rodriguez, Jennifer Schmidt, Niki Starforth, Tiffany
Brovege, Meichele Pittman, and Helena Taylor.

Chapter One

There was a good chance they would die tonight. Tomorrow or next week, maybe months, even years from now, some hiker or explorer would discover what was left of their bodily remains scattered among the massive boulders and prickly cactus. At the very least, they might just disappear without a trace, never to be seen or heard from again, just like all those hundreds who had come up here on this creepy mountain before them.

So what the hell were they doing up here?

Immediately after asking herself that question Dawn was reminded of one of her older brother's favorite mottos, 'If you're not livin' on the edge, you're takin' up space'. Before today that silly phrase had been her excuse for doing daring things like racing dirt bikes and snowmobiles, or hiking to the top of over half of the fifty-eight majestic fourteeners—mountain peaks greater than fourteen hundred feet high—in her home state of Colorado. And most recently, leaving behind everyone and everything she had ever known to start a whole new life here in Arizona.

But now, as she glanced up at the disappearing trail where towering spheres and the jagged peaks of the Superstition Mountains were becoming long ghostly shadows of sinister shapes in the fading daylight, she had no doubt this time she truly was living on the edge…the edge of total insanity.

"Hey, what's up with all those stories about the evil guardians lurking around here in the Superstitions?" Dawn asked. Thank goodness her voice sounded calm and didn't reveal the cowardly thoughts making her feel like she wanted to turn tail and run down off this mountain as fast as her quivering legs could carry her. Still, the carefree chuckle she attempted sounded bogus even to her own ears. "You know, the ones supposed to protect the Lost Dutchman's Gold Mine from treasure hunters, like us?"

"Excuse me, but we're called gold seekers in these parts. Why? Are you scared?" Chloe giggled as she pulled her maroon and gold Arizona State baseball cap lower on her forehead. She strapped her headlamp above the brim of her hat and switched on the light. A thin beam lit the area where the light shone.

"Hardly," Dawn huffed. "But it's getting dark and I'm stumbling all over the place on this rocky trail. I guess I'm not as sure-footed as I thought I was."

Chloe glanced back over her shoulder. "Just stay close to me. I know this trail with my eyes closed. I'll protect you from those creepy demons up here on the mountain, too," she joked in a menacing tone of voice.

"Um? Sorry." Dawn chuckled. "A loaded gun might protect me. One of those buff guys at the gym you made me join, they might protect me. But you…" She shrugged as she gestured at Chloe's slender body. "Sorry, but I just don't feel all that safe with you as my protector." She pulled her own headlamp out of a side pocket in her back pack and strapped it around the crown of the tattered white straw cowboy hat she wore on her head. A long stray tendril of pale blonde hair slipped out of the thick braid hanging down her back and got tangled up in the strap of the headlamp. She tugged the flaxen strand free of the entanglement and shoved it behind her ear.

"Okay, Miss Smart Ass. It's only about another five minutes to the campsite. I think I'm tough enough to protect you for that long."

Dawn shook her head and snickered in spite of her feelings of rampant fear while continuing to follow her new friend farther into the rugged mountain terrain leading to the spooky interior of the Superstition Mountains. She was reminded of how just a short time ago she had been super excited to make this trip.

For a history buff and avid camper like she considered herself to be this was a unique adventure. But it seemed as if all civilization shunned this harsh mountain range and several times this evening she felt as if they were traveling back in time or had been transported to some alien planet. She was finding it pretty hard to be brave right now.

A couple of hours earlier, they left Chloe's SUV at the edge of the wilderness area where the road had become no more than a foot trail. Now, they were miles away from the trailhead, and as the fading sun dropped behind the distant horizon, Dawn was feeling a bit out of her element. The mysterious Superstitions here in Arizona were definitely nothing like the lush forested mountains in her home state of Colorado.

"By any chance, did you remember to bring some matches or a lighter? I used up all my matches the last time I was camping up here, and I can't believe I forgot to pack a new box before this trip. I can never remember to throw a lighter in my camping gear, either," Chloe said sounding thoroughly annoyed at herself.

"I have a lighter and matches. Oh, and I brought a newspaper to use for a starter," Dawn quipped.

"Of course, you did," Chloe replied with a chortle. "I should have known you'd be as organized when you go camping as you are in every other aspect of your life. At school, you put me to shame with the way you have all your lessons planned days ahead and tests graded the day after you give them." She rolled her blue eyes and added, "I'm doing good to figure out what I'm going to do in class five minutes before the bell rings every morning."

"You must be doing something right. Your students sure seem to love you."

Chloe grunted. "Yeah, my kids love me because I let them write about anything they want. You wouldn't believe some of the essays I get from those twelve-year-olds about farting and belching and puke and poop—"

"Ugh," Dawn interrupted, "I don't think I want to know. Now, I know why I chose to be a History teacher. We don't have to write creative essays because we can't change the past."

A sound, similar to a small rock rolling down from somewhere overhead, made Dawn's feet freeze to the spot. As she peered at the dimly lit ridge overhead where she thought she heard the noise, she was gripped by a paralyzing feeling of being watched by someone—or something—from the tower-shaped rocks jutting up from the sides of the trail.

A fleeting image of a castle from an old horror movie Dawn watched years ago passed through her mind—Dracula's castle—sitting high on a remote mountaintop where no one could disturb the undead Count who slept in his coffin during the day and rose up after the sun went down to suck blood from the necks of helpless victims who wandered out in the dark. Just like she and Chloe were doing.

Dracula? Seriously? Where did that ridiculous thought come from? She hadn't watched a vampire movie since high school.

A chill whipped through her body despite the hot temperature of the Arizona night. *Cowboy up, Cupcake,* she told herself in a firm inner voice, recalling another phrase her big brother, Jeremy, always used when she was acting like a big baby about something, like she was doing right now.

Growing up in the Rocky Mountains of Northwestern Colorado had given both her and her brother a hearty dose of outdoor life. There were not too many things about being in the wilderness that scared Dawn, until tonight, anyway.

In the single ray of her headlamp, she could see Chloe marching farther and farther ahead—her long brown ponytail swinging sideways across her back in a carefree motion from the hole created by the back of her baseball cap's fastener. It was apparent she wasn't experiencing any of the terrifying feelings bothering Dawn. But then, Chloe was a native of this area and generations of her family had wandered around in these eerie mountains looking for the Lost Dutchman's Gold Mine. Obviously, they weren't concerned by any of the scary legends about the demons or spirits who were rumored to protect the secrets of the gold mine—the ones that would kill anyone who got too close.

Besides, what were the odds of them finding anything even remotely close to a real gold mine? Still, as she raced up the trail to catch up, she was surprised Chloe couldn't hear the thunderous pounding of her heart in her chest, because Dawn was certain it was as loud as a sledge hammer crashing against steel in the quiet of the night.

"Almost there," Chloe called out as they neared the closest summit. She stopped and turned around just as Dawn came sliding to a halt inches behind her. The bright light from her headlamp momentarily blinded her when it shone straight into her eyes.

"Oops. Sorry about that. I didn't realize you were so close." Chloe giggled as she pushed the light up to the top of her cap.

Dawn instinctively threw her hands over her eyes and told herself she seriously needed to get a grip on her emotions before Chloe realized how big of a coward she could be. But as she blinked and lowered her hands, a shape at the top of the ridge caught her attention.

"Did you see that?" she gasped.

Chloe glanced up toward the area where Dawn's gaze was focused. "I was looking at you. What was it?" She turned back toward Dawn and gave her shoulders a nonchalant shrug.

Dawn's voice wouldn't work for a moment when she opened her mouth to speak. A grave feeling of dread engulfed all her senses. She wrapped her arms around her midsection and held herself tightly as another shiver rattled through her body.

"I-I don't know. It was something tall, a person, maybe?" She refused to look up again, fearing she would see Count Dracula with his black satin cape billowing out behind him gliding down from the jagged towers of his evil abode overhead.

Chloe glanced up at the ledge again. She reached up and grabbed her headlamp, directing its narrow ray along the entire ridge and illuminating the pointy rocks with flashes of light. "I don't see anything. You aren't freaking out on me, are you?"

Dawn took a deep breath and attempted to act normal. "I was a little spooked for a second, but I'm okay now." Her trembling voice betrayed her. Perfect. Chloe really must think she was just a big wimp.

An understanding grin curved Chloe's lips. "I know it can be scary in these mountains at night, but do you honestly think I would have brought you up here if I really believed we would be in any real danger? Seriously, there's nothing to worry about."

"I believe you." She attempted to laugh, but it was more of a weak whimper. So much for bragging about what an experienced camper she had always been back in Colorado.

"The campsite is just ahead. My family calls it our base camp and nothing scary ever happened there for as long as we've all been coming up here," Chloe added with a chuckle.

Dawn exhaled sharply. Yep, no doubt about it. Chloe thought she was a total wuss. She clutched her hand against her crashing heart. Maybe she could still prevent it from jumping out of her chest now they had finally reached the campsite. The limited light from their headlamps did not afford her with a good look at the area where they planned to sleep for the next two nights. But the way she was feeling right now she would be lucky to make it through this first night without crying for her mommy to come and get her.

She squinted and peered in the direction where their lights were pointed. The area appeared to be an overhanging rock ledge at the base of one of the rugged mountain towers; a thought that did not ease her apprehension. It seemed like an ideal place to be trapped by the looming figure she sensed was still up there on that ridge.

Chloe rushed forward without hesitation. She ducked down as she shined her light under the rock ledge. "Looks good under here. No snakes or other unwelcome guests."

"Oh, I feel so much better now," Dawn tried to mimic her friend's enthusiasm and was grateful her voice didn't betray her again.

"And you were worried I couldn't get us here without getting possessed by the scary ghosts of the Superstition Mountains," Chloe said in a teasing tone.

"Ha ha. Okay, I'm better now, really," Dawn said, doing her best simulation of a brave person. *Ghosts or Dracula? Geez. Stop it already*. When she ducked under the ledge and shined her headlamp around, she was surprised to see the little alcove was rather cozy.

A full breath was finally able to fill her lungs. She tossed her heavy green backpack down on the ground and exhaled the breath she just sucked in with one big gust. Thankfully, Chloe didn't seem to notice just how scared she really had been for the past few minutes.

"I hear ya. I'm beat, too," Chloe said as she dropped her own pack to the ground. "Let's get our sleeping bags ready and have a quick bite to eat before we call it a night."

"Sounds perfect." Dawn wasted no time spreading her sleeping pad and bag out on the hard ground, and even less time collapsing down on it. Her beat-up old white straw cowboy hat was placed carefully to the side of her backpack where it wouldn't be crushed. She began to unwind her hair from the tight braid that held her long tresses in place while they were hiking.

"Forget food, just let me sleep, please," Dawn said with a chuckle. Her fingers raked through her pale blonde hair as she pushed the long mass back over her shoulders and let it hang loose and wavy down past the middle of her back.

She had been tired before they even started out on this trip a few hours ago. Her teaching schedule at school had been hectic all week, and they left for this weekend camping trip as soon as the last class of the day ended. All that exhausting terror her wild imagination conjured up out there on the rocky trail stole what tiny bit of energy she had left.

The only thing she wanted right now was to sleep and forget about how big of a chicken she had been a short time ago. She was genuinely disgusted at herself, not to mention so embarrassed. If Chloe never asked her to go anywhere with her again, she would totally understand.

Back in Colorado, she couldn't ever recall a time in the wilderness when she had come close to being as frightened as she had been just short time ago, barring the night when she and the guy she was dating at that time had a mountain lion attempt to tear down their tent, while they were inside, to get at the food they carelessly left strewn around. As unnerving as that experience had been a few years ago, it was now a great story to tell around the campfire about how her boyfriend's .22 rifle saved them when he shot over the big cat's head and scared the hungry predator away.

But what she experienced tonight was in a whole different realm of terror. The sense there was a tangible danger lurking nearby was like nothing she ever felt before and hoped to never feel again.

"We should at least eat a granola bar or something." Chloe dug through her backpack and produced a box of crunchy peanut butter granola bars and pulled a couple out. As she held one bar out to Dawn, she asked, "Are you finally calming down now?"

Dawn accepted the bar eagerly since the presence of food made her ravenous all of a sudden. She handed Chloe one of the water bottles she pulled from her own pack. "Yes, I think so. But I have to admit, there was a moment back there..." She shrugged as she realized there was no way to describe the sense of complete and utter panic she felt a short time ago. She hoped she could block out the image of a man—or something that resembled a man—standing up above them on the rocks or else she was going to be having some serious nightmares.

"I knew you shouldn't have read all that ancient history crap before we came up here."

"I'm a history teacher, that's what I do," Dawn said, laughing. "Besides, I found all the stuff about Jacob Waltz, supposedly discovering the gold mine back in the 1860s and keeping its location hidden until he died in 1891, really fascinating." She realized her hands were shaking a bit as she tried to open the wrapper on her granola bar.

"It was just all the other crazy stuff about how many people have died, or just simply disappeared, looking for the gold mine. Oh, and the ghosts or whatever, that guard the gold mine; those were the disturbing thoughts freaking me out back there."

Her gaze moved of its own accord toward the opening of the overhanging. It was so black outside of the small areas illuminated by their headlamps, which were now lying on the ground beside their sleeping bags, it seemed surreal. She knew once they turned the lights off, they would not even be able to see their own hands if they held them an inch from their faces. If there was anything supernatural, or otherwise, prowling around out there, they would never know until it was too late. It was going to be a seriously long night if she didn't stop this crap right now.

Chapter Two

Sleep would not come easily Dawn assured herself as she snuggled into the comforting depths of her sleeping bag. The strange feelings she had been experiencing since coming up on this mountain tonight would not go away. A gnawing sense of uneasiness churned inside her. There was someone, or something, watching them.

She pulled the top of her heavy Coleman sleeping bag over her head like she used to do with the blankets on her bed when she was a little girl, and imagined there was a scary monster hiding in her closet or under her bed. It didn't help anymore tonight than it did all those years ago. She'd better cowboy up if she hoped to get any rest at all.

It was barely a matter of seconds after she cowered under the covers of her sleeping bag before her lids felt heavy. Now, she was trapped between wanting to fall asleep to escape the lingering memory of her recent unnatural fear and a building sense of anticipation over what awaited her once she lost consciousness. The choice was not hers to make.

It was darker than any night she had ever known. Although she was still in her flannel-lined sleeping bag, Dawn was not alone. Strong arms held her in their embrace. Her head rested in the crook of his neck. The long locks of her hair were spread out beneath her and she could feel the way the strands splayed across the man's muscled chest.

The heat of his breath brushed against her ear. He was whispering something. It was a word she did not understand. Udaya...

She inhaled his musky scent. He smelled like the flowers that bloomed on the prickly cactus covering the desert floor; an intoxicating mixture of sweet succulent floral and the heavier earthy scent of cacti.

This man—he was like a cactus—deceivingly beautiful and dangerous. Dawn knew when she leaned closer to smell the flower, the cactus spines would ensnare her and their daggers would penetrate deep into her skin; deep enough to pierce her very soul.

But it didn't matter. There was a reckless hunger burning in her like nothing she ever experienced before, and only this mysterious stranger could sate her craving.

The man was kissing her neck now. His lips were full and warm; his kisses tender on her fevered skin. His gentle touch promised paradise. She quivered with excitement.

His hand was inching up under her T-shirt and sliding along her taut ribcage, up to the band of her sports bra. He pushed the bra up until he could cup one firm breast in his hand. His fingers gently teased the little nub in the center.

Her body arched up as his mouth stole away the moan building louder in her throat with a kiss that was now demanding and irresistible. His tongue slid between her parted lips. Dawn let her tongue join his in an erotic dance in her mouth that momentarily distracted her from the way his forefinger was flicking the tip of her nipple more forcefully, making it hard and full.

Instinctively, she turned her body toward the man and felt his hard cock press into her abdomen. An internal plea from her body made her grind her body against his. She grew wet with desire and trembled at the thought of having him inside her.

"Please, make love to me," she pleaded. The ache between her legs was becoming a screaming, throbbing pain she knew only he could satisfy. "Plea—"

His mouth covered hers again and stole away her voice and her breath.

When their lips separated, his mouth began to traipse gently along the side of her neck. He pushed her hair back over her shoulders as his kisses left a fiery trail to the base of her hairline behind her ear. Dawn felt an unexpected flash of pain, almost like the sting of a wasp or the prick of a pin, but it was over so quickly, she wasn't even sure if it had really happened.

Waves of pleasure replaced the brief instant of pain and started to reverberate through her body...building and building. She pressed her hips against his engorged cock. She felt the dampness flood between her legs as she breathlessly waited for what she was sure would come next. But—the man was no longer pressing his body against hers. He was pulling away. No.

"I need more," she whispered. So much more, her body begged. She needed him—all of him—and she needed him now.

"Soon my Udaya, my beautiful Dawn," he whispered. Then, he was gone.

Dawn opened her eyes slowly. The hazy glow of

the morning sun was peeking through the entrance of the overhanging. How was it possible it was morning already? She rubbed at her achy eyes. They felt on fire and her body was telling her she needed about ten more hours of sleep.

Her erotic musings began to edge into her thoughts with vivid clarity.

Whoa, that was one hell of a dream. Make that one hell of a wet dream. It seemed so real, seriously real. But it was only a dream, right? Of course it was.

She glanced over toward Chloe, who was burrowed down in her sleeping bag, with barely the top of her head showing. A relieved breath escaped from her. At least, she hadn't woken her up with her wild and weird sexual escapades in dreamland.

As she started to push herself up to a sitting position, Dawn realized her shirt and jogging pants were drenched with perspiration. She was actually wet from her *wet* dream. *How ridiculous and seriously embarrassing was this?* Every detail of her dream began rushing through her mind again. That man in her dream. He seemed so real—way *too* real.

His kisses burned their memory on her lips. All the places he touched her were tingling; her breasts ached and her nipples hardened. Her crotch tightened remembering the way his cock had felt against...*Stop it.*

She wiped her shaky hand across her sweating brow. Granted, she had been lacking in the boyfriend department since moving to Apache Junction a short time ago, but she had been enjoying the freedom of not having a man in her life. Her last brief relationship had been with a fellow teacher in her hometown. He was a nice enough guy, but a bit too clingy and needy. When she made the life-changing decision to move to Apache Junction, she left him behind in Colorado without any regrets. End of story.

Apparently though, she rationalized now as she was sitting here in her sleeping bag feeling very sweaty and uncomfortable, her subconscious mind and body were both trying to tell her she needed more than a camping trip with a girlfriend. A kinky, sexy smelling stranger just seduced her in her dreams, and even when she woke up, her body was still clinging to the incredible sensations she experienced in her sleep.

She reached up and touched her lips, recalling the delicious kisses that were nothing like she ever experienced in real life. She gasped. Her lips felt slightly tender as if she really had been kissed hard and more than once.

"What the hell?" she mumbled. How had she managed to do that to herself? She couldn't even begin to imagine, and she didn't even want to try. She definitely needed to make time to have a social life with the opposite sex again, like real soon.

Maybe it was time for Sluts R Us. In college Dawn and her friends jokingly referred to their sexual antics as the Sluts R Us Club, especially if it involved a one night stand. Of course, it was rare when she actually acted on these slutty impulses, but it happened once or twice when too much alcohol was involved.

"Good Morning," Chloe said, followed by a loud yawn. "I slept like a log. How did you sleep?"

"Um...great, really g-great," Dawn stammered. *A log?* The memory of the man's rock hard cock pressing into her abdomen, in her much too realistic dream reclaimed her thoughts. Flames licked at her entire body as she squirmed uncomfortably in her sleeping bag. *Well crap.* She was trapped her in her own erotic agony. All she could do was hope her flushed appearance didn't give her away. No such luck.

Chloe pushed herself up on one elbow and stared at her friend. "What the hell, girlfriend? You look like you've just been rode hard and put away wet. Who were you screwing last night?"

Another hot rush of blood flooded through her cheeks. "No, I-I— Okay, I admit it. I had a really wild dream. I was making out with some stranger." She shook her head, adding, "At least he smelled good."

"That was one hell of a make-out session." Chloe giggled. "Why can't I have dreams like that?"

Dawn attempted to laugh, too. She would enjoy a dream like the one she just had a lot more if her entire body and lips weren't still feeling as if they were a raging bonfire. Since there was no way she was going to admit any of this to Chloe, she had to suffer in silence and try to push her deviant slumber activities to the back of her mind.

"I'm so excited about our adventure today," she said in an attempt to change the subject.

"Me too," Chloe said in an eager tone. "We're going to an area my dad and I have searched numerous times, because we are certain the clues to the gold mine have something to do with that location." She shrugged, and added, "I just keep hoping I will see something new or notice something from a different angle. A whole new perspective maybe?" She focused her blue gaze on Dawn. "Maybe you'll notice something we've been missing when you see all of it for the first time."

"Oh, wow. That's entirely too much pressure."

Dawn chuckled. "I thought I was just here to be the comic relief." She pulled her tangled blonde hair over one shoulder and ran her fingers through the thick tresses. The slight wave created from her braid yesterday was completely gone now and her hair was back to its usual state of hanging long and straight past the middle of her back. "But I'll try not to get freaked out today, okay?"

She felt completely confident her crazy sense of panic from last night was nothing more than an embarrassing memory.

"Or go to any more wild orgies in the middle of the night without inviting me, okay?" Chloe retorted.

"Deal," Dawn agreed in earnest. She hoped she wouldn't be having any more of those weird wet dreams, either. She forced herself to focus on the real reason she was here. Meeting Chloe at the Apache Junction Middle school where she started teaching a few weeks ago was a stroke of good fortune. An immediate friendship developed between the two young teachers when they chatted in the teacher's lounge, especially once they discovered they both enjoyed the same types of outdoor activities, such as hiking and camping.

When her new friend suggested they go prospecting for gold, she thought it sounded like an expedition she couldn't miss out on. Once Chloe told her they were going in search of the famous Lost Dutchman Gold Mine in the Superstition Mountains, she had really been enthused. She was already familiar with the legendary story about the Dutch gold miner's claim of finding a rich vein of gold ore in this range of mountains.

Now, however, being here in this remote area, she wasn't so sure about this whole thing. Jacob Waltz was considered to be a crazy old man back in the time when he told all those bigger-than-life stories about his hidden gold mine. She was wondering if they weren't a bit crazy to be up here on this dangerous mountain, too.

They had a light breakfast of fruit and yogurt. Well, Chloe had an apple and yogurt, but Dawn's stomach felt a little queasy so she just opted for some yogurt. She was a bit light-headed and dizzy as if she had been drinking last night. *Could you get a hangover from wet dreams?*

Chloe munched on her apple as she showed her the detailed route she mapped out for their hike today. Her knowledge of the area was impressive. At least they shouldn't get lost, or so Dawn hoped.

She grabbed her hairbrush out of her pack and brushed the long strands of her blonde hair smooth before gathering them into a low ponytail at the base of her neck and securing them tightly with a hair band. As she finished twisting the band around her hair, she felt a brief stab of pain behind her ear. She reached up and touched the area where the source of irritation was centered and noticed a slight tenderness. Maybe a spider or bug had bitten her during the night?

No big deal, well, unless it was a poisonous spider and she was going to die. *Could that be why she felt queasy earlier?* She drew in a deep breath. Damn, she just kept imagining the worse of everything on this trip. An aggravated huff escaped as she picked up her old straw cowboy hat and placed it on her head while she waited for Chloe to finish getting ready.

"You know," Chloe said as she pulled the bill of

her Arizona State baseball cap down on her forehead and slid her own long hair through the hole in the back of the hat, "I will not be upset if you would rather we don't spend another night up here and just head home when we get done hiking later today? The Superstition Mountains can be more than a little intimidating if you're not used to this rugged kind of country."

With a shrug of her shoulders, Dawn hoped she sounded sincere when she answered, "Well, I realize I'm not in Colorado anymore, but I'm not going to be chased away by all those scary stories I read about this place or these seriously steep and narrow trails." Chuckling, she added, "Besides, you've been coming up here all your life and you're still alive, right?"

"Alive and well, and ready to be a really rich bitch," Chloe joked as she grabbed her daypack and swung it over her shoulder.

"Oh, now you're talkin'," Dawn chimed in as she followed the other woman out of the campsite.

****

Hours later, just as the sun was starting to drop low on the horizon to the west, Dawn eased herself down to the ground a couple of feet from the small fire they built in a circular pit surrounded by rocks. She ran her hand over the tight muscles of her stomach and gave a tired sigh. The long rigorous hike they had done today kicked her butt big time. Since she walked a lot to stay in shape, and was now doing regular exercise at the local gym Chloe had bullied her into joining a couple of weeks ago, she thought her legs were strong. But they felt like limp noodles right now.

"I'm sort of disgusted with myself. I thought I was in much better condition," she moaned. She placed her cowboy hat carefully on top of her backpack. After smoothing back some of the long strands of hair that had come loose from the ponytail behind her ears, she eagerly reached out to take the can of beer Chloe was holding out to her.

A smile curved Chloe's lips. "You are in great shape, but when was the last time you hiked all day in sun this intense?"

"Well, I did a lot of hiking in Colorado this past summer before moving, but it's definitely a different climate here." She took a swig out of the can of beer, then wiped her mouth with the back of her hand. "I love seeing all this new country, though. Thanks for letting me tag along. I would have enjoyed it more if we were celebrating finding millions of dollars in gold, though."

Chloe nodded her head in agreement and pulled her baseball cap off her head. As she tossed the hat to the ground a heavy frown settled on her pretty face. "I was really sure we would find something new today. I have those old clues left by Jacob Waltz memorized and I've studied that area so carefully; I just don't know what I could be missing." She shook her head and added, "Maybe old man Waltz was just a crazy old fart, after all."

She stood up and stared out toward the distant horizon as she repeated the clues for at least the tenth time today. *"You have to crawl through a hole in the rock. From here you can see the Old Military Trail. You can't see the mine from the trail. If you climb up a short distance you can see Weaver's Needle. The setting sun shines on the gold in my mine. A rock face looks at my mine."*

Dawn forced herself up from the ground and stood

beside Chloe and stared in the same direction where her friend's attention was focused. Off in the distance the sun was nearly gone from the westerly sky as her gaze settled on the ominous shape of Weaver's Needle. The protruding column of massive rock glowed in deep shades of orange and was surrounded by a shadowy purplish haze making it appear almost spiritual.

Today, they had been on the most treacherous trails she ever hiked, crawled through a hole in a huge rock shaped like a natural arch in one of the most rugged and remote places Dawn had ever been; Chloe led them to the barely visible path called the Old Military Trail, and they stared at the huge rock formation called Weaver's Needle from the top of a jagged range of rocks for what seemed hours. But as hard as they tried, they could not find anything resembling a face in any of the surrounding cliffs or rocks.

Chloe continued to gaze off into the distance as frustration and disappointment became evident on her tired face. Dawn felt at a loss for words. She kept thinking about all the research she had done about this area in the past few days, especially the parts about the curse of the Lost Dutchman Mine, and how it was allegedly guarded by unfathomable evil forces that would never allow anyone to live if they should ever find it.

It creeped her out to think of how many lives had been lost in these mountains looking for a gold mine that might be no more than someone's wild imagination. The exact number of missing or dead was not even known for sure, since many explorers and hopeful gold seekers just disappeared without a trace.

Being here in the heart of these hidden recesses and

rugged terrain, however, she could definitely understand how someone might easily become lost or fall into one of the deep caverns and never find their way out of this dangerous rock maze again. But what she still couldn't comprehend was the depth of passion people like Chloe and her family had in their relentless quest to find this supposed gold mine. There really wasn't any solid proof it existed, yet, they never gave up hope.

****

"Hello there."

The two women turned in unison to look in the direction of the unexpected greeting. Dawn glanced at Chloe and was surprised to see she was smiling and didn't seem worried in the least about the approach of the two strangers who were walking their way.

"Looks like you two have been out exploring," the taller of the two men commented as they stopped a couple feet away. He pointed at their discarded hiking gear lying beside the small fire pit. He chuckled and added, "Unless you're looking for a gold mine?"

Chloe's response was quick. "Oh, hardly." She chuckled as she ran her fingers through the long medium brown hair hanging loosely over her shoulders. "Nope, we're just here to get some fresh air and exercise." She gave a nonchalant shrug, adding, "How about you guys? Are you seekers or hikers?"

"Both," the same man replied. "Oh, excuse my manners. I'm Anton Two Moons and this is my brother, Rafael Two Moons."

For the first time since they had arrived, Dawn let her gaze raise up to the face of the man who was doing all the talking. From beneath the wide brim of his tan straw cowboy hat, dark shimmering eyes locked with her gaze for an instant before she was able to look away. There was no denying he was a gorgeous man, but the sense of uneasiness and the heavy knot in the pit of her stomach distracted her thoughts from this man's good looks.

"Nice to meet you," Chloe replied, seemingly unaware of Dawn's apprehension over encountering strangers up here in this isolated area.

She twisted her body in a flirty motion Dawn had never seen her do before now.

"I'm Chloe Webster and this is my friend, Dawn Malone. We're both teachers in Apache Junction."

Rafael Two Moons chuckled, then added as he glanced at his brother, "Wow, the teachers didn't look like this when we were in school, did they?"

Wow, that's original, Dawn thought. She lost count of how many men used that line since she had become a school teacher after graduating from college a few years ago. But Chloe was giggling like a teenager who had never heard it.

Tossing her hair back over one of her shoulders in a teasing manner, Chloe then hooked her thumbs in the belt loops of her low-rise blue jeans. "So, you're hunting for the Lost Dutchman, no doubt?" she asked. "I've heard some people still believe it exists."

Dawn cast her friend a curious glance. Looking for the Lost Dutchman's Gold Mine was practically a national past time in this part of Arizona. What did it matter if these men knew what they were doing here? She turned back toward the two men as she studied each of them and waited for their reaction to Chloe's comment about the gold mine.

They were undoubtedly Native American, around the same age as she and Chloe were, and to say they were both handsome guys would be an understatement. They were taller and leaner than many of the Native Americans Dawn had met since moving here, and their regal features were framed by long flowing locks of shiny thick black hair.

The taller of the two men—the one she locked gazes with—wore the straw cowboy hat and the other man had a folded red bandana tied around his forehead like a headband. Dressed casually, both men wore jeans, dark T-shirts and hiking boots that looked almost brand new. Their backpacks did not appear to be filled with much gear, so she figured they most likely lived somewhere in the area and were just camping for one night.

And luckily, they seemed oblivious to Chloe's little white lie.

"Well, whether or not it exists, we enjoy hiking around in these old mountains," Anton replied as he glanced around at the rapidly darkening countryside. "We have a favorite spot we've been camping at since we were children and it's not too far from here. It's always fun to imagine we might stumble onto a pot of gold or something."

"Really?" Chloe glanced toward the trail. "I wasn't aware there were more campsites any farther up?"

Dawn noticed a strange expression flash across Anton Two Moons' face, but it was quickly replaced by smile. "You must know this area quite well?" He directed all his attention toward Chloe.

"I was raised in the area, so yeah, I guess I know these mountains pretty well." She looked at Dawn and motioned with her hand. "But my friend just moved here from Colorado, so I'm just showing her some of the local countryside."

Dawn's gaze moved to back to Anton's face. He was smiling at her. She was struck by how white his teeth looked in contrast to his smooth bronze-hued skin.

"Welcome to Arizona," he said in a polite tone. He did not let his gaze linger as he turned toward his brother. "We should let these lovely ladies get settled in for the night. We still have to set up camp."

"In the dark," Rafael added with a chuckle. "Oh well, it won't be the first time or the last." He waved goodbye and added, "Maybe we'll see you girls on the trail tomorrow."

"I hope so," Chloe replied as she gave an enthusiastic wave back.

Dawn attempted to be social, in spite of the nervousness she could not ignore. "Nice to meet you both," she called out.

"You, too," Anton Two Moons answered. He did not look directly at either of the women again as he turned to follow his brother out of the camp.

"I hope you don't think I'm terrible for not admitting why we are here?" Chloe said as soon as the men were out of earshot. "It's just easier that way."

"No worries," Dawn answered. She wasn't up for discussing the Lost Gold Mine with those two mysterious strangers, either.

"Well, I have a whole new appreciation for the Indian Nation," Chloe said with a giggle. "I wouldn't mind meeting them on the trail or anywhere else, for that matter."

"For sure," Dawn said with way more enthusiasm

than she felt. There was no denying both men were probably the most attractive men she ever met, and there was a dangerous and sensual aura about them that only increased their appeal. Anton Two Moons, with his towering frame and perfectly chiseled features looked like he could be in the movies, and his brother, Rafael Two Moons was equally as good-looking. So, why did she feel so uncomfortable around them?

****

Mateo Two Moons leaned back against the rock and stared out into the dusky countryside. He was at a loss for words. Dawn, Udaya, in his Apache language, was more beautiful than he could have imagined with her long blonde hair trailing past the middle of her back and her delicate pale coloring. For so long he had tried to picture what she would look like, but he never expected his mate would have blonde hair and be fair-skinned. None of the other men in his vampire Blood Clan had a blonde mate. She would be the only one in the entire village. And she would belong to him for eternity.

"Happy now, Brother?" Anton whispered.

Mateo fought to gain control of the multitude of emotions he was feeling at this moment. He had memorized every inch of her while he watched from his hiding place as his brothers spoke to the two women. Tonight, Dawn Malone—his mate—was wearing her naturally blonde hair pulled into a loose ponytail at the back of her head, and in the waning light the pale wispy strands hanging loose around her beautiful face were shining like a halo of moonbeams. Faded jeans, with a frayed hole in one knee, hugged the slight curves of her narrow hips, and a simple white T-shirt pulled snug across the perfect swell of her breasts completed her casual outfit.

He already knew the way her firm body and soft silken skin felt under those unassuming clothes. She had been under his hypnotic vampire influence and in a dream-like state when he visited her in her sleeping bag last night and held her in his arms and touched her intimately for the first time.

Her eyelids fluttered open long enough for him to glimpse the unique hue of her eyes, and his keen sight had been able to tell they were hazel-colored. But to Mateo the pale brown orbs reminded him of the sand and the flecks of jade that sparkled in their depths were like the deep green cacti that decorated the desert with beauty and wonder. Even her scent reminded him of the fresh clean aura of the Yucca that blooms in early summer, but only releases its scent as darkness descends each night.

One of his own dreams had also come true last night; to see and spend some time with his mate while she was still in her human world—as a *real one*—the term his vampire clan called her kind. Originally, he thought he only needed a few extra moments with her before he made her his mate for all eternity. But in the moment when he tasted that first drop of her sweet blood as he bit the tender spot at the base of her hairline, he also realized there was something else he desperately needed before he followed the rituals of his clan and claimed her in every way...body, mind, and soul.

He had been overcome with a sense of excitement and confusion by this sudden new revelation and the possibilities of what it could mean if his impulsive plan was successful. Although he had no desire to tamper with their ultimate destinies, he knew he had to find a way to change the archaic customs of his people, and the traditions that had been in place since the beginning of their time. He was prepared to tempt fate in his quest to find a way to live with Dawn Malone in her human world, if only for a while, before he took her to live as his mate in his world forever.

Seeing her tonight as she spoke to his two older brothers convinced him even further that he was going to make this plan work. Before he took her to the top of the mountain for the rest of all time, he would know every one of her human desires, and he would fulfill each and every one.

"Yes, I'm more than happy now," Mateo finally answered as his mind filled with the beautiful images of the future.

Chapter Three

Dawn just wanted to get a restful night's sleep. That didn't seem like too much to ask, did it? But she worried about having another explicit dream that seemed far too real to be merely a dream, or even worse, having a horrific nightmare about the malevolence lurking in these mountains that would feel as real as the sensuous dream. Either way, it could mean another miserable night.

The minute she snuggled into the downy comfort of her sleeping bag, her tired lids closed. And it began much the same as it had last night.

The man was lying beside her in her sleeping bag again. The small confines of the tight space were suffocating in the heat of the desert night. His mouth immediately engaged her lips with demanding kisses.

She felt one of his hands move down past the waistband of her sweatpants. That same wandering hand caressed her firm stomach as it made its way lower. She squirmed against the man's taut form as wondrous sensations bolted through her entire body. His mere touch was unlike any she had known before.

She raised her arms up and placed her hands on the sides of his face. His skin felt smooth to her touch. It was too dark to make out his features, but she sensed it was a face nearly perfect to look upon.

Her hands moved up to his hairline. His hair was

long...way past his shoulders. The texture was heavy and full. Her fingers became lost in the infusion of his luxurious locks. From the tips of her fingers to the ends of her toes she thrilled to the image of how this glorious head of hair must look surrounding the flawless face she pictured in her mind.

By now his fingers had pushed her panties out of the way and he was gently massaging the soft feminine folds of her clit. The sweet agony he was inducing escaped in a breathy moan from her lips as he began to work two fingers into her eager pussy. She arched her hips upward and pressed against him like she had last night in an open invitation. Surely tonight he would do more than tease and taunt her to the brink of sexual insanity.

His lips were kissing along the side of her neck, over her shoulder and down along the inside of her arm while she was distracted with the delicious activities in her lower regions. She was slightly surprised to realize his mouth was now kissing her wrist when a quick sharp pain in that area surprised her. She involuntarily flinched. But the man held her wrist against his lips, sucking lightly, as a sweet tempestuous satisfaction began to fill Dawn with euphoria. She could only equate this wondrous sensation to making love for the first time as a virgin. First, the uncertainty, a brief moment of pain, then pleasure; and lastly, a longing for more and more and more.

Dawn had never been so glad to see the sun rising in her entire life. It had been a long torturous night in some ways, and not nearly long enough in others. This latest dream—once again so real it was hard to believe it had only been a dream—could have lasted all night and she wouldn't have minded. But it was much too short, and once the dream was over, she woke up drenched in sweat and with a deep ache between her legs. Wet dreams. Two nights in a row? This was just sad.

If she didn't know better, she would swear the sexy manly scent of the stranger in her dreams still clung to the material of her sleeping bag and the lingering remnants of his touch left its heated mark everywhere on all the intimate parts of her body where his exploring hands had traipsed.

With a weary sigh, she pushed herself up on one elbow to look around. The hazy gray light of early morning glowed outside the cave and afforded a tiny bit of light underneath the overhang. Only a mass of tangled brown hair from Chloe's head was exposed at the end of her sleeping bag. She didn't think Chloe had moved all night. Obviously, she was worn out from the long tedious hike they had been on yesterday.

Dawn was exhausted, too, both from the hike, and now, from lack of sleep, thanks to those stupid dreams. She seriously needed to either get laid, or get mental help. A vibrator might have come in handy last night. The unexpected thought made her snort with disgust. It was going to be a really long day.

"How long have you been awake?" Chloe asked in a sleepy voice. She pushed her sleeping bag away from her face and rolled over to look at Dawn. Rubbing at her sleep-swollen eyes, she yawned loudly.

Her body jerked in surprise at the sound of Chloe's voice breaking into her thoughts of shameless self-pleasure. A hot flush flared through her cheeks. She cleared her throat and once again attempted to sound normal. "Since about ten last night."

Chloe pushed her sleeping bag away from her upper body and looked at her friend with a curious glance. "Weren't we just going to bed about ten last night?"

"Probably." Dawn chuckled. "I fell asleep, I think, but then I woke up almost immediately. I couldn't go back to sleep after that."

"All night?" Chloe sat up and kicked her bag away from the lower part of her body. The sun wasn't even fully up yet, and the temperature was promising to be another blistering day. "That really sucks."

"Tell me about it," she moaned. Those seriously kinky dreams did suck, and not entirely in a bad way. Ugh. It was definitely time for some Sluts R Us action. She pushed herself up to a sitting position. Unconsciously, she rubbed at the tender spot on her wrist. Although it was not light enough for her to see anything, she determined a spider or bug must have taken up residence in her sleeping bag. The sore spot on her wrist felt a bit swollen and tender like the spot behind her ear.

Wait? Wasn't there something in her dream last night involving her wrist? Her mind drew a blank and she was too tired to dwell on the hazy images in her head. "I'm gonna be a total zombie all day," she added as she tried to push the bizarre dreams, along with the worry about a poisonous spider or bug bite, out of her mind.

"We don't have to hike again today. I don't mind heading back to town early."

Dawn couldn't stop the sense of relief that caused her to exhale a big sigh. "Really? Are you sure? I mean,

I don't really mind hiking more today since we're here. But I must admit I'm pretty beat."

Chloe shrugged and squinted in the dull light as she focused her gaze on Dawn's face. "I'm not really up to it, either. And if you don't mind me saying it, you look like crap. Are you okay?"

Dawn chuckled. "Well, thanks." Unconsciously, she traced her fingertips over her inflamed lips. "I'm good, really," she lied. "Maybe lack of sleep is just making me weirder than usual."

"Well, in case you haven't noticed, I'm a little weird myself. Guess that's why we became friends so quickly." Chloe snickered. "Seriously, though, I think we should just head home early today. I'm just so damned disappointed we didn't find anything new yesterday."

"I'm sorry," Dawn answered. She had been so distracted with her own issues of uneasiness and horny musings; she had forgotten what this trip obviously meant to Chloe. "I was hoping I would bring you good luck. I know how important it is to you and your family to find that gold mine."

Chloe crawled to the edge of the little alcove they were sheltered under and stared up at the distant peaks of the mountains overhead. The last of the gray haze was fading as the sun was just starting to cast a brilliant golden glow across the highest summits. They looked as shimmery as the gold she had been hoping to find for all these years.

"For some silly reason I had been more optimistic than usual about finding the gold mine this time." She put her open palm against her chest and gave a heavy sigh. "I had this feeling something really important was going to happen this weekend."

Her gaze wandered out toward the direction they hiked the day before as she added, "It's not even about the gold or becoming rich. I just want to prove that stupid gold mine really does exist. My dad has become very ill recently, and he can't hike these mountains anymore. There's nothing I want more than to find the gold mine for him."

A heavy sadness filled her voice and echoed into the mournful expression on her face. "He's been searching for it his entire life, and my grandfather and great-grandfather before him. I can't stand the thought of another member of our family dying without knowing—" her voice faded away. She shrugged her shoulders and slumped down. "Maybe it's time we all just gave it up and accepted the fact it's just a crazy old make-believe fantasy."

Dawn scooted closer to her friend. "I'm so sorry to hear about your dad. But no, you shouldn't give up. I haven't known you very long, but I do know how devoted you are to finding this treasure. And although I will admit I don't totally understand it, I sure do wish I had something in my life I was so passionate about. You don't want to give up, not really, do you?"

"No, I guess not. But I feel sort of foolish dragging you up here with me. Actually, I've only confided in a couple of other friends about my fascination with the gold mine, and they never showed any interest in coming up here to search with me. In fact, I've never come up here with anyone other than my family until now."

Chloe glanced over at her with a quizzical frown on her pretty face. "I'm not even sure why I felt I could tell you about my family's obsession with this place, or why I felt strongly enough about it to bring you up here with me. Maybe it had something to do with your interest in history. I just don't know."

"Well, now I feel really honored to be here." Dawn grinned. "And sincerely bummed I wasn't able to bring you better luck."

Chloe shrugged and smiled back before crawling out from under the overhanging ledge. She stood up, stretching her arms high up over her head. "So, I guess we won't go back rich bitches, just poor underpaid, but totally hot school teachers."

Dawn giggled as she dragged her stiff body out from under the rock ledge and copied Chloe with a full body stretch. Today she really did feel like she had been rode hard and put away wet. She would never leave home without her vibrator again.

She noticed she had a vague feeling of nausea again this morning. *What was up with that?* Maybe it was just because the altitude was so different from what she was accustomed to. She took a deep breath and looked around. The unforgiving desert floor, spooky peaks and towers of the Superstition Mountains were so drastically different from the lush wooded mountains in Colorado, but this part of Arizona was still a ruggedly beautiful area in a completely different way. She reminded herself this mountain range and its hidden secrets were a part of her new home now.

Luckily she met someone like Chloe who wanted to be her friend, confide in her and take her places she would never find on her own. But she hoped Chloe would understand and still be her friend, if she didn't want to come back up here on this frightening mountain range anytime soon.

****

Home Sweet Home.

Dawn's little apartment on the north end of Apache Junction, and in the hub of a rapidly growing urban area, never felt so welcoming as it did when Chloe dropped her off earlier today from their weekend excursion on the Superstitions.

Curled up on the couch, she settled in for a relaxing evening before the hectic Monday she knew was ahead of her the next day.

She reached for the TV switcher, but put it back down on the coffee table without hitting the power button. It was barely six o'clock in the evening, yet she couldn't keep her eyes open. She had to be at school early in the morning to get ready for a field trip to the Arizona State Capital Museum in Phoenix, which meant an extra-long day with part of it spent on a hot school bus with twenty-four moody twelve-year-olds.

A smile touched her lips. In spite of how difficult it could be to teach pre-teens, sharing her love of history with her students was something she never got tired of doing. It was extremely rare for her not to look forward to being at school every day.

After not sleeping at all the previous night, and very little sleep the night before, added to the queasiness she felt all day, Dawn was prepared to give in to her weariness and head to bed.

Please no kinky weird dreams tonight, okay? She had to get some uninterrupted sleep before school tomorrow, but getting up from the couch to go the very short distance to her bedroom seemed too much of an effort. In a matter of minutes, her eyes were too heavy to keep open and she fell into a deep sleep.

Engulfing blackness drew her in and she was powerless to resist the distant voice she could hear calling out to her. *Udaya...*

Dawn woke with a start; disoriented and gasping for air. Sweat drenched her face and body, but she didn't notice. She slipped her feet into the white tennis shoes she removed from her feet earlier in the evening, and rose from the couch. In a trance-like state she walked to the front door.

The clock on the wall said it was approaching midnight, but it didn't matter. Nothing mattered except going to be with him. He was waiting for her. He had been waiting there, on the Superstition Mountains, for a very long time.

Chapter Four

Just a couple of days ago, she traveled this route with Chloe. But it had been daylight and Chloe had been driving. Dawn hadn't been paying much attention since the entire way they had been talking non-stop about the Lost Dutchman's Gold Mine and their past camping adventures. It had taken them a little over an hour to drive to the location where Chloe parked her truck. Now, even in the dimness of night, Dawn drove from her apartment in Apache Junction, to that exact same spot as if she had been coming here forever.

Wearing the black yoga pants and white T-shirt she had on when she fell asleep on her couch earlier this evening; she had only taken time to put the pair of white sneakers on her feet. Still damp with perspiration, her pale flaxen hair hung limply down past the middle of her back.

Tonight was an unusually cool night for this area, and normally she would have needed a sweatshirt or jacket for being outside in this temperature, but she didn't notice the odd temperature of the Arizona night as she began walking up the same narrow and steep trails she traveled with Chloe.

Not once did she stumble or fall on the treacherous trail. Her feet seemed to move on their own accord, feeling as if they barely touched the ground since she avoided all the rocks and boulders scattered along the trail she was tripping over when she had been here before. She had no idea how far she hiked, but she didn't really care. All that mattered was finding him.

"Udaya."

She gasped when the man's deep voice broke through the silence. She could see him standing at the top of a ridge about twenty feet above her. Although the moon was not quite full, it was bright enough to cast an eerie light across the rugged mountaintops. But there still wasn't enough light to make the features of the man's face visible in this shadowy haze. Even though she longed to see the handsome face she envisioned in her mind, it was her body that clung to the desire consuming her since the first moment this mysterious stranger had come to her in previous dreams.

But this felt more real than the earlier dreams, if that was possible. *Could this really be happening? Of course not. It had to be another dream...another incredibly realistic dream.*

She had just been watching him up on the ridgeline and in less than a flash he was standing just inches in front of her. Where was the panic she knew she should be feeling right now? It was lost to the overpowering turmoil of her desperate desire for this phantom lover.

Some sort of a blanket was draped over his head, hiding most of his face and covering nearly all of his body. She narrowed her eyes and tried to see his features clearly, but his appearance was still a complete mystery when he began to speak.

"I've been waiting for you my entire life," he said.

"I know," Dawn answered, although she did not know why. It was just something she knew.

"My grandmother and my mother told me about

you when I was a child nearly a hundred years ago. Grandmother also told me you would be called Udaya, which means Dawn in my language."

Confusion ruled her thoughts. *A hundred years? Udaya?* His words made no sense. But then, here was no logic to anything happening to her for the past forty-eight hours. And it really didn't matter.

At this moment she only wanted to feel the way she felt in those crazy dreams from the past two nights...the way his touch caused her insides to melt into a cauldron of lust and desire.

"I know you are confused. Your mind cannot grasp what is happening. It's only your body responding to me at this time, because there is no way to resist fate. It was probably wrong of me to bring you here tonight since I'm not ready to take you to the mountaintop to become my mate, yet. But I just can't stay away from you now that I've seen you and held you in my arms. I promise you, I will find a way to come to you in your world before we both must fulfill the destiny set in motion since time first began. You must trust me, Udaya."

More confusion filled her mind. He kept saying words her common sense couldn't comprehend. But he was so right when he said the part about only her body responding to him. There was not one inch of her body not yearning for him to touch her in every intimate way possible.

As if he read her thoughts, he was suddenly holding her in his arms. The blanket he was wearing over his head fell to the ground, and Dawn could feel the hard muscles of his bare body pressing against her. He wore nothing other than some sort of cloth around his hips, but it wasn't enough to contain the hard ridge of his cock, which was once again pressing against her abdomen with demanding intensity. A loud moan escaped from her mouth.

Her hands encircled the back of his neck. Long, thick hair encased her trembling fingers as she buried them deeper into the heavy mass. His lips were kissing her neck and she was sure her knees would have given out if he was not holding her up. Her body was dissolving into a hot mass of shameless needs.

Fiery sensations erupted in her sweating skin as his lips worked their way up the side of her neck and along her jaw line. His devouring kiss encompassed her completely and she opened her mouth willingly, hungrily, for what she knew was about to happen. When his tongue darted into her mouth, she was vitally aware of every exhilarating touch, every heady scent, and every succulent taste. His taste was indescribable; something akin to a sweet and sour candy that made the inside of her mouth convulse with wild explosions of pleasure.

As his lips left her mouth and began to kiss along her neck again back to the hidden area behind her ear, she was prepared, and eager, for the sharp penetration of his bite. When she felt the tiny prick, it sent ripples of ecstasy cascading through her entire being. A climatic explosion ripped through her body. She went limp in the stranger's arms.

****

It was seven-twenty-three. What the hell? How was that even possible? She always woke up by six every morning. Now, she would be seriously late and she had planned to be there early to prepare for the field trip to

Phoenix. Already, she could tell she felt like crap and she hadn't even moved a muscle, yet.

Her mouth was bone-dry and she needed some water and lots and lots of strong black coffee. But when she tried to sit up, her head started spinning so fiercely she fell back against the pillow on the couch where she obviously spent the entire night.

With her hand pressed over her eyes, she moaned. Her stomach was churning and there was a queasy bulk hovering at the back of her throat. If she moved she knew she would throw up. She felt like she had a massive hangover, but the last alcohol she had to drink had been a couple of beers in the campsite with Chloe on Saturday night.

"This seriously sucks," she said out loud, then choked back the urge to vomit, because she didn't think she even had the energy to drag herself to the bathroom. Could this really be the result of a poisonous bug or spider bite she might have gotten when they were camping? Wow, maybe she really could die.

It was more likely she just had a flu bug, which was probably why she had been feeling so strange the past couple of days. Now she would have to call in sick at the last minute. She had only been teaching History at the Apache Junction Middle School for barely a month, so this was not something she wanted to do.

When she was teaching in Colorado before moving here, she only called in sick once in the four years since graduating from college, and that was because she had gotten pink eye from one of her students.

If she missed school today, a substitute teacher would have to take her history class to the Arizona State Capital Museum in Phoenix today, which made it even worse for her to be get sick right now.

Dawn took a deep breath and leaned over to grab her cell phone lying on the coffee table. These slight movements made her feel as if she was going to pass out. Once again, she choked back the bitter taste in her mouth and tried to lay as still as possible until the queasiness eased up enough for her to call the secretary at the school. After she finally managed to make the dreaded call, along with profuse apologies for having to call in sick, she hung up and sank back into the cushions on the couch to try to sort through her confused thoughts. The secretary said she sounded horrible, so Dawn figured she must sound as bad as she felt.

The last clear memory she had of the previous night had been of lying on this couch and feeling too tired to get up to go to bed. That had been ridiculously early in the evening. She must have fallen asleep right afterward, then this lurking and unwelcome flu bug finally claimed her exhausted body during the night.

Without warning, the vivid images of her most recent dream began to flash like disoriented black and white movie stills before her eyes. That man, the faceless stranger, summoning her to the Superstitions, holding her in his strong arms, reducing her to a woman who wanted nothing more than his—and her own— complete surrender. Unconsciously, she raised her hand up and gently touched her lips. She pulled her fingers away as if she had been shocked by a bolt of electricity.

Once again, her lips were tender to her touch, suggesting she been engaged in a fervent make out session. Her hand slid up along the side of her neck where she remembered the man's lips leaving a blazing path of kisses. As her fingertips barely touched the spot behind her ear that was even more painful than it had been before, a blistering sensation fired through her entire body. An urgent yearning between her legs gripped her again. This was insane. She honestly felt like she just had an orgasm and was only recalling the images from her sick dreams.

This flu was making her hallucinate, but what kind of flu would cause that type of reaction? Maybe she invented a new type of flu...the Orgasm Flu. A humorless chuckle escaped from her parched mouth. That would be the kind of flu all women would want to catch. Right?

She should probably call Chloe and get the name of a good doctor in the area, although at this point she wasn't sure if she needed a medical doctor or a shrink. At the rate she was going with these nutty dreams it was probably going to be the latter.

Her sarcastic mirth faded as she tried to concentrate on realistic reasons as to what could really be causing her to feel like she was losing her mind. If she hadn't been bitten by some poisonous bug or spider, then maybe she had some sort of weird illness that really was making her delirious and causing her to have wild dreams about sexy long-haired men who smelled and tasted amazing, and floated down to her from the rocky ledges on the Superstition Mountains. Well, this had to be a new one for the medical books.

Dawn forced herself to sit up, which was a bit easier this time. As she managed to straighten up and put her feet on the ground, she realized her feet felt strange, too. A glance down at her bare feet made her cringe. Both of her feet were covered in dirt, actually they were covered in the fine light brown dust that covered the desert floor throughout this part of Arizona.

Her once-clean white tennis shoes were lying haphazardly on the floor beside the couch as if she had kicked them off in a rush. Last night, right before she laid down, she distinctly remembered removing them from her feet and placing them side-by-side in an orderly manner. Even more puzzling was how her shoes were also covered with the same fine brown sand that matched the dirt on her feet.

Her brow wrinkled in confusion. Those shoes were only worn around the house, to the gym, or whenever she went for a power walk around her neighborhood. Why would they—and her feet—be filthy dirty? She had been asleep on the couch all night, hadn't she?

That crazy vivid dream flashed through her mind again...no way.

Udaya.

A weak gasp escaped from her mouth. There was more, something about centuries and destiny and his grandmother, but his words were shrouded in her foggy memory. She ran her dry tongue over her trembling lips. *Don't remember*, she told herself. *Please don't remember. It was only a dream. No, it was more like a horrible nightmare...*the kind you didn't want to remember because then it would seem too real.

Her body felt as if it had just been wrapped in barbed wire as terror pierced through her waning defenses and wiped out all the sensual overtones she previously felt.

Cowboy up, Cupcake.

As always, when she said that silly phrase to herself, she thought of her older brother. Jeremy was her center point when life got a bit overwhelming and she needed to be grounded again. Maybe she should call him later tonight when he was off work. He was the head coach at the University of Colorado in Boulder and she knew this was a crazy busy time for him as the CSU Football team was starting a new season.

He had also gotten married recently, but always made time for his little sister, and was still the one person Dawn could talk to about anything. But could she talk to him about all this unbelievably weird stuff? The kinky dreams? The sexy long-haired stranger? The Orgasm Flu? Going insane? Probably not.

Before long, Dawn realized she was beginning to feel almost semi-normal, physically, anyway. Mentally, well, she wasn't ready to go there yet. She drew in a deep cleansing breath.

Slowly, she rose to her feet on still-shaking legs. Another relieved sigh escaped her. Five minutes ago, she was certain she would have collapsed or thrown up if she had attempted to stand. In her small apartment it was only a few yards to the kitchen. By the time she got to the sink and reached for a glass of water, she became aware of a throbbing sensation emitting from the sore spot on the back of her neck.

Damn, it was really starting to hurt. She reached around to touch the area again and grew numb. When she pulled her hand away this time and glanced down at her fingers, it was all she could do to keep from dropping down to her knees. A scarlet-colored smear colored the edges of her fingertips.

She grabbed a paper towel from the holder and gently wiped the blood away, then raised her hand up to the back of her neck again. Her hand was shaking in such a ferocious manner her fingertips could only flutter against the swollen area where the pain and source of the bleeding seemed to be located.

The dream—when the man had bitten her neck—dashed through her bewildered thoughts. But that was all it was...a dream. Right? There was absolutely no way she could have a human bite on her neck that was swollen and bleeding.

Don't be ridiculous. This is not real. Now she was becoming convinced she should ask Chloe for the name of a mental health clinic in the area if she really believed it was possible to have a real bite mark at the back of her neck from a dream.

Her gaze was drawn to the spot on her wrist where she faintly remembered the same sensation of being bitten there in one of the dreams. There was a barely visible pink mark that almost resembled a thumbnail moon and there was no pain. But she had only been bitten once on her wrist, and she had been bitten twice in the same spot on the back of her neck.

These had to be spider or bug bites. But did she bring the venous biter home from the mountains with her, and what the hell sort of insect left a mark that looked-more like a human bite than a bug bite?

She knew she should go to the bathroom and look at the bloody area behind her ear in the mirror, but the thought of doing anything else right now made her head spin and her body feel too weak to stay upright for much longer. An overpowering sense of exhaustion controlled her mind and body as she made her way back to the couch.

Sleep was probably all she needed. Lots of sleep to make up for all the sleep she had been missing since she first went to the Superstition Mountains with Chloe. If she could just get some uninterrupted, dreamless sleep, when she woke up, maybe everything would be perfect in her world again.

Chapter Five

"I'm sure glad you're feeling better. You looked like you were gonna die when I dropped you off Sunday after camping, and you didn't look a whole lot better when I stopped by your apartment to check on you Monday night. Have to say, I was surprised to see you back at school on Tuesday morning. At least it was a short-lived flu bug." Chloe reached across the table and scooped up a piece of pizza from the pan.

Dawn nodded as she munched on a piece of pepperoni. She hadn't been worried about dying from the Orgasm Flu nearly as much as she had been worried about going crazy. Those insane dreams, or rather, sensuous nightmares that seemed entirely too real and crossed over into her waking hours were more than a little disturbing. If the strange occurrences hadn't stopped when they had, Dawn was sure she would be in a mental hospital by now.

"And thank you for not giving it to me," Chloe added as she took a big bite of her pizza slice.

"You're welcome. Thank goodness you didn't get that awful flu or whatever it was. It was short, but ruthless." Dawn leaned back in her chair and drew in a deep breath and exhaled slowly. She didn't dare tell Chloe the extent of her crazy symptoms.

When she had time, she still planned to research poisonous spiders and bugs in the area to see if everything that happened to her might have been caused by a toxic reaction to being bitten. But for now, she was just relieved the odd symptoms disappeared. There had been no more nightmarish dreams, and she was back to feeling like herself.

The Arizona evening was a perfect temperature, and filled with the tantalizing aromas from the little outdoor pizzeria where they were having dinner. Everything in Dawn's world seemed perfect again. She reached for another slice of pizza.

"Hey, you girls look familiar," a deep masculine voice rang out.

Dawn pulled her hand back protectively as her gaze rose to the man who had just spoken. The intense gaze of Anton Two Moons met her own. Her mind went blank for a moment.

"Hi there," Chloe practically squealed. A wide smile settled on her lips as she blatantly gave Anton's entire body an appraising scan with her discriminating blue gaze then glanced past him to the other two men who accompanied him.

Anton stepped aside slightly and motioned at the man closest to him. "You probably remember my brother, Rafael, and this is our youngest brother, Mateo Two Moons."

She giggled. "Of course, we remember you, Anton, and Rafael…" Her gaze settled on the youngest of the trio of brothers. "Ni-Nice to-to meet you, Mateo," she stuttered as she stared shamelessly at him. "I'm Chloe. Chloe, um, Webster."

Rafael motioned toward Dawn. "And you are Dawn Malone if I remember correctly?"

Her head nodded in a barely conscious response to

Rafael's question, but she didn't attempt to reply. She, too, was staring shamelessly at the youngest of the Two Moons brothers. Shimmering and dark as night, his eyes were rimmed on top by thick black and perfectly shaped brows. From beneath heavy lashes, his mesmerizing gaze locked with hers.

A strange sense of familiarity floated along the edges of her consciousness. But there was no way they had met before now because there was absolutely no way she would forget meeting a man as mysterious and sexy as Mateo Two Moons.

She didn't even try to stop the smile that came instinctively to her lips. He smiled back. She noticed the way his full lips turned up slightly more on one side, revealing teeth so glistening and white they stood stark in contrast to his golden brown complexion. Raven hair was combed back behind his ears and from her view point it looked as if it was pulled into a ponytail or braid that must hang down his back.

A white western shirt was tucked into faded jeans that hung low on his narrow hips. White pearl snaps running down the front of his shirt were open to mid-chest revealing glimpses of the heavy turquoise necklace he wore around his neck. Pointed toes of scruffy black cowboy boots peeked out from the frayed bottoms of his jeans and completed his rugged look.

As uneasy as she had been when they first encountered Anton and Rafael Two Moons in the Superstition Mountains last weekend, she was now instantly enamored with their brother, Mateo, as she noticed every inch of him in a matter of seconds.

"Would you care to join us?" Dawn heard herself asking without a hesitant thought.

"Yes, please do," Chloe said with another giggle. She motioned at the empty table next to them where they could grab three chairs. As the brothers pulled the chairs over to their table, Chloe glanced at Dawn and gave her the thumbs up sign. Dawn couldn't help but notice how her luminous blue eyes were extra sparkly all of a sudden.

In a matter of seconds, the three brothers were seated around the table. Mateo Two Moons was sitting so close to Dawn she was sure they would touch if she moved even one fraction of an inch. Her body shook slightly with her stanch effort not to move. Unconsciously, she sucked in her breath. As she did, she caught a whiff of his musky cologne.

He smelled like the flowers that bloomed on the prickly cactus covering the desert floor; an intoxicating mixture of sweet succulent floral and the heavier earthy scent of cacti.

She choked back the lump that formed in the hollow of her throat. *Please, don't be crazy now.*

"May I buy you another beer?" Mateo motioned toward her half-empty beer bottle setting beside her plate with the uneaten pieces of crust from her last piece of pizza.

She glanced at him out of the side of her eye. She was afraid to look directly at him again. The memory of the man's cologne from her dreams left her seriously shaken, and sitting this close to a man like Mateo Two Moons while recalling one of those kinky dreams was dangerous to her health—and maybe to his health if she couldn't control herself. She felt as though her entire body and soul had been awakened by some unexplainable force, and it appeared the force was sitting right next to her.

"Um, yeah, sure," she said in a squeaky voice.

He's not the freaky stranger in your weird dreams. But he is seriously, seriously hot. She heard the other men and Chloe talking, but couldn't concentrate on one thing they were saying. Yet, she did know Mateo was watching her every move and could feel his gaze as strongly as if his fingers were traipsing all over her face and body.

"Beautiful night, isn't it?"

Mateo's tone was deep like Anton's voice. Only so much sexier, Dawn thought in a giddy moment. Something ridiculous like butterfly wings were fluttering wildly in her stomach. She was acting like one of her twelve-year-old students discovering she liked boys for the first time.

She gave a quick nod of her head. The night was more than beautiful. Since Mateo Two Moons sat down next to her, the night had turned magical. If she thought everything was perfect in her life just moments earlier, she was positive of it now. *Is this what love at first sight is like?*

The quivering in her stomach grew as she glanced over at the handsome man who was so close she only had to move an inch or two to press her body against his. He was taking two full beers from the waitress. Dawn hadn't even realized he already ordered them.

She had been correct about his hair. A brown band held a thick mass of ebony hair at the nape of his neck and the shiny locks hung past the middle of his back. As he grabbed the beer bottles in each hand, she noticed the way his muscles rippled above his shoulder blades under the thin material of his white shirt.

She clutched her sweaty hands together in her lap. She wasn't sure which she wanted to do most—run her fingers through his long hair or dig her fingernails into those taut muscles she glimpsed beneath his shirt. Of course, to do either, they would most likely need to be engaged in a wild sexual romp.

Wow. Sluts R Us calling. She seriously needed to stop.

She reached out to take the beer he was holding toward her. Her hand visibly shook as she grasped hold of the bottle. She glanced up to see if he noticed. His dark eyes were focused on her face and not her hands. It was impossible to look away.

"Th-Thank you," she stammered in the strange sounding voice again. Well, he surely thought she was a total nutcase now. She couldn't even talk like a regular person.

"My brothers mentioned you and your friend are school teachers. So, what grade do you teach?" he asked as if he didn't notice she was a blubbering idiot.

She focused on speaking, but it was not an easy task. "Middle School, um, seventh grade history." *Please don't say they didn't make teachers like me when you went to school, or then I might think you are an idiot, too, and right now I think you are just perfect, Mr. Two Moons.*

Although she didn't want to look directly at him again—for fear she would do or say something really stupid—she couldn't help herself. He was staring at her with such a tender and almost intimate expression on his face. Goosebumps broke out on her arms. Like his brothers, there was a dangerous aura about him. Only the danger part was seriously over-ruled by his undeniable sex appeal.

Her mind filled with curiosity again as she wondered what it would feel like to release his thick black hair from the ponytail and immerse her fingers in its luxurious mass. A lucid picture of the way the long shiny black locks would look all entangled around his handsome face and spread out on her pillowcase—in her bed—dominated her thoughts.

Unwanted, and unexpectedly, the images from her sensuous dreams began to flash before her eyes in vivid recollections and filled every one of her senses. The indescribable explosion of the delectable way the stranger in her dreams tasted filled her mouth; she inhaled the delicious scent of the man sitting so close to her, and her entire body grew fevered with the image of his hands roving where only a ardent lover would touch.

She was reliving every moment of those tempestuous dreams right now in the middle of this pizzeria, because it felt as if the man from her dreams was no longer a faceless stranger.

Dawn fought to remain in control and not let the outrageous memories of those stupid dreams continue to surface, but it was already out of her power. She gasped and dropped the beer she was holding in her hand. The bottle smashed against the ceramic tiles at her feet and shattered into a dozen pieces as the beer splashed over her feet, the bottom of her jeans, and even on the toes of Mateo's black cowboy boots.

"Oh crap, I am so sorry." She gasped and closed her eyes for an instant in an effort to wipe away the last of the erotic images that were completely consuming her. *Damn!* When she opened her eyes, there was a flurry of activity around her.

"Dawn, are you okay?" Chloe asked in a worried tone. She was already standing next to Dawn with her arm draped protectively around her shoulders. With a glance at Mateo, she added in an apologetic tone, "She's been really sick recently."

Fire erupted in Dawn's cheeks again. *This is your last chance to prove you are not a complete moron.* She drew in a cleansing breath and willed her voice to sound as normal as possible at this humiliating moment, but she couldn't bring herself to look directly at Mateo or his brothers. Focusing her gaze on the floor where the broken beer bottle was smashed, she managed to speak in a somewhat sane tone. "I'm fine, really. I don't know what happened; the bottle just slipped out of my hand."

"Thankfully, it doesn't appear you were cut by any of the broken glass, so no harm done," Mateo said in a soft tone as he knelt to pick up the broken pieces of the beer bottle from around her feet. "Let me buy you another one, that is, if you are feeling up to it?"

At least, she was wearing her nicest black flip-flops with rhinestones and she had painted her toenails a delicate shade of pink before coming here tonight. Did he notice? What had he just asked her? Dawn began to imagine how her toes, with their pretty pink nails, would look as she inched her foot up along his taut muscled thigh, headed toward his...*focus. What had he just asked her?*

"I should probably call it a-a night," she mumbled as she once again attempted to rein in her slutty thoughts. She still avoided looking at Mateo, because she didn't dare chance another fanatical episode like the one she just experienced. But when she glanced at Chloe, it was obvious by the expression on her face she was disappointed the night with these three gorgeous hunks was coming to an abrupt end after such a short time.

"Of course," he said in a worried tone. "I hope you don't have a relapse of whatever it was that made you sick." He held his out-stretched hand to her.

She hesitated for a second. If only being this close to him induced such a foolish reaction, did she dare touch him? But how could she not?

Her trembling hand slipped against his palm as he pulled her to her feet. He was taller than she by several inches she realized as her gaze was drawn upward. His dark shimmering eyes focused on her face. Their gazes met; her mind went blank once more.

"I would like to see you again if you'd be up for that?" he asked in a hushed voice as if he wanted only her to hear.

"Y-Yes," Dawn stammered. Her voice sounded far away. "I would like to see you again, too." *As soon as possible. Like in five minutes in my bed.*

"Tomorrow night?"

She tried to concentrate on his suggestion. It was Friday, tomorrow was Saturday. Tomorrow night was so far away. Should she suggest breakfast? Her voice didn't work. She nodded her head.

He smiled, exposing those perfect teeth again. Their stark whiteness made his skin look like rich bronzed satin. She was distracted by his enticing mouth for only a second before looking up and locking gazes with him once again. His fingers tightened around her hand, but she was only vaguely aware because she was lost in his hypnotizing gaze and nothing outside of this moment in time existed.

"Should I meet you here around this same time tomorrow night then?" he said. "We can grab a beer. I owe you one. Then maybe go dancing, a movie, or something if you would like?"

Dawn nodded her head again and stared mutely up at him. He was looking at her as if he didn't notice she was not able to speak, or unable to think, or be coherent in any ordinary way as long as she was in his presence.

"Same time, same place tomorrow then." He leaned down and whispered against her ear before he gently slid his hand away from hers and stepped back. The smile on his lips seemed to extend up to his shimmering gaze. *He smiled even with his eyes*, her entranced mind thought as she stared wordlessly up at him.

A return smile came naturally to her lips. If she was able to move, she just might reach out and grab his hand again and never let go. But as he backed up and turned to leave, she could do nothing more than stare numbly at his back as he walked away. It wasn't until Chloe grabbed her arm that the trance she seemed to be in began to crumble.

"What the hell was that all about?" Chloe giggled.

Dawn shrugged with an unconscious gesture. "What?"

"You and the sexy Apache stud. I thought he was going to do you right here in the pizza joint, right in front of God and everybody."

"I-we—nothing happened, really," she wasn't going to try to explain what actually happened, because there was no rational explanation.

Mateo Two Moons just invaded every one of her most intimate senses and stolen her mind and body. He'd basically rocked her world in every way, and that had been in the few short minutes he had been here. She was pretty sure nothing in her life would ever be the same again after tonight.

Chloe was practically shaking her by the shoulders as she stood in front of her and continued to talk excitedly. "Come on, girlfriend, you have to tell me what just happened here. That was like the hottest thing ever, right? I mean, was that some sort of mind-fucking telepathic sex going on there or what?"

All of a sudden, she remembered they were standing in the middle of a public establishment, with hordes of other people who might have witnessed the same sensual episode Chloe was talking about. She groaned inwardly. *Just kill me now.* She grabbed Chloe by the arm and pulled her along until they were out of the pizzeria and away from the curious stares she was certain were directed at them.

"It wasn't that obvious, was it?" she said in a whispered voice, even though they were alone out on the sidewalk now.

"Oh, hell yeah. It most certainly was." Chloe gasped. "So obvious and so incredibly hot. I started sweating and getting all horny just watching the two of you stare at one another like you were about to jump one another's bones right there. But his two gorgeous brothers didn't seem to notice at all, which is weird because, I mean, how could they not? They just paid the bill—even for the pizza and beers we had before they got there. Then they politely said goodbye to me like I was no longer worth their time, and waited out here on the sidewalk until he finished screwing you with his eyes and talking dirty in your ear. They all took off while you finished having a Mateo-gasm back there in the middle of the restaurant."

Dawn threw her hands over her face and groaned out loud. She knew Chloe wasn't exaggerating, because she had never experienced anything even as remotely erotic as what had just taken place between her and Mateo Two Moons with no more than their brief encounter, and in a crowded public place, no less. Well, except for her recent wet dreams, but she didn't want to go there again. Look at what happened when her thoughts wandered there earlier?

Still, her rebellious mind began to recall the arousing details of how the dangerous long-haired stranger in her dreams touched her mind and body as intimately as Mateo had done to her tonight with nothing more than his mere presence. Only with her crazy dreams, she almost convinced herself she had been sleep walking and hallucinating because she was ill, or bitten by a rare poisonous spider, or even that she was just losing her mind. But what happened tonight had taken place in front of Chloe and the entire patronage at the pizza place. This one wouldn't be so easy to explain to herself or anyone else.

"I don't know—that was just so—" Dawn still couldn't find the words to explain what had just taken place. She shook her head and shrugged in defeat. "Nothing like this has ever happened to me." But there was no denying the way her body and mind were still clinging to the mad sexual attraction she had for Mateo Two Moons. Life-changing might be a better way to describe how meeting him affected her.

Chloe chuckled, and tossed a long strand of hair back over her shoulder. She focused her gaze on Dawn and asked in an innocent tone of voice, "Um, so was it like lust at first sight? I mean, I don't think I've ever seen anything like that happen before, either. And I'm a little pissed it happened to you and not me, especially since there were two spare Apache sex gods who could have easily had their way with me."

Another shrug lifted Dawn's shoulders as she chuckled and tried to appear nonchalant even though there was nothing calm about her raging emotions. She stared back at her friend wishing she could confide in her about all the outlandish things that had been happening to her in the past week since they went to the Superstitions to hunt for the Lost Dutchman's Gold Mine. But there was no rational explanation for any of it, including the way she was feeling about meeting Mateo Two Moons tonight.

"Geez, I think I might be too embarrassed to come back here tomorrow night."

"But you will."

"Oh, hell yes," Dawn said without an instant of hesitation. Twenty-four hours from now she would be here or anywhere else Mateo Two Moons wanted her to be. But tomorrow seemed like forever right now.

****

"She is already under your spell," Anton Two Moons said to his youngest brother. "This silly game you are playing is all a waste of time. First, you make us go out to meet her and her friend at their campsite on the mountain so you can look at her from afar," he swept his hand through the air in a theatrical gesture. "And now, you talk us into pretending to be a bunch of yuppies carousing around town. And for what? What more do you need to know about her besides the fact she is your mate?"

Mateo retorted in an indignant tone. "How is it you consider this wasting time when time is all we have?"

A snide chortle escaped from Anton. "Guess you got me there, little brother. We do have a lot of time, as in forever."

"Well, it's still her destiny to be your mate. No amount of time can change that," Rafael added. "Why prolong it? It's great to have a mate to look after all your needs and well, you know, all that other stuff." Rafael chuckled when Anton punched him playfully in the arm.

Mateo shook his head and cut in, "It's not about some game or about that other stuff." He rolled his eyes. He heard both his brothers make exasperated noises. "I don't even know how to begin to explain why it's so important to me to be down here in Dawn's world with her, even if just for a little while before I take her up to the mountain. It just is."

He didn't grasp any of it yet, so how could he make his brothers understand? He had no doubt Dawn was partially under his vampire spell already—this was proven when she had come to the mountain in the middle of the night after he telepathically summoned her to him. As far as he knew, no one in his clan ever attempted to use their vampire power to beckon a real one to come to them, and he still had a hard time believing it worked. But it was then he realized how powerful and unbreakable their connection truly was, and how there was no changing their ultimate fate.

He didn't want to alter the fact she would become

his mate and bear his children, he just wanted to discover all there was to know about her as she was now—just a woman—and he desperately wanted to love her in the way a man is meant to love a woman. There would be so much more between them than there had been with all the other clan males and their human mates. He was determined he and Dawn would have a real love story first and he would do everything in his power to make that happen.

He found it hard to believe no one in his clan or any members of other Blood Clans in different locations ever questioned if it was possible for their kind to expand beyond their current limitations and outdated beliefs. They knew nothing of how the old traditions had come to be and if there could be a safer or easier way for the clans to survive in the modern world around them.

The males did not even know how their mates were chosen. Anton's woman, Nita, came from the Navajo tribe in Southern Utah. She had been a student at the University of Phoenix when she made her trek up to the Superstition Mountains to fulfill her destiny. Anton had been waiting for her and without hesitation he drank the blood from her neck, wrist, and lastly and most importantly, from the large artery in her thigh...the final phase of the mating process before he led her from her previous life as a twenty-year old college student to a life of obscurity with her immortal mate.

Nita gifted him with three sons and three daughters in the past fifteen years. Their oldest son, Chaz, was fourteen, and he would be the next dhampyre—half-human, half-vampire—in their Blood Clan to claim his mate when he reached maturity at one hundred years of age.

Lydia, Rafael's mate, had come from much farther away—from the Algonquian Indian tribe in Canada. The delicate beauty had shown up on the mountain eleven years ago. On a camping vacation with friends, she disappeared on the first night and was never seen or heard from again. As was usually the case, it was assumed she wandered out into the rugged terrain and fallen into some hidden cavern or abyss where there was no chance of finding her. But she had been spirited away to her destiny on the highest peaks of the Superstition Mountains to live out what remained of her human life at the side of her vampire mate.

Their first born dhampyre children had been twin daughters, then eight more years passed before she had given birth to a male. He was a handsome three-year-old who would someday follow in his father's footsteps among the ancient clan. Lydia was soon due to give birth again to their fourth child and already special ceremonies were being conducted in their village with the hopes she would produce another male dhampyre.

It was during this process when real ones, the term used to describe humans since the beginning of their time, were in the most danger from the clan, because more blood was needed than usual for the primeval rituals held before an impending birth.

Now, at last, it was Mateo's time to fulfill his destiny with the woman who had been preordained to spend eternity at his side. His mate, Dawn—Udaya—was so drastically different from the other eternal mates in his clan...she was older and not of Native American descent. Although he couldn't explain it, he believed she was also the beginning of a new way of life for his clan.

He knew he didn't need to drink the blood from her thigh to make her his...nothing could have stopped their fates from entwining once she had been drawn to the mountain. But meeting her in the restaurant in Apache Junction tonight only proved to Mateo they belonged together in both of their worlds.

Maybe his brothers and the rest of his clan did feel it was foolish to waste time with mere human traditions. But they did have forever to live their immortal lives hidden in the shadows and caves of the Superstitions, and for now, Mateo loved being here with her in her world. What would a few days or even a few weeks matter?

Chapter Six

Mateo clearly remembered the day his grandfather, Drago, told him what was known about the history of their clan. Mateo had been only fifteen years old—over eighty-five years ago. He could recall every word, and there had not been a day since when he had not contemplated the many unknown facets of his ancient breed. Their past, however, seemed to hold very few clues to what could be done to improve their future.

"This is the story of how our people came to be and it has been passed down through the generations. It is a fact, my grandson, that since the beginning of mankind, there have been mysterious societies and hidden tribes living in total seclusion; some because their secrets are too terrifying, and too unbelievable to reveal to the mere mortals who would prefer to never know of their existence. For this reason, and for our own survival, the Blood Clan chose to dwell in the most secluded places around the world, where we can live in peace and total isolation.

It is believed that centuries and centuries ago, somewhere in a European country, a relatively young male vampire—only a hundred years old—bit a human woman in the neck. This was a normal thing for his breed to do. But for some unknown reason he didn't drain her of all her blood and kill her as is the usual process when a vampire drinks the blood of any human.

Instead, he drank only a small of amount of blood from her neck, then another small amount from her wrist, and finally more blood from the large vein in her thigh. He forced himself to stop after drinking these three small amounts of blood from these different parts of her body. No one knows why he did this, but this process induced a trance-like state that put the woman completely under the vampire's control.

He took her to the top of the mountain where he dwelled in the deep caverns since he had been turned into an undead being by another vampire who had bitten him back in the beginning.

The human woman was cared for by the vampire, and in return, she was completely devoted to him in every way. When he awoke from his daytime slumber, he would descend from the mountain to quench his thirst for human blood so he would not be tempted to drink more of his mate's and possibly kill her. But he did give her droplets of his own blood to drink occasionally, because he hoped his immortal blood would keep her strong and healthy so he could enjoy her human companionship for as long as possible.

Every morning at dawn, before he went back into the cave to sleep during the daylight hours, he would make love to her. Although it seemed impossible for a vampire to sire a child, she became pregnant, and nine months later she gave birth to a female child that seemed human in all ways. A year later, she gave birth to a healthy baby boy. As their vampire father slept in the dark cave on the top of the mountain during the day, their human mother cared for these miracle children in the hidden encampment they called home.

At night, while their immortal father hunted for the

blood of humans below the mountain, they slept beside their mother peacefully unaware they lived an unusual life unlike any other children in the world. They existed on the meat of wildlife they killed, and berries or roots when available and created the most basic type of life from the land they lived upon.

Three other sons and five more daughters were born over the ensuing years and as the brood of dhampyre—half-vampire, half-human—children grew into young adulthood, it seemed none of them inherited any of their father's vampire traits. The girls became women, maturing into their twenties and beyond in a natural human way.

But as each of the male children approached their quarter-century age, noticeable changes began to occur with them. Sunlight began to burn their eyes and skin. During the day they slept beside their father in the secluded cave. Their throats burned with an intensity no amount of water could quench. Under the cover of night their father would take them to the villages below the mountain so they could satisfy their unnatural cravings for human blood without harming their human mother and female siblings. Like their father, they never appeared to look any older than men in their mid-twenties.

As the years passed, the human mother grew too old to bear more children; she eventually became elderly and frail. Her vampire mate couldn't bear the thought of losing her, so he bit her in the neck again. This time, he drained enough of her blood so she would become an immortal and they could spend eternity together. She grew young and beautiful again. Her need for human blood was minimal, so her vampire mate *would bring her small vessels of blood from his hunts in the human village below the mountain.*

Those first females born to the original vampire and his human mate remained at the hidden encampment their entire lives. They continued to grow older in typical human ways. Worried they would die the father bit the oldest of the girls in the neck and drained her blood like he did their mother. But instead of growing young and beautiful, she died. He attempted to save another daughter, and she died after he bit her, too. Then, he killed a third daughter by biting her neck and draining her blood.

The sire vampire realized only his mate and sons were destined to live for eternity. The remaining three daughters lived for many years until they died of what appeared to be natural causes associated with old age. The male offspring continued to age in years, but not in appearance.

As each of those four sons born into this original clan turned one hundred years old, another strange phenomenon occurred. For each of them, a human woman traveled to the mountain, draw by some unknown compulsion to seek her vampire mate. These women would submit willingly to the dangerous immortal men who came to them while they were in a dream-like state.

The vampire would bite them first on their neck, then on their wrist, and finally on the large vein at the top of their thigh just as their vampire father had done to his human mate when he first started their unique clan.

Afterward, the women would accompany their vampire mate to the top of the mountain where they would be completely devoted to their mate, give birth to his dhampyre children, and live out their human lives until they were no longer fertile. Like that very first human woman of the Blood Clan, each of the women were bitten in the neck one last time and drained of nearly all their blood by their vampire mates until the instant their hearts would stop beating. They, too, would now become immortal—returning to the youthful state they had been when they were first drawn to the mountain—becoming forever, and in every sense of the meaning, an 'eternal mate' to the vampire who claimed them decades earlier.

The first clan grew in numbers, and as the village filled with children and the human women who mated with the male vampires, it became apparent they needed more from the villages of the real ones than just blood for the male vampires. They also needed food, blankets, clothing, and other necessities for the real ones who lived among them.

The original vampire traveled down to the settlement at the base of the mountain and chose five men he felt were trustworthy. He placed them under his vampire spell, compelling them to bring necessary provisions to the mountaintop village for the growing brood of dhampyre children and their human mothers. These men were called the Clan Society and it was considered an honor to be a member of this ultra-secret group. The elite membership was passed down through the generations and none of them ever betrayed the Blood Clans they served.

In time, male vampire descendants began to take their mates and offspring to other parts of the world to start their own clans. Now, many Blood Clans exist around the world...hidden in their secluded mountaintop villages, concealed encampments, or secret jungle compounds; living much the same as they have since the very beginning when the original vampire first began his clan."

Mateo knew the time for change was imminent. He was prepared to be the trailblazer for the new life he envisioned for his kind if he could only convince his grandfather.

"This is the most ridiculous thing I've ever heard," Drago said in an aggravated tone. "She is your eternal mate. Nothing else matters except that she is here, and she is fertile and will bear you many sons." He stared at his youngest grandson, disbelief on his face.

"I realize we are destined to be together forever, and I would never think of not fulfilling my obligations to my clan. But, Grandfather, times are so much different now than they were when you left your original clan in Mexico over two hundred years ago to come here."

Mateo summoned more courage as he spoke in their native Apache language to his elder relative, the noble chief of their secret vampire clan, and a man he never wanted to anger or disappoint in any way. This speech had been rehearsed over and over in his mind for the last few days. He had to get it right the first time, because he knew his grandfather's decision would be final and uncompromising.

"Back then, there was no other way of life for our kind other than living here on the mountain in complete seclusion. But now," he continued, sounding much more confident than he felt, "We have learned to walk among the real ones without being detected during the nighttime."

Mateo met the unwavering ebony gaze of his grandfather. Although Drago was over two centuries older than Mateo, the two men looked as if they could be twenty-five-year old twins. "I feel there are many changes coming for our kind," Mateo added. "And if we are open to accept them, our clan can only grow stronger. Because of the Clan Society from the reservation who provides us with learning tools from the real ones, we are well-educated and can speak several languages. Although our book knowledge is vast, we know little of the world beyond these mountains. But I know there is more than just existing in the caves and shadows in the darkness of night. I just need to find a way to prove it."

He mentioned the Clan Society, because their obligation to the vampire clan had expanded over the centuries. Now these select few did even more than provide the vampire village with necessities for living or tools to advance their knowledge of the world below the mountain.

As the modern world had become more dangerous for the vampires to hunt for their own prey, the Clan Society had also begun to provide the mature male vampires with fresh blood sources to fuel their need for blood. Born as dhampyres—the children produced from a vampire father and human mother—their appetite for blood was minimal, but it could not be denied or their thirst would become uncontrollable and they could be capable of killing even a loved one to satisfy their unnatural cravings.

Most of the blood sources brought to the mountain by members of the Clan Society were homeless alcoholics and drug addicts who lived on the streets of the reservation or in the slums of nearby Phoenix. They were for the most part deemed by society to be non-productive members of the human race whom no one missed once they disappeared.

But occasionally, in between the arrival of the Clan Society with hand-picked blood sources, there was always the tempting lure of the gold seekers and hikers who wondered much too close to the caves at the top of the mountain. These curious real ones provided an additional feast of blood the vampires could gorge themselves on for days or even weeks if they were young and healthy.

Mateo placed his hand over his heart and continued to speak to his grandfather, who had hardly said a word so far. "For all eternity we will be the honored Blood Clan of the Apaches, and I am a proud member of this clan. Once we learn how to use all the knowledge we've gained from the world of the real ones, we will be able to ensure a better and safer existence for our kind." Mateo paused, expecting his grandfather to disagree or at least say something, but the elder vampire remained silent.

"You have always said that as our population continues to grow, so must our ability to learn how live among the real ones without being detected. I know we are able to be with them without arousing suspicion because my brothers and I have been doing it for many years now."

"I have worried much about this," Drago finally said. He shook his head slowly. "Sometimes I think I was wrong to let the Clan Society bring us all those books and modern gadgets from the world of the real ones. They should have just provided us with blood sources and nothing more. Now, we—you younger ones—take so many risks with the knowledge you have gained."

"It's not feasible to think we can continue to exist without advancing along with the rest of the world. We walk such a fine line of trying to remain hidden in these mountains and blend in with the world down below. I believe there will come a time when we will have to learn how to live among the real ones all the time if we are to survive," Mateo added.

A heavy sigh fell from Drago's mouth. "I have thought much about this, too. But it really worries me, Grandson. I don't know how this would be possible. Our survival up to this point has only been because we have been able to remain hidden from the rest of the world down below."

"But, Grandfather, eventually modern technology will catch up with us. Every time a jet flies over the tops of the mountain I wonder if we will be discovered. Every day the real ones discover new ways to search the hidden places of this earth. There will come a time, when someone—somewhere—discovers one of the secret villages of a Blood Clan, whether it will be ours or one of the others in a different part of the world, then all of our kind will be exposed because they will hunt for us until they find every one of us."

Mateo saw a flash of alarm flare up in his grandfather's gaze. The older vampire's jaw grew rigid as he considered the truth Mateo had spoken. "But I can promise you this," he rushed on, "I will never stop looking for ways to protect our clan. My desire to spend time with my mate in the world of the real ones will only help with this quest, although this is not the only reason I am asking you to give me time to be with her in her world." He stressed the depth of his devotion to his clan by reaching out and placing his hand on his grandfather's bare shoulder as he went on with his prepared speech.

Drago smiled down at the spot where his youngest grandson's hand rested against his shoulder. "Help me to understand why you ask for this time to be with her then. You could mate with her in the ways of our clan and still continue with your research to learn of ways to protect our future."

Mateo sighed. "I realize I am asking to go against the customs of our clan as far as the mating process is concerned, but only for a little while. I just want to know this woman as she is now—a real one. I want to learn all her human desires and needs. Because, as you and I already know, once she is brought here to the village under my spell, she will be little more than my love slave and the mother of my children until she is no longer fertile and I turn her into a vampire to be at my side for the rest of eternity."

Drago remained silent for a few moments. He stared intently at his youngest grandson.

Mateo could tell his grandfather was processing all he said. Drago was an ancient vampire, but as far as his grandson was concerned there was no man—real one or immortal—who was as wise. Even though he might wish it wasn't so, Drago understood they must always strive to expand their knowledge of the modern and evolving world below if they had any hope of protecting their clan and their secret way of life here in the Superstitions, as well as the other clans all over the world. Mateo also knew regardless of the decision his grandfather made today, nothing would change Dawn Malone's eventual fate.

Mateo's grandmother, Raven, had not had a choice, either, as did any of the human mates. His grandfather told him when he first arrived here in the Superstition Mountains after leaving the Blood Clan of his birth behind in old Mexico, Raven had been waiting here on the mountain for him.

After he made her his mate, he descended the mountain to select their Clan Society. They were all members of the Jiricalla Apache tribe who lived in Raven's village at the base of the Superstitions. The Clan Society escorted Drago back up the mountain to where his mate waited for him to return. Then they had taken the couple to the highest summit of the mountains so they could make a home in the sacred caves hidden deep in the mountaintop.

Those caves also contained strange shimmery veins as bright as sunrays lining the rock walls. At the time, none of those tribal members understood the extent of the wealth contained in the secret caves, and although the Apache tribe did benefit some from the gold in the cave through the years, their main objective was to protect the Blood Clan at all costs. Much of the treasure was used to provide protection for the dangerous secrets concealed at the top of the Superstitions.

After Drago and his mate settled into their home on the mountain over two hundred years earlier, she gave birth to fourteen dhampyres—thirteen daughters and finally one son. Had they not had any sons, Drago's clan would have ended with him.

When years passed and Raven bore no more

children, and her body grew ravished with age, Drago bit her neck and drained her of blood so she would become his eternal mate. She sat at Drago's side now looking as youthful and lovely as the day he had come to her, nearly two centuries earlier, even though she had been a middle-aged woman when she had become an immortal.

The thirteen daughters born to Drago and Raven Two Moons moved down to the Apache village below when they become young adults. The children these female dhampyres gave birth to, whether male or female, also were real ones in every way and lived human lives like their mothers.

Mateo's father, Antonio, was the one son Raven had given birth to. Producing more male dhampyres for Drago's clan rested solely on Antonio's shoulders. Over a hundred years ago, he had come of age and found his chosen mate, Rosa. She had come to him from the Mescalero Apache tribe in New Mexico at the young age of sixteen. Six dhampyre children within sixteen years had been the result of their mating; three daughters, and thankfully, three sons.

But she had not borne any more children and had become Antonio's mate about forty years earlier. Once the three girls, Mateo's sisters, were mature enough to begin their own lives, they moved to the village below, lived their normal human lives, grown old and died of natural causes in the past couple of decades. The responsibility of saving Drago's clan from extinction was passed to Antonio and Rosa's three sons.

Since there were no guarantees when it came to the sex of dhampyre offspring or how many children each mate would conceive, and because it took a full century before the male members of the Blood Clan were mature enough to seek their own mates and produce offspring, the survival of all clans were always in peril. Some ancient clans in other parts of the world now existed with only the original leader and his mate, because they had not been able to produce any male dhampyres.

Since Mateo's two older brothers, Anton and Rafael, found their mates, the dhampyre children their women had given birth to so far romped freely around the mountaintop village until they were old enough to seek their own destinies. They dressed in the old Apache style of loincloths, and spoke a mixture of English and Apache when they were in the hidden encampment. But like every member of Drago's clan, they were also well-educated in the modern ways of the world below.

On the occasions when they would go down to the world of the real ones, they looked and acted like any other children of Native American descent. The Clan Society from the Apache Reservation took the dhampyre children to movies, museums, libraries or anywhere else they desired to go during the daylight hours. Long before sunset, however, the children would be returned to the mountain.

Unless there was an extreme emergency and they were forced to come to the top of the mountain, not even the members of the Clan Society, who were promised safe passage at all times, wanted to be caught in the vicinity of the Superstitions at nightfall when the mature male vampires awoke and left the caves.

Now, at last, Mateo's mate had arrived. He had waited a bit longer than his brothers. Their mates had shown up at almost the same time as their century birth date. But Mateo's hundred-year date happened almost two months ago, and it had been a long agonizing couple of months until Dawn Malone finally appeared on the mountain.

He had been consumed with seeing her for the first time and spent most of his time trying to imagine what she would look like. There had even been times when he thought of going in search of her. A couple of weeks ago he actually brought this idea up to his grandfather. After all, he had come here to meet his mate when he had become old enough, hadn't he? But Drago told him to be patient. Now that his mate was finally here, ironically, it was Mateo who was asking his grandfather to be patient.

"I know you would never put the clan in intentional danger. But it could still be risky if you spend so much time in the world of the real ones," Drago finally said. "We have not survived this long by being careless."

"If there is any chance of that happening, I would immediately finish the mating process and bring Dawn—my mate—to the mountain."

Drago's thick brows raised in surprise. "You have started the process, but stopped? Why would you do that if you wanted to wait to bring her up here?"

"It was not until I began the mating process I realized how badly I want us to spend time in her world before I bring her to ours for the rest of eternity."

"Did you drink the blood of her thigh?"

Mateo drew in a heavy sigh and shook his head. He knew sucking blood from their chosen mate's large artery in their thigh was the final step in producing complete control over their woman's mind and body.

Once he pierced this major artery with his teeth, he would suck Dawn's blood until she lost consciousness. When she awoke a short time later, her body, mind, and soul would be completely under his control for the rest of her mortal life, then for all eternity once he turned her into a vampire when she grew too old to bear his children.

"No, only from her neck and" Mateo hesitated, before adding, "And that's when I realized I wanted to wait." He didn't dare tell his grandfather already sucked the blood from her neck twice and once from her wrist without completing the mating process. Even now, just recalling how intoxicating Dawn's blood tasted on those three occasions caused Mateo's mouth to water with the desire to sample her sweet blood again soon.

Drago played idly with one of his long thick braids. "This starting and stopping is worrisome. It's never been done before as far as I know. We don't know how it might affect her. It could make her weak and sick at the very least. What if she remembers something about being bitten? It could have dangerous consequences for us if she remembers anything and tells other real ones." He chuckled. "Not that anyone would believe her."

"I won't let anything happen that could even remotely draw attention to our clan, Grandfather, and I definitely won't let anything happen to her." Mateo recalled Dawn's friend saying she had been sick…could that have anything to do with him biting her? He wouldn't risk her health because of his own desires. Until he was ready to complete the mating process he had to be strong and not allow himself to bite her again.

His gaze moved to the large cavern where so many

more secrets were concealed. He hoped he could convey how dedicated he was to his clan, and yet, still make his grandfather understand how important waiting to make Dawn his mate was to him.

Drago focused his dark eyes on his grandson. "I can't help but wonder how you will be able to hide what you are from her and other real ones if you try to spend too much time with her. You can't chance being caught out in daylight. So much is at risk for you in her world. It would be disastrous to our entire clan if anything happened to you."

"I won't let that happen, Grandfather," Mateo said with determination.

Drago's gaze moved out toward the hidden encampment as if he was assessing the private world he protected for so long here in the Superstitions. Unlike the Apache reservation in the valley below where the real ones lived in prefab housing and drove expensive pickup trucks, nothing had changed here on the mountaintop since the Clan Society first accompanied Drago and Raven here. Wickiups made of sticks and clay provided housing for the dhampyre children and their human mothers. They slept on animal skins just as their Apache ancestors had done from the beginning of time.

"Help me to understand why this is so important, Grandson." Drago asked. His thick black brows drew together in a quizzical expression.

Mateo shrugged his shoulders. "I wish I could. I don't even understand why this is so important to me. But I do understand how desperately important it is to keep all of this—all of us—safe." He waved his hand out toward the encampment.

Once again, he wished he could explain it better to his grandfather, to his brothers and parents... and mostly, to himself. But he had always been curious about the world below and the real ones, more curious it seemed than anyone else in his clan. Ever since he could remember he wanted to explore this other world, which was so drastically different from the secret world of the Blood Clan. As a very young child he constantly pleaded to go down to the Apache village to learn first-hand how the real ones lived. His grandfather had given into him and commanded members of the Clan Society to take him down to the village.

Mateo's curiosity continued to grow as he matured. He ventured out beyond the Indian village on his own once he was old enough not to draw any attention to himself. Occasionally, his older brothers would join him, but they did not share his intense curiosity about the real ones.

He discovered libraries containing books on subjects he had never known existed, because the only books brought to the mountain by the Clan Society were educational ones or classic novels they felt would be interesting. At the library, he poured over books about ancient legends involving his kind—the myths about half-vampire half-human children—dhampyre—only they weren't just myths that existed only in horror novels and scary movies. He began to question the phobias and old superstitions that kept his clan prisoners in their secret world. But so far, he had been too worried about risking the safety of his clan to test out any of his theories.

It was also at the public library where he first met and interacted with real ones who were not a part of the

Apache tribe. He realized he could easily blend into their world during the night time. Even more importantly, he seemed to have no problem controlling his urge to drink blood when he was with humans as long as he drank a small amount from the blood sources in the village before he descended from the mountain top.

That had been before he tasted the decadent blood that ran through the veins of Dawn Malone. Since that first drop of her sweet blood, he had a constant and unnatural craving for more. But maybe he could control his longing to drink her blood now that he knew there was a chance of putting her health in danger. Finding the strength not to bite her still might prove to be his greatest test. Mateo hoped it was one he could pass.

Raven remained quietly at Drago's side throughout this conversation, but now she held her hand out toward her youngest grandson. Mateo took her out-stretched hand without hesitation. Her head tilted to the side and her long ebony hair fell across the side of her face and cascaded over one of her shoulders. Even though she was ancient in years, with her smooth high cheekbones, full lips and sparkling black eyes she was the epitome of a beautiful young Apache woman.

A worried frown creased her brow as she asked, "So, you want to be with this woman while she still has a will of her own, before you put her under your vampire spell? But what if this woman does not want to be with you in her world? I cannot imagine anyone would not love you as much as we all do, but what if she doesn't? How would it make you feel when you must bring her here to be your mate? You cannot change the destiny set in motion since the day you were born."

Mateo drew in a heavy sigh. His grandmother was a wise woman. She would always think of the rational things he never considered. But since meeting Udaya at the pizzeria last night, he was fairly certain he did not have to worry about being rejected. She seemed every bit as enchanted with him as he was with her.

He shrugged and smiled at his grandmother. "Well, I guess if that were to happen, I would welcome the challenge of making her change her mind about me." He winked and added with confidence, "But I have a feeling she will be begging me to make her my mate."

Chapter Seven

Tonight Dawn wanted to revisit the crazy dream—
or trance—or whatever it was that led her to the
stranger on the Superstition Mountain. She needed to
see the man's face, so she could prove once and for all
it wasn't Mateo Two Moons in those bizarre episodes.
But she had fallen into a deep dreamless sleep and
awoken feeling the most rested she had in days.

For a brief moment, she thought about getting up
and doing her usual Saturday morning chores, which
included cleaning her small apartment, doing a couple
loads of laundry, and weekly grocery shopping. But this
was not an ordinary Saturday morning. There was no
way to define the way she was feeling since meeting
Mateo last night. She felt as if she was teetering on the
edge of a massive black abyss, but rather than keeping
away from the dangerous rim, she couldn't wait to
plunge into the unknown.

How crazy was it that she had only been in his
presence for less than half an hour last night, yet, the
excitement of seeing him again tonight was actually
making her feel giddy? She grabbed the extra pillow on
her bed and hugged it to her chest as she smiled. This
was seriously insane and the last thing she needed right
now. She tried to remind herself the move to Arizona
was so she could concentrate on herself and her
teaching career. Just a week ago, she thought all she

needed to make her life perfect was to get laid.

But that was before Mateo entered her life. Now everything was different.

Whoa. Slow down, girlfriend. She reminded herself she knew nothing—absolutely nothing—about this Mateo Two Moons. They had barely met, and except for the fact he was the sexiest, hottest, most gorgeous man she had been privileged to meet up to this point in her life, and probably for the remainder of her life, they might not have anything in common. She hugged the pillow tighter and grinned in spite of the absurdity of it all.

His shimmering dark gaze flashed before her eyes and the sizzling memory of his smile echoed through her mind. An undeniable flame flared up in the core of her female parts and inched through her belly. There was obviously of some sort of connection going on between them and it had been strong enough to be obvious to everyone else, too. She didn't want to think about that embarrassing episode last night, especially since she would be returning to the pizza place again tonight.

That reminded her...how much longer until she saw him again? She giggled and glanced at the slow moving hands of the clock sitting on her night stand, then shook her head and rolled her eyes. Good thing her middle schoolers couldn't see what their teacher acted like outside of school.

Maybe they could go someplace besides the pizza parlor after they met up tonight? They could always come back here? For a drink or something? She should definitely put clean sheets on her bed. Just in case. Maybe buy some condoms? No, the way Mateo looked he was probably prepared for everything. Would she even be able to please a man like him in bed? What the hell was she thinking?

He said a beer and maybe dancing or a movie; yet, she was already planning some serious sexual activity. If she appeared to be too anxious, she might end up being a one-night stand, and already she knew she was wanting so much more from this man than one night.

Dawn pushed the pillow away and bolted up in bed as the shocking revelation hit her. She wanted Mateo Two Moons in a way she had never wanted another man before...like in forever. Last night that little four letter word filtered through her mind unexpectedly— love. *Wow*. She had met him less than twelve hours ago and she was already in way over her head. She glanced back at the clock, and got giddy all over again.

Over eleven hours to get ready before she saw him, and she had nothing to wear. Well, nothing that seemed perfect enough, anyway. She should go shopping for something new since it was such a special occasion; maybe buy some new sheets for her bed, too. Just in case. *Stop it.*

Ten and a half hours later, Dawn stood before the full-length mirror hanging on her bathroom door and scrutinized every inch from her head to her toes. Although she did not think she was beauty pageant material, she didn't think she was all that bad, either. Tonight she wanted to be beautiful, though, and she had gone to extra lengths to look her very best.

Her naturally straight pale blonde hair was now hanging in soft waves to the middle of her back and she had parted it on the side so her long chin length bangs curved teasingly over her right eye. She had taken more time with her makeup, too.

Normally, she wore only mascara and lip gloss. But she had given herself the works; an extra spritz of her new cologne, aptly called Scents of the Desert, a light layer of foundation, powder, blush, two coats of mascara, as well as a trace of green shadow to enhance the flecks of jade in her hazel eyes. Instead of her usual colorless lip gloss, Dawn decided to wear a shimmering deep mauve gloss she thought made her lips look extra kissable. That is, if Mateo Two Moons should get the urge to kiss her tonight.

Hey, a girl can hope, right?

Her wanton thoughts were off and running again, imagining how his mouth would descend down upon her anxious lips, claiming them in a devouring kiss that would leave her breathless and hungry for so much more. *Damn.* She just might have to start writing romance novels now that she had met Mateo Two Moons. He seemed to inspire her to be very prolific and creative…in a sexually explicit way.

Uninvited, and for just an instant, the memory of the weird neck and wrist biting incidents in her unsettling dreams wafted through her thoughts. She forcibly pushed all the bad thoughts out of her mind as quickly as they entered. After tonight, she hoped all her realistic-like dreams or horrifying nightmares of strange encounters with faceless men on mountaintops would be replaced with something real; something she sensed she had been waiting for her entire life.

This had to have been the longest day in history, Dawn determined as she glanced at the clock on her bedside table again. She looked back at her reflection in the mirror and gave an affirmative nod of her head. To her surprise, she found the perfect outfit in her closet earlier today, so she didn't need to go shopping for anything new. For this special date, she had chosen a tight-fitting pair of indigo denim jeans that accentuated her long legs and hugged her in all the right places.

Her high-heeled black western style boots made her legs look even longer and thinner than her five foot six-inch frame. She topped her outfit off with a silky white tank and a cropped black blazer. Just a tiny bit sexy, but not too much for their first date, Dawn decided as she turned away from the mirror and took a deep breath.

As she pulled the door shut to her apartment, she realized her hands were shaking. It wasn't like she had never been on a date before. Well, actually she had never been on a date with a man like Mateo Two Moons before now. Her heartbeat pounded wilder against her breast with each step she took as she walked the few blocks from her apartment to the place where they were meeting. When she turned the last corner to the street where the pizzeria was located, her excitement began to turn to panic. Now her frantic heart nearly stopped beating altogether.

What if he didn't show up? She was stood up by a blind date once and suffered quite a blow to her ego, even though she had never even met the no-show loser. But this would be different. This would be devastating, like the end of the world devastating. If Mateo Two Moons stood her up tonight, she would surely die. *Geez. Stop it, already.*

She was acting like a teenager who had fallen in love for the first time. There it was again, that four letter word. Or maybe it was just lust, like Chloe suggested last night. Before she had a chance to analyze the crazy notion, Mateo was there. She skidded to a stop only a few inches in front of him. Once again, her breath stopped short in her throat.

"Dawn, you look so beautiful tonight," he said in a husky voice.

"So do you. I mean—" words failed her as her gaze locked with the glistening raven eyes looking down at her from within the most amazing face she had ever glimpsed. Did women in this day and age still swoon, she wondered? That old-fashioned word might be the only one to describe what she was feeling right now, and she knew about these old-fashioned things because, after all, she was a history teacher.

Her knees felt as if they would buckle at any second. A wildfire erupted from somewhere inside her and was shooting sizzling flames through her entire body, leaving her nothing more than a melted puddle at his feet. The breath was still caught in her dry throat and she couldn't form one coherent thought. Yes, she was fairly certain this was called swooning, with a side helping of that little four letter word called love.

A tender smile curved his mouth. He reached out with his fingertips as if he just needed to touch her. It was just a light brush against her cheek, but it vibrated through Dawn's entire body.

"Are you hungry?" he asked.

Speak, she commanded—her mind appeared to be frozen in dumb ass mode. *At least try to act like a sane person.* Would that ever be possible when she was in this man's presence? "Um? Not really," she managed to say without stuttering. *Well, not for food anyway.* And she did put clean sheets on her bed. You know, just in case.

If there was one thing she was certain about right now, though, it was she did not want to return to the very public scene of last night's crime of passion. "But if you are, I'd just go for a salad or something light. There's a quaint little restaurant down the street. I've never been there to eat, but it looks nice." Three normal sounding sentences in a row. *Wow.* Maybe, she was regaining control of her mind again.

Her wandering gaze automatically scanned his entire body of its own accord. He was wearing a white shirt again, but not a western one tonight. This shirt was loose fitting and looked to be made of a fine silk material with tiny buttons rather than snaps running down the front. It was tucked casually into the low waistband of a pair of black jeans. Encircling his neck was a thick silver chain that shimmered each time his shirt collar parted. He wore the same black cowboy boots he had worn last night, but they appeared to have been given a polish and shine for tonight.

Their outfits almost matched, she realized. *Together we are perfection* was the only thought that flitted through her mind before his deep voice brought her back to reality.

"I know of a place. We can start with drinks and conversation. Then we can have a late dinner afterward if we get hungry."

"Perfect," she said with a nod of her head. *Yes, he is.*

"Did you walk here?"

She nodded her head. "I don't live far," she added. He slid his arm around her shoulders as if they had known one another forever. Yes, they felt perfect together.

Being this close to him she could smell his musky cologne, but tonight it only reminded her of how sexy he smelled. Dior? *Maybe.* Intoxicating? *Definitely.* Her knees grew weak again. Thankfully, she was leaning into him and his body supported her as they walked. They were headed away from the pizzeria now. She had no idea where he was taking her, but it didn't matter. She knew she would follow him anywhere.

All those silly clichés about romance and love at first sight might have some merit after all. Maybe she really should write a romance novel.

"There's this little out-of-the-way place on the edge of the reservation. It's my favorite place to stop for a beer, but it's not a dive or anything." His voice grew almost apologetic as if he worried she would think a restaurant on the reservation was beneath her.

"I would love that," she answered without hesitation. "I've been hoping to check out some of the local hangouts now that I live here. I hate feeling like a newcomer or tourist."

They stopped beside a big dark colored pickup. She had no doubt this truck belonged to Mateo. If there was one thing she already learned about the locals in this part of Arizona, it was that almost all of them drove huge trucks decked out with every fancy adornment possible.

Even in the dim glow of the streetlight, she could tell this extended cab truck was no exception. The rims on the oversized tires were shiny silver spokes, running boards of heavy stamped silver ran beneath both the front and back doors, and beefy silver bumpers guarded both the façade and rear of the truck. As he opened the door for her, she gratefully accepted his hand to help boost her up so she could climb into the tall cab. A distinct odor greeted her nose.

He closed the door and hurried around to the driver side before she had a chance to comment. But once he was seated next to her, she couldn't refrain from saying something. "This has a new car smell or, I mean, new truck smell. Did you buy it recently?"

He chuckled as he started the engine. "I was just thinking of how intoxicating your cologne is. It reminds me of Yucca blossoms."

"Thank you. I bought this cologne at a little boutique in town. It's made locally and it's called 'Scents of the Desert'. Seemed perfect."

A smile curved his lips as he turned toward her. "It is perfect. As for the truck, I bought it earlier this evening."

Dawn giggled although she knew he was serious. *This evening? Like right before he met me earlier? Would he buy a brand new pickup just for our date? Of course not. Maybe he ordered it a long time ago and it just arrived today, so he picked it up tonight. That's probably it.*

The cab of the luxurious truck came alive with mystical acoustic guitar music when he started the engine. Its hauntingly beautiful chords filled the interior of the vehicle and Dawn's senses with a feeling of enchantment. So far, everything about this night felt like a fairy-tale.

"That's really beautiful," she whispered, pointing toward the blue lights of the truck stereo.

"That's Joseph Red Feather. He's a very talented Apache musician. Have you heard any of his music before?"

"No," she answered truthfully.

"I'll take you to see him play in person sometime. If you would like to go?"

Her heart skipped a beat. He was already talking about another date. Could he be feeling the same crazy emotions about her as she was feeling about him? "Yes, I would like that very much."

"It's a date then," he said with a smile as he turned to look directly into her eyes.

She was helpless to resist gazing back at him. His grin was infectious and a smile came easily to her lips as her eyes peered into his glistening gaze. The cab was lit with a dim overhead light and his eyes were filled with such an unexpected look of tenderness she was instantly overwhelmed with intense feelings she could not understand. A tear appeared in the corner of her right eye and began rolling silently down the side of her face.

He reached out and gently wiped the rebel tear away before it rolled to the edge of her jawbone. His touch snapped her out of the trance his gaze had drawn her into. "I-I'm so sorry to be so emotional. I don't know what came over me," she murmured as she fought to control her wayward emotions.

In a hushed voice, he replied, "I felt it, too. It was so powerful." His palm rested against the side of her face. "We can't deny it, Udaya—Dawn. I am your destiny and you are mine."

He pulled his hand away from her face as if he had been burned and looked away. "Now, it's my turn to be sorry. I shouldn't have said that. We've just met. You must think I'm a crazy Indian."

Dawn sat unmoving and unable to think straight. Udaya? That was how her name was pronounced in Apache, wasn't it? But how did she even know that? It wasn't like she spoke any Apache, because she didn't. His words were spinning through her mind.

He was her destiny? She was his destiny? Those words seemed vaguely familiar, but who even talked like that? Yet, even though his choice of words sounded so old-fashioned and strange in this day and age, the meaning was clear. She felt it last night when they first met, and obviously, so had he. If there was such a thing as destiny, then she had been destined to move here to Arizona just so she could meet this man.

Chapter Eight

The little pub at the edge of the White Mountain Apache Reservation was perfect. The entire evening was turning out to be perfect. No one could be more perfect than Mateo Two Moons. Perfect was the tone of the entire night so far.

He requested a cozy little booth at the back of the room. They sat across the table from one another so they could look at each other. Several times he reached across the table and lightly touched Dawn's hand as they talked.

Since she had a deep love of American History, which was obviously why she had become a history teacher, and he knew as much about history as she did, they had lots to discuss. She was amazed at how much they seemed to have in common, besides of course, the physical attraction they couldn't deny. Each time he casually touched her hand or brushed his fingertips along the side of her face as they were talking or just gazing into one another's eyes, it was as if a high voltage was shooting through her entire body.

"Tell me about your work," she asked in the course of conversation. "You mentioned you were on the Apache Tribal Council? Is that what you do for a living?"

"Yes. It keeps me busy. I, um, I travel a lot during the day."

"Sounds interesting," she said, ignoring the way he fidgeted in his seat and glanced away from her for a second. "I would love to hear more about it."

She pushed the last of her bacon cheddar burger plate to the edge of the table. It was a massive serving of burger and fries and she had barely eaten a fourth of it even though it was delicious. "I have to admit I haven't taken time since moving here to learn much about the local politics of the area. But I have been studying up on the legends surrounding the Lost Dutchman's Gold Mine. What's your opinion of the whole secret gold mine thing?" She wasn't sure if she imagined Mateo's strange expression or not, because he seemed to lose then regain his composure within a matter of seconds.

He pushed his mostly uneaten plate of food to the side, too, and reached across the table again. This time he intertwined his own fingers in the fingers of the hand she purposely placed within his reach. "I heard you were exploring the Superstition Mountains, or so my brothers told me." He chuckled. "I, personally, think old man Waltz might have found a cache of gold supposedly left up there by Spanish Conquistadors centuries ago. But his tale of endless veins of gold was probably exaggerated. How is it no one has ever found even a clue to its existence?"

He shrugged his shoulders. A crooked grin curved his full lips as he asked, "So, do you believe in the legends and what did you think of those rugged mountains when you were up there?"

Dawn was having a hard time concentrating on his questions because her entire body was being affected by the intimate intertwining of their fingers. She was imagining their bare legs being all tangled together among the freshly-washed purple flowered sheets covering her bed back at her apartment. *It's a good thing I took the time to change those sheets today. He surely has condoms with him tonight? Just in case.*

"Um? Oh, the Superstitions? Well. They absolutely terrified me," she managed to say even as the sensuous thoughts ruled her mind.

A look of surprise claimed Mateo's face. "Did something happen up there? I mean, terrified is a pretty strong reaction."

She forced herself to concentrate on the conversation, but without thinking about how weird it might sound, she began to expose her true feelings about the Superstitions to him. "Actually, terrifying is a huge understatement. I felt as if someone was watching me when I was up there. And if I didn't know better, I would swear I went sleep walking up there a few nights ago. That incident was as scary as it was ridiculous. Then, I had this really weird illness and some strange bite marks on my neck and wrist. Even worse, I've had these crazy wet dre—er—some really strange dreams since going up there on that creepy mountain."

Oh my God, she did not just say all that crap out loud? *Just kill me now.* She moaned inwardly. She could tell by the strange expression on his face he was probably thinking she must be completely insane. He cleared his throat and stared at her oddly.

"W-Well, that all sounds really terrifying. You said you were having dreams? About w-what?"

She hesitated before answering him. Had he caught the 'wet' part? His voice sounded strange. Maybe he was rethinking this entire date after her rambling craziness. He probably wanted nothing more than to high tail it out of here. Before she could reply, though, he reached out with his free hand and placed his palm gently on the side of her face and saved her from making a bigger fool of herself.

"I know those mountains can feel pretty threatening. I've had some strange experiences up there myself. And I hope you know you can talk to me about anything," he said quietly.

She stared back at him, and was overcome with a complete sense of security. She swallowed hard and nodded. "I know."

His hand slid away from her cheek as he gave her a reassuring smile. "These dreams? Are they frightening?"

After a heavy sigh, Dawn chuckled and rolled her eyes, hoping she could lighten the mood. "Actually, they weren't scary. They were more mysterious and sensuous and they left me totally turned on." She gave a nervous giggle. She did it again. *Too much information.* There was no hope for her.

His grin widened. "So, sensuous dreams? There must be a hidden meaning in there somewhere."

"Yeah right. If only my real life could be as exciting as my dreams have been lately." *Seriously? Shut up already.* Flames burned the hollows of her cheeks. Would he be offended by this subject? At the very least, he would surely think she was a horny nutcase after this conversation. She really had no idea what Apache men considered appropriate, but it was too late now to retract her last statement. The sound of his deep laughter did not clear her confusion, but the meanings of his next words were perfectly clear.

"I would like to help remedy that situation if it is within my power," he said when his mirth subsided. His grip around her fingers tightened, but she barely noticed. His voice was huskier as he added, "Tonight."

Her gaze once again locked with his and the unspoken thoughts in his raven eyes were as obvious as his suggestive comments. "I-I would like that, too." He only needed to squeeze her hand and gaze into her eyes and she was so ready to jump into those fresh sheets on her bed. She squirmed awkwardly on the seat of the hard wooden chair as the inferno between her legs burned out of control.

"Let's get out of here," he whispered as if he was afraid of being overheard.

She managed a weak nod of her head. *Yes, please get me out of here before I climb across the table top and rip your clothes off.* The image of shoving the remains of their barely eaten dinner onto the floor so the table could provide a crude platform for them to have animalistic sex on was making her female parts convulse against the heavy material of her jeans.

Within a matter of seconds, he tossed a wad of bills on the table—the same table where she just pictured the two of them naked and getting it on like wild animals—pulled her to her feet and was leading her out of the restaurant.

Dawn eagerly lengthened her steps to keep up with his long strides. He unlocked the passenger door when they reached his truck and lifted her in before she had a chance to step up on the running board. Her head spinning and her body felt as if a zillion pins were pricking lightly at her skin. It was a sweet, strange mixture of excitement and anxiety. She was certain she had never wanted anything more than she wanted to make love to this man, and she already had so many emotions invested in this new relationship she couldn't help but worry about seeming, well, just plain slutty.

She should have asked Chloe if there was some old-fashioned rule with Apache men about dating women who put out on the first date. Oh well, too late now, because she had no intention of changing her mind.

The truck engine roared to life and Mateo wasted no time in getting out of the parking lot and heading back into Apache Junction. Once they were on the highway, he reached over and grasped her hand, which had been lying limply in her lap. His touch made her entire body quiver uncontrollably with the exhilaration of what they were about to do. She wrapped her fingers around his hand. Soon she would be wrapped in his arms.

They drove in silence. The mystical sounds of Joseph Red Feather's guitar music filled the cab of the truck once again. Dawn was still having the minor conflict with her conscious.

"Are you okay," he asked. "You are very quiet over there."

She exhaled the breath she had been holding and nodded. The old cliché, 'I don't usually do this sort of thing,' was the only thing that came to mind. But she was afraid it would sound as if she was trying to make herself sound more saintly than she was, and she could not chance saying something stupid about her past sexual encounters, so she just mumbled, "I'm good." Unfortunately, she couldn't stop the awkward-sounding chuckle that escaped from her. She turned to smile at him in the hopes of appearing more confident. "I'm great, really. Well, maybe a little nervous. Things are happening pretty fast."

He leaned toward her. "Too fast?"

The slight movement sent the manly odor of his cologne Dawn's way and she was flooded with the memory of the musky scent she smelled in her dreams. The now familiar phobia that kept gripping her in its frosty clutches returned and she began to recall every intimate detail from her insane dreams again.

"No, not too fast," she answered quickly, trying to think of something other than the ridiculous notion Mateo was the man in her weird dreams. She realized he was driving down the street that led to her apartment. Had she told him where she lived? She must have, although, she couldn't remember when. It didn't matter. What mattered was she knew she was going to make love to him soon regardless of the consequences. Yep, the one night stand option had definitely won this first round, hands down.

He pulled up in front of her southwestern style two-story apartment building and parked in a vacant spot as if he knew exactly where he was going. But once he climbed out of the truck and rushed around to the passenger side to help her out of the truck, he waited for her to lead the way.

"Lower level, apartment nine," she offered as he draped his arm around her shoulder and they started walking toward the building. It felt so natural to be next to him; to have him holding her as if they had known one another for much longer than twenty-four hours. She glanced up at him. The breath caught in her throat.

His bronzed skin seemed to shimmer in the

artificial glow of the street lights and his hair appeared bluish black. That dangerous aura about him was more apparent than ever at this moment, and although there was a tiny nagging sense of unease in the pit of her stomach, she was far more excited than she was afraid.

Dawn led him to the door of her apartment. Her hand was shaking when she tried to insert the key into the keyhole, and even though she tried to hide it from Mateo, he noticed.

"Are you cold or afraid," he asked. He placed his hand over her trembling one, but did not attempt to unlock the door for her.

"Seriously turned on," Dawn whispered.

He wasted no time helping her turn the key in the lock after her last comment. With one hand he pushed the door open before she could say or do anything else. The quiet dark interior of her small apartment felt strange. She hadn't brought a man here since moving in a couple of months ago, and bringing Mateo Two Moons here now made the cramped one bedroom apartment feel stifling and even smaller.

She had this unexplained notion they should be making love for the first time under the stars—on the highest mountain summit; somewhere wild and open. The bed of his shiny new truck, maybe? She didn't mind roughing it once in a while. They could have gone to his place. Where did he live anyway? These disoriented thoughts hurdling through her mind were quickly overruled by the feral out-of-control sensations claiming her body. A weak gasp escaped from her mouth as she was unexpectedly swept off her feet. The sudden gesture startled and thrilled her at the same time.

Wow. What man in this day and age picked a woman up and carried her to bed? Mateo Two Moons, that's who.

He seemed to know exactly where her bedroom was located. Not hard, Dawn reminded herself, since the doorway leading to her bedroom and bathroom was the only exit from the living room and kitchen area in her small apartment.

His mouth began to rain fiery kisses on the side of her neck, causing a mini bonfire to erupt in each spot his lips touched and it was spreading out of control throughout her entire body. As he placed her on the bed, she wrapped her arms around his neck in an enslaving hold. His nearness was the most over-powering aphrodisiac she had ever known and she was sure she would die if she turned loose of him now.

"Mateo," she moaned. "I want you so much."

"You have me, always and forever."

His whispered words filled her with a sense of magic. *Always and forever.* Her entire being stirred with yearnings she never experienced before with any other lover. This was more than merely anticipating making love to the hottest man she had ever known...this felt as if she was about to begin on a sensuous journey beyond anything she ever imagined. A journey that would truly last forever.

He joined her on the bed. They were lying on their sides, facing each other and his arduous kisses were once again devouring her mouth, while their tongues twisted together in fanatical devotion. Fleetingly, she thought about how exquisite his mouth tasted, and how she hoped she didn't taste like cheese burger and fries. But that thought was gone almost as quickly as it had appeared.

One of his hands was tangled in her long hair, cradling her head as he hosted more demanding kisses on her lips; his other hand had worked its way up under her white lace bra, and was kneading one eager nipple, which was responding by standing swollen and firm against his fingers.

Her free hand slid down his side until she came to the waistband of his jeans. The black leather belt he wore unhooked with little effort. His silk shirt was easy to pull free of the jeans, and in no time she was working on the buttons that ran down the front of his shirt. But she had only unbuttoned a couple when he sat up and pulled her to a sitting position with him. He pushed her black blazer away from her shoulders. She shrugged the jacket away as his mouth began to draw a trail of fervent kisses along her bare shoulder and upper arm. Electrifying currents launched her body to a new level of desire.

Her trembling fingers began to finish the job of unbuttoning the rest of his shirt. She wished they had turned a light on so she could see his bare chest. In the darkness of the room only his shiny silver necklace glistened. The feel of his skin under her fingers when she splayed them across his biceps was as smooth as velvet and hard and developed as a bodybuilder.

Mateo did not give her time to explore his well-defined muscles as he anxiously began to undress her. She lifted her arms up over her head and let him pull her white top off. His kisses began to nip gently along the rise of her breasts above the top edge of lace that adorned her bra. His lips against her fevered skin sent bolts of ecstasy through her.

Reaching back, she quickly unhooked her bra so he could engage her breasts properly. He wasted no time in pulling the bra straps from her shoulders and discarding the undergarment somewhere among the rest of their rapidly disappearing clothes. His lips encircled one taut nipple and he began to suck gently.

She moaned softly and leaned forward to allow his lips full access to the inflated bud. When his mouth moved to give the other breast equal attention, Dawn reached behind his head and pulled the band down from his long ponytail. The heavy locks tumbled free and loose down his back and around his shoulders. She could feel the silken strands floating over her upper body as she immersed her fingers into the luxurious thickness.

Indescribable arousal deep in her core caused a flood of warmth and dampness between her legs. She had never been with a man who had long hair and the feel of Mateo's nearly waist-length hair brushing softly against her naked skin as he continued to suck gently on her nipple was one of the most exhilarating sensations she had ever experienced.

She imagined how beautiful her pale skin melded against his bronzed body must look. Contrasting, complimenting, and in perfect harmony in every way. Next time they would have to turn on the lights or make love in the daytime so she could see the unique beauty of their bodies blended together.

He was already unsnapping her jeans and pulling the zipper down as she fumbled with the snap on his jeans. When she was finally able to slide his zipper down, she realized he wasn't wearing anything underneath as his rigid cock was released from the confines of his jeans.

Commando. Damn. This was so seriously hot.

Mateo was working diligently to pull her jeans down and she eagerly followed his lead as she slid his jeans past his hips and down his muscled thighs. They both stopped long enough to pull their boots from their own feet, then each of them finished discarding their pants. In just a matter of seconds, the last of their clothes were gone and forgotten.

He lowered his body and Dawn's legs parted effortlessly to make way for him to settle between them. The touch of his rock-hard cock brushed against the inside of her thigh. An anxious moan escaped from her. He positioned his hips between her legs and with a gentle push against her opening slid inside of her. For an instant he made no movements.

Pulsating throbs deep within her body made the anticipation unbearable. Her pussy tightened around his cock with commanding urgency. His first plunge deep inside took her breath away. There was a slight resistance to this intimate intrusion as her body arched up to accept all of him. She clasped hold of his tight muscled buttocks and pulled him into her as deep as she could handle.

They began to move together as one, losing sense of time and reality. The escalating pleasure was so engulfing, so fulfilling, it nearly rendered her unconscious. Shooting sensations of rapture fired through her body and made her feel as if her insides were about to detonate.

Mateo pulled her up to a sitting position without freeing her body from his and with her legs wrapped tightly around his waist he pulled her to the edge of the bed where he knelt on the floor and began to delve his hips against her as he continued to move in and out of her like a perfectly oiled machine. She threw her head back, unaware of the hungry whimper that escaped when the rising climax was almost more than her mind and body could endure.

His energy seemed boundless as their bodies pounded together, wanting—needing—all this impassioned indulgence could render. She drew on every reserve in her body in an effort to last as long as he did, but she couldn't stop the drowning waves of ecstasy that kept washing her over the edge of the sensual pinnacle time and time again.

When she was certain she could not stand the intensity of these delicious sensations a second longer, and she was yet again at the highest mind-boggling summit she was convinced her body could climb, she felt his body give a heavy shudder as his fiery essence spilled into her. His movements started to slow, but she couldn't control the strong tremors still shaking through her body for a few more moments even after he no longer moved.

He picked her back up in his arms without dislodging the intimate tangle of their bodies and lay down on the bed with her still impaled on top of him.

Dawn drew in an unsteady breath as her sanity began to seep back into her spinning mind. Her sweating body still boiled over with sizzling remains of their powerful love-making as she continued to lay face down on top of him. The apartment could fall down around them and she wouldn't have enough energy to move.

This man was definitely like no other lover she had

ever known. They had gone far beyond physical contact. When he entered her, Dawn felt he claimed more than her body; it was as if he possessed her very soul. She wasn't a very spiritual person, but she was certain she just had a revelation of some sort. The connection she felt with him was almost unearthly. She wished they could remain linked together like this for the rest of forever. But even forever wouldn't be long enough.

****

Mateo closed the front door of the apartment as quietly as possible. Dawn had not moved a muscle the entire time he had been getting ready to leave. They had spent the entire night engaged in such deep intimacy that it felt as though their spirits had become fused.

The image of her sleeping alone in the bed when he left her caused a strange lump to form in his throat. She reminded him of an angelic being with her long blonde hair spread out in wild profusion along the top of her flowered pillow case. The matching sheet covered her firm luscious body all the way to her chin, but he didn't need to see more to remember she was not so angel-like last night. His Udaya was the precise mixture of angel and hot temptress. The erection this thought aroused reminded him how much he wanted to stay here with her forever.

He climbed into his truck and drove off as soon as he started the ignition. He couldn't chance she would come out of her apartment and detain him. The sun would be up soon. He should have left earlier. But he lingered, wanting to spend every possible second with her, even if it was only lying next to her watching her sleep. The consequences of being caught away from the mountain once the sun rose, though, were not an option.

Driving back to the reservation, Mateo was lost to the amazing experience of making love to his mate. A smile claimed his lips. He could still smell the succulent scent of her desert-scented cologne in his truck. The hardness of his cock was more than a little annoying now that he was no longer with her. But it was a small price to pay for all he discovered in her loving embrace.

The first night with her had been more exciting, erotic and romantic than he could have ever imagined. Had she realized it was the first time he ever made love? There was no way she could have known, he told himself smugly. He had no doubts he had been a gifted first-timer by the way she responded to him.

His smile widened. It had been so worth the century-long wait. It saddened him to think if he had completed the mating process as soon as she arrived on the Superstitions to camp with her friend that first night, he would have never known the extent of her real passion because she would have been completely under his vampire spell and compelled to make love to him whenever he desired it.

Now, he had no doubt she was as excited to be with him as he was to be with her in every way. When the time came to make her his mate for all eternity, they would have experienced so much more than his grandfather, father, or brothers had ever known with their mates.

A deep sense of relief filled Mateo for the strength he had been able to exhibit while they had been in the throes of such intense love-making. His mouth and throat felt as though they had erupted into blistering coals with the thought of being so close to her and not drinking more of her blood, but he fought the consuming urge with every reserve he could muster, and he prevailed. If he had been able to control his vampire urges during such electrifying intimacy, he was confident he could pull off his plan without any trouble.

But he reminded himself he still had to be careful while he was coming to see Dawn in her human world. There was too much at stake...his entire clan's existence for one thing.

Mateo parked his truck in a secluded location on the reservation. He did not have to worry about leaving it there, because the Clan Society protected everything associated with the secret vampire clan from the mountain.

It was nearly daylight, and Mateo had to hurry to the caves before any light of day touched his nocturnal skin and reduced him to a blackened spot on the ground. As he traveled quickly up the mountain with his sure-footed immortal ease, he thought about the admission Dawn made regarding her dreams. Of course, they weren't dreams, and he was surprised and more than a little worried to know she was able to remember anything about those events.

He recalled the concerns his grandfather mentioned when he told him he started the mating ritual, but hadn't completed it. Could the strange illness she mentioned be a result of his bites? If there was any chance he was putting her health at risk, he would not hesitate to make her his mate immediately. But she seemed okay now. She had been better than okay tonight.

As long as he remained strong and resisted biting her again, hopefully, they wouldn't have to rush the inevitable. They would spend eternity in his world, and he really loved living in hers, even if it was only for a little while longer...and if he could deny his ravenous hunger for her blood.

Chapter Nine

Dawn wished the night would never have to end. But there was no ignoring the sun shining through the bedroom window and hitting her smack in the face with its bright rays. She felt a smile touch her lips; lips that still clung to Mateo's demanding kisses. Her hand impulsively rose up to touch the area at the back of her neck where she had been bitten in those bizarre dreams. *Don't start with that crazy stuff again.* She sighed with relief to discover that—of course—there were no new wounds.

Before opening her eyes, she reached over to the side of the bed where she was sure he would still be sleeping. The feel of cool sheets greeted her hand. Her eyes flew open. She was alone among the tangled mess of sheets.

One night stand echoed through her mind. Then she noticed the note lying on the empty pillow beside her. As she grabbed the piece of white paper, she was growing more anxious by the moment. The note was written on a piece of paper torn out of the tablet she kept in the kitchen for writing her shopping lists and notes.

She grunted with aggravation. She knew how men usually were when they first got up in the morning. Mateo had most likely gotten up from the bed and sauntered into the bathroom to take a pee. Flushing the toilet was optional when it came to men, which probably explains why she hadn't heard him in the bathroom. Then, he must have dressed, roamed through her tiny apartment looking for pen and paper, written a note, and placed it on the pillow before leaving. And she hadn't heard one damn thing?

Well, they hadn't gotten much sleep last night, so she was obviously exhausted. She couldn't stop the silly grin that claimed her lips. Oh, it had been so worth the loss of sleep.

She pushed up to a sitting position, aware of the slight tenderness between her legs from their exuberant night of making love; it was a pain she didn't mind at all. Her goofy grin widened. The way this man made her feel was unreal. She rubbed her sleepy eyes and tried to focus on the note. *Please don't let it be filled with bad news like, 'Dear Easy One-Night Stand, Wish you had higher morals, but you don't, so I won't be seeing you again. Bye Bye.' Ugh.* She forced herself to look down at the carefully written words on the note paper.

My beautiful Dawn,

There is nothing I would like more than to wake up this morning with you in my arms. Unfortunately, I have commitments I am unable to ignore and had to leave early. I didn't want to wake you. Please forgive me for not saying goodbye. I will count the minutes until I can see you again. I will call you tonight and I hope you will be looking forward to it as much as I will be.

Love,

Mateo

Love? Love. Love Mateo? Damn.

This was crazy. She barely knew anything about him, other than he was gorgeous to look at, and a magnificent lover and just about perfect in every way, but she knew without a doubt that she loved him. She pressed the note against her bare breast. It was the closest she could be to him right now. She would be counting the minutes until she heard from him tonight.

"Mateo Two Moons, I love you, too," she said softly.

Since there was no need to get up yet, she leaned back on her pillow. She hugged the note a few minutes longer then put it back on the pillow in the exact spot where he had left it earlier. A fleeting thought passed through her mind and made her gasp out loud.

They hadn't used any protection last night. She vaguely remembered thinking about that very important issue as he had been carrying her to the bedroom, but it passed through her mind as no more than a nonexistent whisper and she had completely forgotten to mention it to him. So why hadn't he said something? No one made love for the first time without talking about that stuff these days.

But they made love last night over and over and over again without even thinking about it. Oh well, too late now. Damn.

Her brows drew together as a heavy frown settled on her face. She tried to care more about the fact they had been so careless, but for some reason it just didn't seem all that important in the big scheme of everything else she felt when she thought about that man. The panic she knew she should be feeling was nothing more than a minor aggravation. Next time they would have to talk about using protection. And she was fairly certain there was going to be a next time.

Another grin came to her lips before a huge yawn reminded her of how tired she still was. She thought she'd just rest in bed for a bit longer before she got up and did something to pass the time before Mateo called her tonight.

But it was barely seconds before she was sound asleep, and lost to another strange world of dreams...real dreams.

She was following a trail on the Superstition Mountains. How odd she was not afraid at all this time. Instead, she was trembling with excitement. Ahead, she sensed there was something so amazing she couldn't wait to see it.

This trail was familiar. The setting sun was shining along the tops of the mountain, and on the shapes of jagged rocks and scraggily pinion trees along the sides of the trail. She remembered all this from the hike she had taken with Chloe.

As Dawn approached a towering expanse of the mountain, a small opening became visible at the base. She did not hesitate to kneel down on her knees and crawl through the dark hole.

Rising up to her feet, she realized she was in another familiar area. She had been here with Chloe, too. The Old Military Trail. But they hadn't been on this high of a ridge when they were here before. The lower ledge where she had been standing with Chloe last weekend was barely visible and she had no idea how she had gotten up here on this higher ledge. From here she had a clear view of Weavers Needle. The tall pointy sphere was glowing red in the fading sunlight. Still, she wasn't frightened at all.

She glanced down and noticed a shape began to form on the desert floor below the Needle in the dimming light. The last rays of sun sparkled along the edges of the silhouette spread out below her. The outline highlighted by the fading sunlight began to take on a recognizable form. It resembled the profile of an old man's face. Indentations along the barren ground clearly outlined his features, and rocks formed his nose, mouth and eyes. The eyes appeared to be staring at a particular spot on the mountain behind her.

Turning slowly her gaze followed the same path as the unmoving stone eyes. A gasp caught in her throat as her disbelieving mind fought to comprehend what she was seeing. The entrance to the cave was massive and resembled a gaping mouth. Dawn was sure this was the jaws of Hell. Although she was afraid to see more, she couldn't look away. Her gaze was drawn past the terrifying image of the heinous gateway, to the interior of the enormous cavern. She gasped and drew in a trembling breath.

The walls of the cave were filled with glistening veins of gold and the fading rays of the setting sun made them cast blinding spheres of light across the land. Dawn threw her hands over her eyes to block the piercing glare of the gold. She shook with a mixture of awe and disbelief. It really did exist.

The Lost Dutchman's Mine was no longer lost. She had just found it.

The sound of someone knocking on her door woke Dawn from her most recent and extremely detailed dream. For a moment, she was still mired in the vivid images of finding the Lost Dutchman Gold Mine. This dream was so detailed. Maybe not as intense as the others—the kinky ones—but all her dreams lately had been a bit too real. She glanced at the clock on her night stand and was shocked to see it was almost three-thirty in the afternoon.

Another knock sounded from the front door. "Coming," Dawn called out and jumped up to grab her blue satin robe from the hook on the bathroom door. What if it was Mateo? She probably looked like crap. She haphazardly ran her fingers through her tangled hair as she rushed toward the door.

"It's Chloe. Are you okay in there?"

Whew. As much as she couldn't wait to see Mateo again, she would prefer to not look like something the cat drug in when he came back. Pulling the door open, she was immediately aware of how she must look by the knowing expression on Chloe's face.

"I was worried you were sick again. But damn. That must have been one super-hot all-nighter. Is the Apache stud still here?" Her gaze moved past Dawn toward the open bedroom door. Her eyebrows rose up as she whispered, "In there?"

Dawn had to giggle at the way Chloe was acting. Her cheeks were slightly flushed and there was an asinine grin curving her lips. Not that she could blame her. Mateo Two Moons would cause any woman to get excited at the thought of him lying in her bed. "Nope. He had something to do today and left early this morning."

Chloe walked into the apartment and snickered. "And you're obviously still trying to catch up on sleep. He must have worn you out, big time. Seriously, you look like hell. But in a good way, of course." She smiled and shook her head. "Wet dreams. Pizza Porn.

And now this." She gestured toward Dawn's tangled hair and scantily-clad body.

"I can't even believe any of this is really happening," Dawn replied. She pulled the tie around her waist tighter and smoothed down the front of her short robe as she motioned for Chloe to have a seat at the kitchen counter. "Coffee?"

"Thanks, but it's kinda late in the day for coffee, and I have no reason to be up all night." She chuckled dryly. "Okay. Details." She climbed on one of the two bar stools at the small kitchen counter.

Dawn began to dump scoopfuls of ground coffee into the coffeemaker. "Well, we met in front of the pizza parlor like planned, but he suggested we go to this place at the edge of the reservation. It was perfect, and he looked so seriously hot. And he's, um, he's just about the most wonderful man ever." She poured water into the top of the coffee pot. "I think I'm totally, madly in love with him." There, she admitted it out loud to someone else. There was no denying it now.

A loud gasp escaped from Chloe. Her blue eyes widened as she stared back at Dawn and shook her head slightly. "You barely know him." A worried frown tugged at the corners of her mouth. "You're moving way too fast. You know that, right?"

Turning away Dawn stared at the coffee dripping into the pot. "I know." She shrugged. "Two days ago I didn't believe in love at first sight, either."

"Two days?" Chloe repeated in a stunned voice. "So, you were feeling like this since Friday night when you first met him, and you didn't tell me?"

"Crazy. I know." She opened an overhead cupboard and grabbed a large white coffee mug with the words Colorful Colorado written around its circumference in a rainbow of colors. "Sure you don't want some?

Chloe gave her head a negative shake. "I need a beer." She headed to the refrigerator to help herself. "Sure you don't want one of these instead?" she asked as she grabbed a bottle.

Dawn laughed. "After the coffee I might." She pushed a long strand of loose blonde hair back from her forehead. "I can't believe I've practically slept all day." She smiled when she noticed the knowing smirk on Chloe's lips. Their gazes met, and Dawn giggled as she looked away, feeling once again like a teenager who had just had her first sloppy wet kiss. "He's just, well, amazing in every way." The words just fell out of her mouth without conscious thought.

"Okay, I'm officially jealous now," Chloe said as she plopped back down on the stool. She took a big gulp of the beer she just opened. "So—think he feels the same?"

Wrapping her hands around her coffee mug, Dawn took a sip of coffee, then slowly nodded her head. "Yeah—yeah, I really think he does." She looked directly at her friend again and added, "This is going to sound really insane, but I have no doubt I am going to be with him forever."

Chloe took another big drink then sat the beer bottle on the countertop. "You're right. It sounds so insane. It's only been two days since you met him. One spilt beer on his feet. One display of public porn. One perfectly hot date. One all-night fuck."

Another giggle escaped from Dawn. "Oh, trust me, it was so much more. It was making electrifying love over and over like I've never done befo—"

"Okay, enough," Chloe interrupted and held her hand up in front of Dawn's face. "I was just jealous before, now I'm getting sort of pissed." She smiled to counteract her words. "You really do have it bad." She shook her head from side to side in a slow gesture. "So, when are you seeing Mr. Perfect Everything again?"

She shrugged as a childish smirk curled her lips. *See? Even Chloe had noticed Mateo Two Moons was perfect,* she thought smugly as she sat down on the other stool.

"He's supposed to call tonight. So, maybe later? I hope." She turned and grabbed Chloe's forearm. "Oh, I almost forgot. I had the craziest dream about your gold mine right before I woke up a little while ago."

"My gold mine?"

"The Lost Dutchman's Gold Mine," Dawn retorted with a roll of her eyes. "I found it. Well, in my dream, anyway."

"You and your crazy dreams." She glanced down at her beer and began to chip at the label on the bottle with the nail on her forefinger. "You didn't mention anything to the Apache stud about the gold mine, did you?"

Dawn shook her head, aware of Chloe's strange tone of voice and obvious change of demeanor. "We talked a little bit about the legend, but I didn't tell him anything about you or your family's quest to find the mine. Why?"

Chloe rolled her eyes this time, and attempted to sound nonchalant when she spoke again. "Oh, I'm just being paranoid. I don't want people to think I'm one of those totally obsessed gold seekers that really think the mine and the gold exists."

Confusion clouded Dawn's thoughts. She had no doubt Chloe really did believe the Lost Dutchman's Gold mine existed. Her entire family was dedicated to finding that mine. So why was she denying it all of a sudden?

"Okay, tell me about this dream?" Chloe asked as she pulled the label all the way off the face of the beer bottle and wadded it up in her hand. She turned to face Dawn and downed the last of her beer with one huge gulp. "So, since you had a dream about the gold mine after making wild savage love to Mateo Two Balls all night long, did your dream involve gold dildos?"

Dawn nearly spit out her mouthful of coffee at the image Chloe's suggestive words presented. "Oh yeah! Massive ones of rare metal...rock hard," she answered through her laughter after she was able to gulp down the coffee without choking. "Now, I think I'm beginning to understand what you're looking for up there on that mountain."

"Okay, well I'm totally horny now," Chloe said as she joined her in a round of giggling. "I think I need to go home and dig out the old faithful vibrator, Mr. Peter. He's not made of gold, but he is rock hard."

Dawn laughed as she shook her head, not wanting to envision Chloe with her battery-operated friend. "You'd be really turned on if you found the massive cave filled with gold I dreamt about," she added.

Chloe grew more serious immediately and her voice held a note of suspicion when she spoke again. "A cave? With chests of gold? Or with veins of gold? You know, it was rumored by some that Jacob Walsh might have actually found a cache of gold hidden in the

Superstitions by Apaches after they massacred a group of Spaniards traveling through the area with bags of treasure."

Dawn gave her head a negative shake. She briefly recalled Mateo's comment about a cache of gold supposedly left up there by Spanish Conquistadors hundreds of years ago. "No, not chests of gold. It was, well, let me start from the beginning." As she began to recount all the details of her strange dream, Chloe remained silent until Dawn was finished telling her everything she remembered from her dream.

"Don't you think it's a pretty vivid dream considering I've only been to the Superstition Mountains once, and I was scared shitless the entire time, so I really wasn't noticing much of anything except the imaginary images of Count Dracula lurking in the shadows?"

For a moment, Chloe didn't reply. She stared at her with a deep frown drawing her brown brows together to the point they were nearly touching in the middle. Finally, she exhaled heavily as if she had been holding her breath. "Count Dracula? Really?"

A sheepish grin touched Dawn's lips before she opened her mouth to speak again. But Chloe didn't give her a chance to respond.

"Yes—yes, that is really detailed. Um? I'm guessing it's just a result of all the clues I told you about when we were camping."

"Oh, for sure," Dawn agreed. "I'm sure that's why I even dreamed about the gold mine in the first place." She remembered Chloe telling her about the confusing clues the old miner, Jacob Waltz, had left regarding the location of the gold mine. *"You have to crawl through a hole in the rock. From here you can see the Old Military Trail. You can't see the mine from the trail. If you climb up a short distance you can see Weaver's Needle. The setting sun shines on the gold in my mine. A rock face looks at my mine."* Just like in her most recent dream.

Chloe's expression remained serious. "Was there anything else you remember from the dream? You said you crawled through a hole, but I remember my dad also mentioned another clue from one of the old miners who searched for the Lost Dutchman mine suggesting the sun shining through the hole in the rocks reflected off the gold in Waltz's mine. Did you see anything like that?"

"I don't recall seeing anything like that in my dream. But the reflection of the setting sun shining through the cave opening and hitting the veins of gold around the entrance was blinding." She shook her head as she tried to recall more of the details she had seen in her dream, but there wasn't anything else she hadn't already told Chloe.

"As crazy as it sounds, do you think I had some sort of weird premonition and saw the real location or something in my dream?"

Chloe gave a careless shrug. "Oh, of course not. It's just curious you would have such a detailed dream about the gold mine. The location of the face on the desert floor is an interesting theory." She drew in a heavy sigh, adding, "Hey, I'm sorry if I involved you in my family's harebrained obsession." She added a weak chuckle that sounded forced.

"If I get a cut in the proceeds, I will keep those dreams coming," Dawn joked. Chloe's weird mood was not lost to her, so she attempted to change the subject. "But truthfully, I would rather just dream about Mateo."

"Okay. That's my clue to leave," Chloe retorted. "Any more of this mushy love stuff and I might puke." She pretended to poke her finger down her throat and gag as she jumped from the stool. She leaned over and hugged Dawn, adding, "I guess I'll see you at school tomorrow if you don't decide to run off into the sunset with the Apache stud."

That image was really appealing to Dawn…sitting next to Mateo in his big shiny black truck, driving West down the open highway toward the setting sun, while the hauntingly beautiful songs of Joseph Red Feather filled the cab. Yeah, that might even be preferable to sitting in front of a classroom full of twelve-year-olds who thought History class was the most boring subject they had ever been forced to learn.

"I'll see you tomorrow," she said in a resigned tone as she followed Chloe to the door.

Chloe waved as she headed down the sidewalk toward her older model SUV. "Have fun tonight," she called out without looking back.

Dawn smiled as she watched her drive away. With her long shiny brown hair, deep blue eyes and tall, slender figure, Chloe was a stunning woman. She was almost always happy and seemed to attract positive attention wherever she went.

There were a couple of the men teachers at the middle school who were completely smitten with her and flirted shamelessly whenever they were all in the teacher's lounge together. Chloe flirted back, but never encouraged anything more. She told Dawn she had been engaged when she was in college to a grad-student whom she was madly in love with at the time. The engagement ended horribly when her fiancé slept with one of their college professors.

That traumatic experience seemed to have left Chloe pretty jaded about getting seriously involved with anyone again. She did date, though. Just in the past few weeks since they had been friends, she mentioned a couple of different men she was seeing on a casual basis. Still, at other times it seemed as if Chloe wished she could let go of her painful past, and fall in love again.

Dawn closed the door and sighed. Enough sleeping for the day. She had to get a shower, get dressed, and be ready for Mateo's call; a thought that made her squeal out loud, again, just like one of her students. She sighed. It was useless to resist. She loved that gorgeous hot perfect Apache stud. And she could not wait to see him. Hopefully, he would want to get together with her tonight. He only said he would call. But a simple phone call just didn't seem like enough after what they discovered in one another last night.

After grabbing a banana to ward off the growling noises coming from her stomach, Dawn headed to the bathroom to take a shower. As the hot water washed over her, the air grew fragrant with a heady mixture of Mateo's earthy cologne, and her own rich floral fragrance combined with the undeniable scent of body odor still lingering from their night of heavy sex. It filled her nostrils and made the area between her legs grow wetter than the water flooding over her body from the showerhead.

Sensuous memories of the previous night and thoughts of what she wanted to do with him in the future claimed her mind while she slowly washed her hair and body with her soapy hands. This shower would be absolutely perfect if Mateo Two Moons was taking it with her.

Her fingers tingled with the thought of how she would run them through his long hair, and down over his sleek muscled body. She imagined how the little droplets of water would hang from the pointed tips of his thick hair cascading over his muscled shoulders. The water would trail down his bronzed skin, still glowing from making love to her all night. Her loins throbbed ruthlessly with eager anticipation of what they would do the next time she would see him. They definitely needed to take a shower together.

Hopefully, he would call soon. Maybe she should wash her sheets to pass the time? Maybe she would just put clean sheets on the bed and save those purple flowered sheets forever without washing them. Then, when he wasn't here with her, she could just roll herself up in them and get turned on all over again to the clinging smell of their hot sex last night. *Wow, kinky.* These kinds of thoughts had to be Mateo's fault.

Once she dried her hair and pinned it loosely to the top of her head with a brown hair clip, applied minimal makeup and dressed casually in a pair of faded blue jeans, black flip-flops, and a white T-shirt with a picture of one of her favorite rock bands on the front, she waited impatiently for Mateo to call as she paced back and forth in the limited confines of her small apartment. The beer she refused when Chloe was here earlier was now accompanying her relentless prowl from wall to wall. But she drained it of its contents on the first few strides.

If he didn't call soon, she would surely have a panic attack and die. She was once again being reduced to acting like one of her middle school students. This was definitely Mateo's fault.

Another agonizing thought came to mind. Her heart began thudding frantically against her breast. He said in his note he would call, so she must have given him her cell number. Why was it she could not remember anything lately? Like birth control for one thing…one really important thing. Oh right, it was all because of sexy Mateo Two Moons, and the way he made her lose control of every rational thought and reaction with just the mere thought of him.

So, why hadn't he called yet? She was seriously going to die here.

Chapter Ten

If it weren't for the minutes ticking away on the digital clock on her microwave, Dawn would swear time just stopped. But at last the loud ringing of her cell phone snapped her out of the hypnotic state she had been in as she sat on one of the tall stools at her kitchen counter and stared at the time. She grabbed her phone from her lap where it had been lying for what seemed like forever. It was a number she didn't recognize. She drew in a big breath and pushed the answer button.

"H-Hello?"

"Hello, beautiful."

It was a voice she would recognize anywhere now; his voice—so deep and seriously sexy. There it was again. She was pretty sure now the intense feeling of light-headedness she just experienced at the sound of his voice was what women in olden times had been talking about when they said someone made them swoon.

"Hi," she replied in a voice that sounded high-pitched to her ears. "Mateo, right?" No way did she just say that? After last night? *Seriously? Just kill me now*.

A soft chuckle came from the receiver. "I hope you weren't waiting for someone else to call. I could be the jealous type where you are concerned, Miss Malone."

"Oh, no. Just you." Thank goodness, he could not see the heat she could feel flaring up in her face right now. Unless something drastic happened to change things, ever since last night, Sluts R Us and everything it entailed, was reserved just for Mateo Two Moons from now on. "I—I—"

Gratefully, he saved her from embarrassing herself any further. "Can I see you tonight?"

She tried to clear her throat as quietly as possible, and attempted not to respond like a total idiot. "Yes."

"I'll pick you up in about thirty minutes, then, if that will work for you. Dress casually. I thought we'd go for a drive."

"It sounds perfect," she answered in a tone of voice a bit more natural. Just perfect, like everything else that concerned this man. "See you soon."

"Not soon enough."

The phone receiver went silent. But Dawn's excited childish squeal filled the quiet room. Should she change into something more date-suitable? Maybe not, she determined as she glanced down at her clothes and decided she was the right kind of casual for an evening drive. Just a squirt of her new desert-themed cologne, another touch of lip gloss, some mascara and she would be good to go. Mateo might as well see her in her usual weekend attire anyway, since she hoped he would be seeing her day—and night—for the rest of her life.

But thirty minutes was way too long to wait to see him again. It would be nearly dark by the time he got here. If he arrived just a little earlier, they could have ridden off into the sunset together. She gave her head a shake and shrugged in defeat at the mushy way her mind was working lately.

She heard the big truck coming before she saw the headlights shining down the street. The roar of the engine sounded powerful, sort of like the driver, she thought as her excitement grew. Should she wait for him to come to the door, or should she just race out to meet him on the sidewalk? She should probably wait for him to come get her.

She quickly backed away from the window. Mateo seemed to be an old-fashioned guy. Maybe it was because of his Native American heritage. The idea of being a bit old-fashioned with a man like Mateo was very appealing. And swooning was always appropriate with old-fashioned type guys, right?

She held her breath as she waited until she heard the knock, then she forced herself to wait a moment longer so he wouldn't know she was just standing there waiting for him. When she did open the door, his perfect smile—those glistening white teeth between those tempting lips she couldn't wait to kiss again— were the first things she saw.

"Hello," he said in a voice that sounded like a soft caress to Dawn's ears. His gaze never left her face, and once again, she noticed how his smile appeared to be as much in his dark shining eyes as it was on his mouth.

"Hi," she said as an instant smile parted her lips. She could just stand here and stare at him forever and all would be perfect in her world.

"Are you ready to go?"

"Oh-oh yes," she stammered trying to find her brain. "Well, unless you would like to come in for a drink or beer or something?" She realized she said the last word in a lower tone—something? More like a suggestive invitation. Did he notice?

One thick brow lifted in a suggestive arch. "I would like to come back later for—something." His tone mimicked hers. "But first I thought a moonlight drive might be nice since there is going to be a full moon tonight. I have a six-pack of beer and some sandwiches in the truck for the ride."

She gulped much too loudly. *Something* was still on her mind as she gave her head a weak nod.

"That sounds perfect," she murmured. Mateo Two Moons in the romantic glow of a full moon. That sounded—what had Chloe said?—Mateo-gasmic or something similar. Food or drink was not even necessary.

She grabbed her purse and let him wrap his arm around her waist as they headed to his truck. A deep sense of comfort washed through her body. They really were perfect together.

"Rock music, uh? Joseph Red Feather is probably way too tame for you," he said in a joking voice after they had climbed in the cab of his truck. He motioned toward her shirt.

She chuckled. "I love all kinds of music. But I must admit, hard rock is one of my guilty pleasures. I would never admit it to my students, even though wearing this shirt probably makes me look like I'm trying to be one of them. So, this shirt is reserved only for very special non-school related activities."

Soft laughter came from Mateo's side of the cab. "I'm honored. I want you to take me to a rock concert, okay?"

"It's a date," she answered without hesitation. Add that to the list of endless things she could not wait to do with this incredible man. "So, where are we going tonight?"

He reached over the leather console in-between the seats and picked up her nearest hand. "There's a lake about fifteen miles from here. I thought we could watch the moon rise over the canyon walls surrounding the lake. I didn't want to share you with anyone other than the moonlight tonight."

Swoon. Oh yes, those women in the olden days definitely must have known men like Mateo Two Moons, and that is how swooning came to be. Did they still make smelling salts, she wondered?

She almost said his plan sounded perfect, but she was fairly certain she had said that particular phrase a few too many times already, out loud, and in her head. But when she was with him, everything was perfect.

"I haven't watched the moon come up for many moons," she said instead. *Oh God.* She just should have said it sounded perfect. Now it sounded like she was making fun of his culture. "I mean—wow—I mean, that was a really stupid thing to say," she gasped. Her hand went limp in his tight embrace. His hold tightened.

A hardy laugh escaped from him. "Stop worrying about offending me. I've gotten over the fact your people stole my people's land away from us a long time ago." He squeezed her hand again when she didn't laugh with him. "Miss Malone, when I look at you I don't see a 'white woman' or a woman of any race. I only see the woman I've been waiting to meet my entire life. I see the woman—the beautiful woman—I love and will spend eternity with."

Her entire body went limp this time. Her brain turned to a glob of mush again. "Love?" she whispered, but continued to stare straight ahead. That four letter word—coming out of his mouth—was the sweetest sound she had ever heard. She didn't want to look at him, because she was afraid she would start to cry again like she had last night.

She was so overcome with emotion she wasn't even aware he pulled his hand away from hers, or that he stopped the truck on the side of the road, until he was leaning over the center console. With his hands gently turning her face toward his, she had little choice but to return his intense gaze.

"I know it's probably too much, too soon, and probably way too overwhelming." His dark gaze held her captive. "I felt it from the first moment I saw you, but I wasn't going to say it, not yet, anyway. I'm sorry if I have I ruined everything by being so impatient to tell you how I feel. I just don't want to waste one minute of our time together." His voice was almost pleading, and even in the dim lighting in the truck cab, Dawn could see how desperately he implored her to speak the words he was hoping she would say.

She stared into those iridescent black eyes and lost all train of thought. *Come back brain, I need you now.*

"I have ruined it," Mateo said in a low tone as he continued to hold her face captive in his hands and stare into her wildly blinking eyes.

"H-Hardly," Dawn finally managed to gasp. She reached up and imitated him by placing her hands on each side of his face. "It's just I was so afraid of the way I was feeling about you in the short time we've known one another. I worried if you knew how I really felt I would scare you off. But now—" She swallowed hard, thinking carefully about what she wanted to say.

"Yes?" Mateo asked in a worried whisper.

"I've never believed in love at first sight until two nights ago," Dawn continued in a hushed tone. Her mind had graciously returned to a more natural state, and her heart was overflowing with undeniable love for this man. Now, if she could just relate her feelings to him without sounding like one of her twelve-year old students.

She heard his relieved sigh. She drew in a quivering breath. Her heart thrashed in her chest. This moment in time, this first moment when they were professing their love for one another, felt so magical it didn't even seem real. It was almost like a dream, only this one was beautiful and filled with promise and love. *Please, please let this dream last forever.*

He didn't give her a chance to say the rest of the words spinning through her mind as his lips descended on her mouth in a tender kiss. She returned his kiss with a depth of emotion that made her heart ache in her breast. When the kiss that sealed their declaration of love ended, they pulled apart and continued to gaze into one another's eyes.

As hard to believe as this all was, she knew there was no use trying to make sense of any of it anymore. In barely forty-eight hours, the life she previously lived was behind her, and from this moment on, every breath she took would be for Mateo Two Moons and the future she knew they would share.

"We should probably get to the lake if we want to see the moon rising over the canyon walls," he finally said as he reluctantly released his loving hold on her face.

Her head nodded in agreement as she let her hands slide away from his smooth cheeks. For a moment longer he continued to stare at her with such an obvious look of love upon his handsome face, she couldn't breathe.

There was no denying he loved her as much as she loved him. A tender grin curved his mouth as he finally turned away from her to focus on driving the rest of the way to the lake.

It was full-on nighttime engulfed in total darkness outside of the cab of the truck, but at this moment, Dawn was certain they were riding off into the sunset.

They drove in silence for the few remaining miles, with only the sounds of the mystical guitar music playing on the truck stereo. Words were not necessary since the most important four letter one had already been spoken. As they pulled into a secluded cove beside the lake, a slight breeze was blowing over the glassy-topped water, causing mini ripples that mimicked tiny waves along the surface of the water.

Mateo parked his truck close to a towering rock wall located several yards from the sandy shore of the lake. There were no other vehicles or people in the entire area.

"Perfect timing," he said as he jumped out of the truck and rushed around to open the door for her.

Yes, perfect. She seriously loved being an old-fashioned kind of girl, she thought as she took his hand and allowed him to help her out of the truck.

"I'll grab the blankets," he announced as he reached into the back seat and pulled out a six pack of beer and a couple of folded woven blankets. "Hungry?"

She shook her head and smiled. "Not yet, thanks. But I'll take one of those beers." Once again, she was impressed with this man; he even remembered her favorite beer.

"It's really beautiful here," she said glancing around and nodding her head in approval. "This is a very romantic spot." She reached out and took the beer bottle he had opened for her. "I bet you've brought a few girls here over the years," she added in a teasing tone of voice.

A quick chuckle was his only reply. He spread one of the brightly colored Indian blankets out on the ground, sat down, and patted the empty spot next to him. "Want to hear about all the girls I've brought here in the past, or would you prefer to make me forget all about them?"

The indisputable tone of his voice made Dawn's limbs turn to rubber. She responded by rubbing her hand up and down her beer bottle in a sexually suggestive gesture. "I think we can wipe all those past memories completely out of your mind." She slid down to the ground next to him and set her beer in the sand off to the side of the blanket. She had something else in mind to rub and she needed both hands to accomplish the task.

As she eagerly unsnapped his jeans, he leaned back without a moment's hesitation on the blanket to give her easy access. Her eager fingers slid his pants zipper down. His erect cock flagged out from between his open zipper like a glorious beacon.

Commando. Yes!

It was so convenient, and damn, it was so seriously hot, she thought as her pussy throbbed and everything between her legs grew saturated with impatient and blatant desire.

Lowering herself, she took his inflated cock in her sweating hand. It was hard as stone beneath the smooth silken skin that moved slightly under her gentle stroke. She took a deep breath and leaned farther down. Her entire body was trembling as her lips gently encircled his member. The heat from him radiated inside her mouth as she opened wider to accommodate all of him. She heard him moan as she let her sodden tongue lavish and tantalize him with unadulterated devotion. Her other hand tenderly held his balls, massaging gently, sensually. They moved in unrestrained rhythm within the cradle of her cupped palm.

She was vaguely aware of his fingers entangled in her hair as he discarded the hair clip she had used to hold the long tresses on top of her head. The freed mass of hair fell over her face and spread out over his sculptured abdomen.

Her lips sucked with more dedication and his torso moved in tempo with her sucking motions. Small droplets of his fluid leaked into her mouth as she relished his unusual manly taste, a delectable flavor she could not even begin to describe as it slid effortlessly down her throat.

Eventually, she had to cease the erotic act for a second to catch her breath. The fervent groan that escaped from Mateo again only served to increase her desire to finish what she started and give him even more pleasure. For the first time in her life, she didn't even mind swallowing. *Wow.* What this man did to her. But before she could continue, he reached down and gently pulled her up so she was lying on top of him.

His kisses entertained her mouth as he slipped his hands between their bodies and unsnapped her jeans. He began to push them—along with her baby blue G-string panties—from her hips. They parted only long enough so he could kick off his boots and they could both remove their denim jeans the rest of the way.

Her flip-flops had already fallen off her feet sometime during the initial round of foreplay. Neither of them, it seemed, wanted to waste any more time with the dispensing of clothes. She pulled her T-shirt over her head, and as soon as she had tossed the shirt to the side, he was unhooking her bra. Her freed breasts were held tenderly in his palms as he lavished each one with kisses and teasing nips, switching between one attentive nipple, then the other.

She reclined back on the soft blanket, thoroughly enjoying the individual attention he was giving each breast again tonight. She could so get used to living in this fantasyland. Overhead the ebony sky began to fill with sparkling clusters of stars. Could they just stay here forever and never return to the real world? Because this was the way it was meant to be when they made love—as wild and free as the untamed Arizona night.

When he was finished ravishing her breasts, he slid up her body until his thick rigid shaft was situated between her legs and he was able to slide into her. She clasped her legs around his waist and they made slow easy love, moving in tempo with the gentle sound of the water lapping against the shoreline. A deepening sense of bonding enhanced their ardent love-making, created by the love they both confessed to one another...a love that would last forever and beyond.

The first glow of the moon peaking just barely above the tops of the high canyon walls looked enormous and mysterious. Snuggled in Mateo's strong embrace under the second blanket he brought along, her head rested on his muscled chest. His raven hair and her pale blonde hair were entangled in wild profusion.

Their naked bodies concaved and melded together almost as intimately as if they were still making love. The only sound other than their soft satisfied breaths was the rhythmic sounds of the rippling water in the lake.

Dawn was still in awe of the fact she was here in this amazing place, with this perfect man, and he seemed to love her as much as she loved him. Perfect no longer seemed significant enough to describe the way she was feeling about life right now.

"Happy?" he asked in barely more than a whisper.

A soft sigh escaped her mouth. "I've never imagined I could be this happy." He began to stroke her hair tenderly. The night fell back into silence.

As the enormous moon began inching higher above the peaks of the stone cliffs, the entire landscape lit up in its soft silver glow. The shadowy waters of the lake hosted a million sparkles along its crest and the sandstone canvas of the surrounding canyon walls were streaked in shades of rich rust, pale tans and browns.

Dawn was lost to the wonder of it all. The more she saw of Arizona and the natural beauty of the desert and surrounding areas, the more she fell in love with this place she now called home. It was almost as beautiful as Colorado.

In that instant she decided that someday she was going to take Mateo to Colorado. The image of him standing among the tall shadowed pines of her home state created an image that took her breath away. Yes, she was definitely taking him to Colorado someday.

Time seemed suspended as they continued to lounge on the sandy shore. They made love again, relishing in the exploration of each other in the most personal ways. She was certain there was not one inch of one another's body they did not know intimately by the time they were through making love on this second night of unequaled passion.

The moon had been up for what must have been hours when he finally spoke of leaving. "Although I would like to stay here forever, I suppose I should get you home," he said in a mournful tone.

She hated the thought of leaving here, or of being separated from him again, but she knew Monday morning would come far too soon, and she had another busy day at school ahead of her. "I have an Open House tomorrow night at the school," she announced with a deep tone of regret, which surprised her, because ordinarily she looked forward to the first Open House of the school year.

She sighed heavily. "I can't believe I'm saying this, but for the first time I'm wishing real life wouldn't get in the way of my fantasy world."

"Do you think this is just a fantasy?" Mateo asked in a surprised tone as he secured his hair in a ponytail at the back of his head again. He then focused his full attention on Dawn.

"Well, it's sure not my normal life," she joked as she gathered her own long hair in her hand and held it over one of her shoulders so he could snap the back of her bra.

He helped her pull her shirt back over her head, then he tossed her the delicate blue panties she had been wearing earlier. She caught them in mid-air and stifled a giggle. Maybe she should copy his style and do away with unnecessary undergarments. She grew wet again with just the thought and considered seducing this gorgeous man one more time before they left. But she refrained. They had to go home sometime, right?

"Mine either. But it's the most alive and happy I've ever felt."

She glanced at him as she yanked her jeans over her hips, and nodded her head as a poignant smile curved her lips. "That makes two of us."

As they headed back to the truck, Dawn wondered how she was going to be able to return to the common tasks of her regular life after the incredibly erotic and romantic weekend they spent together. She didn't want to think about that, yet.

"I should have special-ordered a bench seat when I bought this truck," Mateo said in a slightly aggravated voice as they drove back toward Apache Junction. "Then you could sit right next to me. You're just way too far away right now."

She chuckled and squeezed his hand, which always seemed to have a hold of hers when they were in this truck. A bench seat would be nice, and seriously redneck. It had been a long time since she had seen a vehicle that didn't have bucket seats, but she wished Mateo had a bench seat right now so she could be snuggled up next to him with her head resting on his broad shoulder like in the old movies from the nineteen fifties and sixties. Then it would only seem natural to ride off into the sunset and live the fantasy forever.

"I'm not coming in," he said when they reached her front door. He chuckled when he saw her lower lip protrude slightly. "What grade did you say you taught? First grade? I think your student's habits are rubbing off on you with that cute little pouty frown."

"This weekend went by way too fast," she said in a

tone that mimicked her pout. She wrapped her arms around his neck and let her fingers slide into the thickness of the long ponytail hanging down his back. Once again, she was tempted to lure him inside and back into her bed. But he was right, of course, this perfect weekend had to end sometime.

Mateo's arms held her tight against his body as he leaned down and gave her a kiss filled with as much emotion and promise as seemed humanly possible at this moment. She returned his kiss, prolonging the inevitable for as long as she could without needing to breathe. How was it that his mouth always tasted so amazing? She needed to ask him what brand of toothpaste he used.

"You'll call?" she asked instead as they finally pulled apart.

"Every night, my love," he promised. He kissed his fingertips and touched them lightly to her lips then took a step backward. His brilliant smile lit up his dark shimmering eyes before he turned and walked away.

My love. How perfectly romantic. A happy sigh escaped from her parted lips.

She remained in her doorway until he had driven out of sight. A quote from Romeo and Juliet's balcony scene popped into her mind; 'Parting is such sweet sorrow.'

So sappy love clichés really were her natural state of mind now. And it was all Mateo Two Moons fault.

She walked into her quiet apartment, still tasting his last delicious kiss on her mouth. She ran her tongue over her lips hoping to savor every tiny remembrance of him. Tomorrow she would go to school like it was any other day. She would try to act like she was the same person she had been last week and she would pretend she hadn't just spent the past couple of days in a state of erotic bliss so overpowering she found it hard to believe it really happened.

Tomorrow was seriously going to suck.

Chapter Eleven

Chloe knew she should wait until tomorrow morning before heading up to the Superstitions. But since she wasn't going to be able to sleep anyway, she might as well go up there tonight. If she hurried, she should be in her usual camping spot by nightfall. By early morning, she could be on the Old Military Trail.

Then she would just have to wait for the sun to set tomorrow evening, so she could look for the new clues Dawn had seen in her dream about the Lost Dutchman's Gold Mine. Of course, it had only been a dream, she reminded herself for the umpteenth time. But Dawn's dream had presented her with a fresh insight and a new enthusiasm to check it out.

In the dream, Dawn said she had been standing in a spot high up on a ledge Chloe or her father never paid much attention to when searching for the gold mine in the past because from the trail below it appeared that ridge did not lead anywhere. Even more importantly, the graphic dream placed the face Jacob Waltz talked about on the desert floor at a location they never thought to check. The face was only visible when the sun was setting. Chloe, her father, and even grandfather always assumed the face that supposedly looked at the mine was somewhere on the surrounding walls of rock.

If there was any chance at all the dream could reveal a new clue to the location of the Lost Dutchman

Mine, she had to know, and she had to know now.

Her hands shook as she tossed her camping gear into the back of her SUV, but she wasn't sure if that was from excitement or something else. A nagging guilt was making her edgy and uncertain about missing school the next couple of days when there was so much going on with the first Open House of the year. With any luck, though, she would be back fairly early on Tuesday.

With even more luck, she might be coming back with millions of dollars' worth of gold in her possession and she could retire from teaching altogether. The thought made her entire body shake, and that was undoubtedly from excitement.

She considered calling Dawn to tell her she was headed up to the Superstitions tonight, just because of the remote possibility she could run into trouble and might need for someone to know where she was. But when they were up here last weekend, she admitted she didn't understand the obsession gold seekers had in their relentless quest to find the gold mine, so Chloe didn't really want her to know she was off on another wild goose chase to search for something Dawn had seen in a dream.

She was also worried Dawn might mention her dream to her Apache stud. She already knew they talked about the gold mine. Mateo's brothers, Anton and Rafael, admitted they were searching for the gold mine the first night they met them on the Superstitions. She couldn't take the chance anyone would get up on the mountain with this new information ahead of her, so she had to go tonight.

The sun was hanging low in the westerly sky by

the time she parked her SUV in her usual spot at the base of the Superstitions. The narrow trail she always took was heavy with shadows from the tall rocks and low brush along the sides. Although she had come up here and searched around by herself during the daytime many times over the years, she had never come here alone at night. When a weird slow-moving coldness inched down her spine and made her footsteps halt only a couple of yards from her vehicle, she realized the shadowy trail was freaking her out more than just a little bit.

She glanced around nervously. She could always sleep in the back of her SUV. That idea made more sense than trying to hike up to the campsite this late in the evening. It would be completely dark long before she was even halfway to the camp. Another frosty chill raced down her spine. She wrapped her arms tightly around herself and looked around again. Beads of sweat broke out along her upper lip.

This was so ridiculous. Before now, she had never been afraid of these mountains, and she never thought much about all the stories of people who had gone missing in this remote mountain range. But she was thinking about all of them now. Rumors had the dead or missing head count at over six hundred since the mid-eighteen hundreds. Who knew how many more disappeared before anyone was actually taking a head count?

"Okay, staying in the car tonight," she said out loud as she opened the back hatch. She folded the rear seats down and unrolled her sleeping bag. Luckily, she thought to bring her tablet along and it was loaded with unread books she never had time to read at home. She could pass the time reading while she cowered in the back of her SUV until daylight.

She chuckled and shook her head at her silly case of the willies. At least, Dawn wasn't here with her, because she had been a total scaredy cat when they had been up here last weekend. The two of them together acting like big cowards wouldn't be a good combination. But if the new clues from Dawn's dream proved to be helpful in locating the Lost Dutchman, Chloe would gladly share the wealth with her new friend. Well, some of it anyway.

After locking all the doors and leaving just a tiny crack at the top of all the windows for air, Chloe settled into her sleeping bag with her headlamp strapped around her head. She tried to focus on a mystery novel she downloaded months earlier. But every faint noise made her jump, and she kept imagining things darting around outside her vehicle.

There was a huge full moon tonight so the landscape was lit up with the natural glow of the bright orb, and she knew if there really was something out there, she would surely be able to see it. But every time she attempted to read a few lines of her book, she thought she caught something from the side of her eye moving around behind the rocks or bushes.

"Fuck," she mumbled after nearly jumping through the roof when she thought something had just rubbed against the side of her vehicle. Slowly, she glanced out the window, expecting to see an animal lurking outside. There were plenty of cougars, wolves, coyotes, and even panthers were known to roam around in these rugged mountains. A relieved sigh escaped from her when she didn't see anything close to her vehicle. She needed to get a grip on her out-of-control emotions since she was obviously imagining things. What was it Dawn said? Oh yeah.

"Cowboy up, you big fat chicken cupcake," Chloe said in a loud aggravated voice.

Flipping off her headlight and shutting down her tablet, she decided she needed to get some sleep and quit scaring the crap out of herself. Something else Dawn said echoed through her mind.

Count Dracula.

"Seriously?" She attempted a weak laugh. She yanked her sleeping bag over her head and sunk farther down into its comforting refuge.

The sun coming up in the desert sky was more than a welcome sight. Chloe barely closed her eyes all night. But unlike Dawn, when they had been camping, she wasn't plagued by dreams that woke her up feeling hot and flustered. Instead, she had been shrouded in a suffocating fear that would not give her a moment's peace, and she didn't even know what it was she was so afraid of. But she was certain of one thing, this terror was like nothing she ever experienced before, and never hoped to experience again.

"Just my shitty luck...no wet dreams," she mumbled in a foul tone as she kicked her sleeping bag away from her feet.

It was early, barely six a.m. She glanced around as the sun cast its first golden rays over the mountain peaks and began to fill the desert floor with the hazy light of the new day. She should have waited to come up here this morning. Last night had been a complete waste of time, and it only proved to her she wasn't as brave as she always believed. She shook her head in disgust as she recalled the ridiculous thoughts in her head last night, mostly about Count Dracula.

"Thanks for putting that stupid idea in my head, Dawn," she muttered as she opened the back hatch of her SUV and climbed out into the open.

The morning was cool and calm. There were no sounds or signs of anything moving for as far as she could see in any direction. She felt alone—really alone—and defenseless in a way she never felt before. She wrapped her arms tightly around herself and glanced out at the barren desert landscape as an uneasy sense of growing panic began to consume her.

"What the hell is wrong with me?" she asked as if someone would answer her. It had to be sleep deprivation making her so jumpy and stupid. She just needed to focus on the reason she was here, and get started on the hike up to the Old Military Trail. It wouldn't take her long to get there, though, so it would be a long day of waiting until the sun set this evening. But what else was she going to do all day now that she was here?

A sensation like tiny knives cutting away at her skin rippled through her body. She shuddered and thought about climbing back in her SUV and getting the hell out of here before anyone knew how crazy she had been. If she went through with this plan, tonight she would have no choice but to spend the entire night at the location where she would be looking for the gold mine. It was way too dangerous to attempt to climb down from the Weaver's Needle trail after the sun went down.

A deep sense of foreboding settled in the pit of her stomach. Maybe she should wait until she could bring someone else up here with her. But who? Her dad had been diagnosed with cancer recently, so he probably would never come back here to the mountain with her, and Dawn was most likely going be too busy with her Apache stud to want to spend time with her anymore. She doubted she could even convince her to come back up here after their last excursion, anyway. It had been more than a little obvious how nervous this area made Dawn and how anxious she was to get away from these mountains.

Chloe drew in a nervous breath. She truly was alone in this quest. She either needed to get over this silly phobia she recently developed or just give up her search for the Lost Dutchman's Gold Mine altogether. If she left now, she could almost be to her classroom on time, and no one would ever know she spent the night up here cowering in her sleeping bag imaging who knows what lurking outside her vehicle. She wiped her shaking hand over her sweating brow and stared at the handle on the driver's door.

Just go home.

Before it's too late.

An exasperated huff escaped from her lips. She never believed any of the scary stories about the ghosts or demons that guarded the treasure and kept gold seekers from getting too close to the mine, assuming them to be the result of someone's overly active imagination. So now, of all times, she sure wasn't going to allow herself to start believing them.

She grabbed her backpack, and stuffed her tablet in the side pocket. It would be a long day, and hopefully she would be able to concentrate on reading rather than spooking herself out while she passed the endless hours until sunset.

Hiking up to the Old Military Trial in the coolness of the morning was enjoyable and gave her a chance to calm her nerves and clear her head of all those daunting thoughts. By the time she arrived at the general location in Dawn's dream she was laughing at her earlier feelings of doom and gloom. She knew these mountains so well, and the idea they might hold endless riches somewhere deep in their hidden interior only increased their lure to Chloe and her family, just as they had to countless other gold seekers.

It was not evil spirits she needed to dread. It was her own carelessness she needed to worry about. If she didn't watch every step she took along the steep trails; if she became distracted, slipped and fell into one of the deep gullies or canyons, she would become just one more of those hundreds of casualties claimed by these unforgiving mountains. Even a step too close to one of the rattlesnakes concealed and coiled among the rocks or hidden under a bush could be a deadly mistake.

These mountains really were filled with endless dangers, but it wasn't from horned demons or ghostly specters, she told herself as she settled in for the long wait until the sun went down.

Considering it was almost the first of October, and the day started out at a cool comfortable temperature, by mid-day it was scorching. She was grateful for the baseball cap she had worn today to keep the burning sun off her face, but the long sleeve cotton shirt and jeans were way too heavy. She took her shirt off and tied it around her waist, leaving only her yellow sports bra to cover her upper torso. She thought about stripping down to just her bra and panties, but modesty and the thought of having a caravan of hikers appear on the trail before she could cover herself, kept her from taking any more clothes off.

Still, she was miserable. Rivulets of sweat ran down her neck, the length of her backbone, between her breasts, and made her entire body drenched. She was too hot to even read. Packing the tablet had been a complete waste of time. She spent the entire day moving from rock to rock in an effort to find the teeny bits of shade they offered at their bases, and having daydreams about what she was going to do with all the gold she was about to find. Everything from the cruises she would take to exotic lands to the charities she vowed to donate to if she could find this gold mine dominated her thoughts during the long tortuous hours until sunset.

When the sun finally began to drop lower in the sky, Chloe was once again rethinking her plan. She was surprised she hadn't dropped dead from a heat stroke, and she had already drunk most of the bottled water she brought with her. There was more water in her SUV, but she wouldn't get back to it until tomorrow sometime.

If she found something here tonight, she might not get back even then. She could be spending—who knows how much time—chipping and digging out gold ore from the Lost Dutchman's Gold Mine to haul back so she could finally prove to everyone, to the entire world, it really did exist.

She carefully made her way through the boulders along the bottom of the mountain as she tried to analyze all the clues again. Most of Dawn's dream held the same clues to the mine's location Chloe and her father followed every time they came here. The only differences were that in the dream she climbed higher on the overhanging ledges so she could see the face Jacob Waltz mentioned in his clues, and that face was on the desert floor below Weaver's Needle.

To see an open expanse of the ground below the towering sphere of Weaver's Needle, Chloe realized she had to climb up farther up on the mountainside than she and her father ever considered in their previous hikes. The route to that higher ledge was going to be more than a little treacherous.

Even though it was slightly cooler as she hiked up the side of the mountain in the early evening, she was still sweating like a pig. Every couple of minutes she had to stop to wipe the river of sweat from her eyes so she could see where she was going. Blinded by the sweat, she slipped a couple of times on the loose rocks where she was trying to find secure footing. Each time, she froze at the possibility of tumbling down the side of the mountain, and falling into some deep crevice, never to be seen again.

After what felt like forever, she finally pulled herself up to the jagged ledge about two-thirds the way up this side of the mountain where she was sure Dawn described she had been standing in her dream. With a sense of relief, combined with an invigorating feeling of anticipation, she turned slowly around to look at the valley below.

The sun would be falling behind the uneven peaks of Weaver's Needle in a matter of minutes. Since it had taken her longer than expected to climb up here to this higher ledge she worried she missed the critical window of opportunity to find the rock face below on the desert floor. As she exhaled the breath she had been unconsciously holding, she gazed down.

"Oh my God," she gasped as the shapes of the prestigiously situated rocks Dawn talked about seeing in her dream, caught her attention. The last rays of the sun were settling along the outline of the rocks, making the face an obvious sculpture on the desert floor. Her entire body began to shake. She had to lean against the rock wall behind her to keep from falling to her knees.

A rock face looks up at my gold mine.

All these years—so many trips up here—endless hours studying Jacob Waltz's clues, and not once had any of them thought to climb up high enough to look down upon this narrow expanse of the desert floor for the rock face. Evidently, all the other gold seekers through the years made the same mistake, searching for the face along the walls of Weaver's Needle or surrounding cliffs and towering rocks of the Superstitions, because no one ever suggested the rock face was a scattering of rocks on the bottom of the canyon below the Needle on the desert floor.

Her gaze grew blurry as she focused so intently on the visible face spread out below her. The desert ground clearly outlined the shape of a man's face with a rock mouth in a barely curved grin, and nose with two nostrils. Nearly identical brown hued rocks formed the man's eyes and a couple of dark spots on the sides of the rocks resembled pupils in an eyeball. They were directed at an angle, which appeared to be looking at an area to the right of the Needle, and farther up the mountain behind where she stood now.

She exhaled sharply, not even aware she had been holding her breath again, and began to turn slowly in the direction of the rock eyes' unwavering stare. Scanning the area above her head, she couldn't see anything more than the menacing ledges of sharp stone. Growing shadows of the rugged mountains were swiftly cloaking the entire area in gloomy shroud.

But a single ray of the fading sunlight shone along the ridge where the rock eyes were pointed...*the sun sets on the gold in my mine.* She had no doubt the last beam of the setting sun would lead her directly to the Lost Dutchman's Gold Mine.

Her heart beat frantically against her breast as she wiped away the thick gummy layer of sweat along her upper lip. Somewhere up there on that narrow-looking ledge, where she couldn't see from this location was the one thing she and her dad had been dreaming of and searching for their entire lives. She imagined her father's face when she told him and showed him the proof she had found the Lost Dutchman's Gold Mine, at last. There would be no greater joy in her life.

She wished her grandfather and great-grandfather were both still alive so they could share in this amazing discovery. They had all believed unconditionally and been ridiculed for that belief. But now, at long last, she was going to prove to the world their devotion had not been in vain.

A panicked sense of urgency overcame every other emotion she was feeling. Darkness was closing in fast. She had to get up higher—hopefully high enough to reach the cave that supposedly housed the gold mine Dawn had seen in her dream, and she had to get there before it became too dark for her to see where she was climbing.

There was no trail to follow and her headlamp

would not afford much light. Once again, she reminded herself of how one wrong step could be fatal. Maybe she should just spend the night here on this ledge and climb up the rest of the way in the morning? It would probably be safer to be in the cave than out here in the open all night. Besides, there was no way she could wait until morning to see those rich veins of gold Dawn described in her dream, and she had no doubt they were there, because everything else in the dream had been spot on.

The hammering of her heart was deafening in the stillness of the dusky mountaintop. Her entire body was trembling with an overpowering sense of excitement. The Lost Dutchman Gold Mine was real. She had really found it. Her life would never be the same again.

She reached up to grab on to a protruding rock to begin the last of the precarious trek, but the feeling she was no longer alone made the blood grow cold in her veins. Her hands began to slide down to the sides of her body as her recent excitement began to turn into a paralyzing sense of dread. The breath she tried to inhale hung up in her parched throat and made her feel as if she was strangling on her own terror.

She was only afforded a brief glimpse of the man as she turned to look at him. A fleeting, disjointed realization crowded in with the all-consuming terror ruling her mind and body. She almost smiled in relief because he seemed vaguely familiar.

This dark dangerously handsome stranger who just appeared out of nowhere was as gorgeous as the three Two Moons Brothers. How odd? There must be another one of them. It was her last conscious thought.

Chapter Twelve

Monday had been horrible—even worse than she expected.

Dawn's students were cranky and difficult all day, and the Open House with their parents had been long and boring, although, she tried really hard to be enthusiastic about meeting with all of them. She felt a little guilty, because usually she really enjoyed school-related events. But today she couldn't concentrate on anything other than the next time she would see Mateo. Occasionally she would be reminded of the little nagging fact they made love over and over again throughout the entire weekend without even thinking about or discussing any sort of protection.

When they were together, it was like a sexual frenzy stole away all their common sense. A shit-eating grin claimed her lips for about the hundredth time today…every time she thought about Mateo Two Moons. Once again, she forgot all about the little issue of birth control, and all she could think of was how long it had been since she had seen Mateo and how eager she was to get lost in that uncontrollable frenzy again.

Making everything even more unbearable was that Chloe had taken the entire day off from school without even telling her. She stopped by the principal's office to ask if anyone knew why Chloe wasn't here, and was told by the secretary she left a message on the answering machine saying said she had to deal with a personal issue. Dawn's repeated calls and texts to her cell had been useless.

At first, her feelings were a little hurt Chloe wasn't answering her calls, because even though they hadn't known one another all that long, it seemed like they were already pretty good friends. By the time she got home late Monday night, however, she was more than a little worried about her friend and what sort of personal issue caused her to disappear on such an important day at their school.

The first Open House of the school year was kind of a big deal, and she knew Chloe had been looking forward to it. Something major must have happened to cause her to miss it. Could her father's condition have worsened? Chloe mentioned he was too sick to go camping or hiking anymore, but Dawn didn't know how serious his illness was. All she could hope for now, though, was she would hear from her soon and everything would be okay.

But Chloe's call wasn't the only one she was anxiously waiting for. She quickly got ready for bed, so she could wait for Mateo's call. No sooner had she changed into her pink polka dot pjs, washed her face, brushed her teeth, and climbed into bed, when her cell began to play the enchanting guitar chords of a Joseph Red Feather song. She spent part of her lunch hour today setting her ringtone for calls from Mateo to play his favorite musician. Now, she would always know when he was the one calling, and the song she had chosen was a beautiful love ballad called In My Perfect World. It was just perfect.

"Hello, I missed you so much today," Dawn said in

a rush. His deep soft laughter on the other end of the receiver made her heart feel like it was bursting open with happiness.

"I missed you more. How was the Open House?"

"Exhausting. I thought it would never end. How was your day? Where are you? Want to come over for a little while?"

He chuckled and sighed loudly. "My day was missing you, and there is nothing I would love more than to come over, but unfortunately, I'm in Tucson for a couple of days."

"Tucson?" she moaned. That was so far away. Her previously happy heart dropped down to the pit of her stomach. "On business, I'm guessing?" She hated the idea of him being out of town. She hated him being anywhere other than with her.

"Yes. It's business," he replied. "But I would like to see you tomorrow night if you aren't busy?"

Tomorrow night? Oh, hell yes. But that was twenty-four long hours away. "I would like that," she replied trying not to sound too anxious and crazy. "How about if I cook dinner for you?"

"Can you cook?" he asked in a teasing tone.

She giggled. "Cooking is only one of my many talents, Mr. Two Moons."

"Well said, my love." Mateo cleared his throat, and added, "I am already aware of some of your other talents, so I am definitely down for dinner."

Another giggle escaped from her. Oh, how she loved it when called her, 'my love'. She wished she could gaze into his eyes right now, because she knew they were twinkling like ebony diamonds as he smiled suggestively at their conversation. "Anything I should not make? Like are you allergic to any certain food?"

"I'm easy," he said with another chuckle. "But then, you already knew that," he added.

Dawn laughed, but refrained from commenting on his remark. She had been rather easy herself lately where he was concerned. "I guess I'll see you tomorrow night. I can't wait."

"Me either," he agreed. "Oh, and Dawn?"

"Yes?"

"I love you," he said tenderly.

"I love you," Dawn said in an equally soft tone. A feeling of complete and utter bliss spread through her entire body, and lasted long after he was no longer on the other end of the phone. She physically felt the extent of his love for her, even now, when he wasn't here with her, and she knew it was only going to grow. Love at first sight was just the beginning for the two of them. Forever echoed through her mind again.

****

Mateo put his new cell phone down on the console in the center of his truck seats. He had gotten the phone the same night he bought this truck. All these things were necessary if he wanted to fit into Dawn's world, even if it was for only a short time. He even rented a place so he could have somewhere of his own to take her when they weren't at her apartment.

The luxurious fully furnished condo was not far from where she lived. It was an expensive rental, but his family didn't have to worry about money. Drago's clan had an endless supply of gold in the big cave up on the Superstitions. The Clan Society handled all gold transactions, and they learned long ago there were always ways to secretly launder the precious metal in exchange for a hefty fee.

A weighted sigh escaped from Mateo as he slumped down in the seat. He hated lying to Dawn about everything, regardless of how necessary it was for the safety of all who were involved. But then, wasn't his entire existence here in her world a deception? It started when he lied about his job on the Tribal Council to cover up why she would never see him in the daytime.

Now, he was pretending to be in another town so he could hide something else from her, which seemed ludicrous when the whole idea behind this sham was to spend time with her before he took her to the mountain for all eternity. Still, concealing the truth about where he really was seemed easy compared to the secret he had to keep from her now.

Something devastating transpired last night— something he never would have expected to happen in a million years. But there was no way to undo it, and it was a horrible tragedy that complicated everything.

He kept telling himself he should just go to her apartment tonight, suck the blood from her neck, wrist, and thigh until she passed out, and make her his mate forever. This would be the easy solution. Even though he knew this was exactly what he should do before anything else occurred to jeopardize the welfare of his entire clan and the secrets they had hidden in the gold-laden cave, he was still not ready to give up the life he envisioned and just started living here in Dawn's world.

He tried to swallow, but his mouth was bitter and dry. His thirst for human blood was unusually desperate tonight. Although he did not need to feed on blood from real ones often since he had been born a half-breed vampire, when the urge did overcome him, it was powerful and consuming.

He couldn't stop remembering how sweet and satisfying Dawn's blood had tasted on the nights when he had drunk from her neck and wrist. He was afraid to even think about how succulent the blood from her thigh would taste when he was ready to go that far.

The urge to drink more of her blood had become so strong on the drive back from the lake last night he had been afraid to go into her apartment when they returned, even though he wanted nothing more than to spend the rest of the night lying beside her in bed like he had done the previous night.

The memory of watching her sleep in his arms that first night after they made love brought a poignant smile to his lips and caused his arms to ache with the yearning to hold her close again.

Mateo also knew there was another reason he was craving human blood so strongly. There was a fresh young blood source in the village on the mountain. She had come too close to the hidden village of the Blood Clan, as had many gold seekers in the past. Mateo's father sensed her nearness as soon as the sun dropped low enough in the sky for him to awaken and leave the caves.

Antonio couldn't believe a real one was so nearby just when they needed extra blood to use in the special rituals they were conducting for the impending birth of Rafael and Lydia's child, and he wasted no time in bringing the welcome intruder back to the village.

Mateo had also been aware of a human presence when he exited the cave where he spent the daylight hours since he had turned a quarter of a century over seventy-five years ago. He knew his father had gone out to hunt for the real one, but he had been so anxious to get to Dawn he hadn't waited around for Antonio to return. He didn't learn who the new blood source was until he came back up to the village after dropping Dawn off at her apartment last night.

As he ran his tongue over his brittle feeling lips again he tried to focus on something—anything—other than drinking blood. He gritted his teeth tightly together and headed back to the village at the top of the Superstitions where he knew he could quench his evil cravings without harming someone else.

As much as he wanted to resist these demonic urges right now, he knew it would be useless. When the vampire part of him thirsted for blood, the human part would never win.

Chapter Thirteen

"What do you mean, she's gone missing?" Dawn tried to keep the rising panic out of her voice. She could tell the man on the other end of the phone was already worried enough without her adding to his panic about his missing daughter.

"Her car was found this morning at the base of one of the hiking trails. It's where we always parked when we went up there to scout around. A search party went out this afternoon to look for her." Mr. Webster choked back a sob. "We believe she went up to the Superstitions sometime Sunday evening, but I can't believe she went up there alone at night. She knows how dangerous that could be." He couldn't hold back the sob this time and it accompanied his next simple questions, "Why? Why do you think she would she do that?"

For a moment Dawn was too shocked to speak. She felt numb and terrified at the idea of what might have happened to her friend. Even worse, she knew why Chloe had taken off to the Superstitions Sunday night. Guilt was nearly as strong as her panic right now.

But it was only a dream.

"Did she call you be-before she left Sunday?" She finally managed to stutter. "Do-do you think she was searching for the gold mine?"

There was a long pause on the other end of the

phone before Chloe's father spoke again. He sounded as if he had gained some composure back. "I spoke to her Sunday morning, and she didn't mention anything about going to the mountain. In fact, she talked about the Open House at school on Monday night—last night. She was looking forward to meeting with the parents of her students."

He was quiet for a few seconds, and Dawn heard a heavy trembling sigh on the other end. "If something has happened to her, it's my fault. My stupid obsession with finding that gold mine is to blame. I will never forgive my—" His voice cracked and another loud sob echoed through the receiver.

"Please, Mr. Webster, it's not your fault," she attempted to console him. *It's my fault.* Should she tell him about the dream? Her chest felt as if a boulder the size of a house had just rolled over it. Another wave of crushing guilt left her unable to breathe for a moment. She wouldn't mention the dream to Chloe's father yet, she decided as she finally took a gasping breath.

There could still be a good, if not great, outcome. Maybe Chloe had fallen on one of those narrow steep trails and broken a leg or something even less serious. There were lots of people looking for her and they would find her before it was too late. She just had to be alive. Dawn had to believe that, because she couldn't bear the alternative.

"I will be in touch," she said quietly. "I have to go right now. But I-I—" She wished she could tell him she was confident his daughter was okay, but saying it out loud might sound as false as it was beginning to feel. The crushing boulder rolled back over her chest and was now holding her heart prisoner under its monstrous girth. "I'm so sorry," she said softly as she pushed the end button on her phone.

She sat in her white pickup staring blankly ahead, yet seeing nothing, even though school had just let out for the day and she was surrounded by students and dozens of other people. Parents were picking up their kids; big yellow buses lined the edge of the parking lot filling up with the students who lived too far to walk home from school. Normal life was going on as usual, in spite of the fact a beautiful vibrant woman was missing and her disappearance might have a tragic ending.

An invisible icicle formed along Dawn's spine as the unforgiving terrain of those jagged mountain peaks crowded into her mind. The stories she read about all the people who vanished somewhere along those spooky trails joined her dreaded thoughts. Chloe had been gone since Sunday night and it was late Tuesday afternoon. That was a long time—far too long—to be in the dangerous conditions that existed in the Superstitions, especially alone, and possibly injured. An entire night among the towering rock walls of Dracula's evil lair. *Don't even go there.*

A nauseated heaviness settled in the pit of her stomach. If something really horrible happened to Chloe, she would never be able to forgive herself.

But it had only been a dream. Had Chloe seriously believed it meant something more? She choked back the bitter tasting lump in her throat; it felt like it had settled on top of the sick mass already filling her stomach. She recalled the way Chloe responded Sunday afternoon when she told her about the dream. Although she tried to act as if she didn't think it meant anything,

Dawn hadn't missed the way her blue gaze sparkled with unspoken curiosity as she considered the vision about the rock face on the desert floor.

Mateo was coming for dinner later this evening, but she needed him now. The worry over her friend's fate had driven a stake of foreboding through her heart, and his strength and love was the only thing that could even begin to sooth her pain.

She felt as if the rest of life wasn't happening outside of the cab of her small pickup truck as she drove out of the school parking lot. She knew she should stay in her classroom for at least another hour or so, grading papers and preparing a new lesson for tomorrow's classes, but there was no way she could concentrate on anything other than her missing friend and talking to or seeing Mateo as soon as possible.

She had to tell him about the crazy dream she had about the Lost Dutchman's Gold Mine. Maybe he knew something more? The Apaches had been living here far longer than anyone else. Perhaps they had some theories about the location of the mine that weren't mentioned in the history books and could give them a clue as to Chloe's whereabouts.

But he wasn't answering his cell. She called him at least a dozen times and texted as many times since she had gotten home. Although she assumed he was probably traveling back from his business trip to Tuscan, she couldn't imagine he didn't get cell phone service somewhere along the route. She was leaving him a frantic message every single time. *'Call me right away. It's an emergency.'* Why wasn't he answering?

To pass the endless panic-filled time, she finished putting together the lasagna she planned for dinner, and popped it in the oven to bake. Meanwhile, she tore up lettuce and chopped veggies for a salad, then slathered butter and fresh roasted garlic on a loaf of bread to accompany the main course. This dinner was her specialty and everyone who had ever eaten her lasagna said it was the best. Making this special entrée for the man of her dreams was—an ominous feeling whipped through her body at that thought.

No. Not the man of her dreams. She firmly reminded herself Mateo was not the faceless stranger who ravished her body and bitten her in those weird kinky dreams. He was the real man she loved more than life itself. Although that sounded obsessed and extreme, it was true.

As the tantalizing smells of the baking lasagna filled Dawn's little apartment, her anxiety grew. She knew she would not be able to force a single bite down over the sickening lump that refused to dissipate from her throat, but hopefully, Mateo would eat.

He still wasn't responding to her urgent calls and texts. What if something had happened to him, too? An urgent sense of foreboding clutched at her heart. Her hand instinctively covered the spot over her left breast when it felt like her heart ceased to beat for a moment. *Stop it…*he was fine. Chloe was fine. Soon, everything in her world would be perfect again.

She switched on the ceiling lights and stared out the kitchen window above the sink. Nighttime was closing in. She always loved this time of the evening, just as the last glow of the sun was about to fade from the horizon; the beginning of the end of another day, then the misty shadow of the moon as it began to form a faint outline in the velvet haze of the night—right before the sea of stars began to dot the sky with their sparkling display.

But right now she was only recalling the horror she felt on that night a week and a half ago when she and Chloe had been hiking up the trail on the Superstitions. Twilight on that night had not felt so enchanting. Her eerie feeling had been so consuming that something—or someone—was watching them. Or stalking them? The terror she felt had been so strong she vowed to never go back up there on those scary mountains again.

With her arms wrapped tightly around her midsection, she remained frozen to the spot as the fading landscape outside her window became a blur before her eyes. Her own embrace around her body tightened, but the shivers wouldn't cease. Her teeth began to chatter as if the temperature had dropped to minus zero, even though it was still sweltering.

Chloe was somewhere up there among those menacing dark shadows and deathly trails, which had led to so much tragedy and loss of lives since the beginning of history. She was helpless and alone—and someone or something—was watching her.

Dawn couldn't breathe. Her blurred vision began to fade to black and her legs felt too weak to support her.

She could not allow herself to believe there was actually neck and wrist-biting, blood-sucking monsters waiting to attack innocent people along the sinister trails of the Superstitions, or anywhere else in the world.

But she permitted those horrifying thoughts to seep into her mind and now there was no escape. She reached out to grab the edge of the counter, because she felt herself spiraling downward. But before everything went completely black, a pair of strong arms prevented her fall.

****

"Udaya!" Mateo pulled her to him. He could feel the violent shakes rattling through her body. He tightened his hold on her. "I received all your messages once I was in cell range, and I rushed here as fast as I could."

Her arms wrapped around his neck. She buried her face against his chest as loud gasping sobs shook through her body.

When he first turned her around and gazed down at her, he glimpsed a look of complete and utter horror in her hazel eyes and in her expression. A jagged pain tore through his heart.

For several more minutes, he held her as they leaned against her kitchen counter. Her uncontrollable crying made her entire body convulse and her tears soaked the front of his black western shirt. Remorse washed over him as her inconsolable state of anguish seeped into every pore of his being. Her pain was now his pain, and it was more gut-wrenching than he ever could have imagined.

In his secluded world atop of the Superstitions, they did not have to deal with this sort of sorrow. Now he was wondering if he made a grave mistake by not making Dawn his mate from the first moment she had come to the mountain. She could have been spared all this grief.

"Something terrible has happened," Dawn managed to say through her sobs.

He kissed the top of her blonde head and tenderly rubbed her back with his hand. "I'm so very sorry about

172

your friend, my love."

A couple more sniffles escaped from her before her weeping began to subside. "You know a-about Chloe?"

"It's, well, I heard about her disappearance on the radio—on my way back from Tuscan this evening," he lied.

Dawn remained in his arms with her face still pressed against his chest, unmoving, except for the continued tremors shooting through her body. Her intense crying jag seemed to be over for now. But his anguish was only increasing by the second. He did not want to continue to lie to her, but in her fragile state of mind, there was no way she could handle the unbelievable truth of what happened to her friend.

"Let's sit down and talk," he said quietly. His breath brushed lightly against the loose strands at the top of her head and he noticed her blonde hair flutter slightly. Right now, Mateo felt like a complete contradiction in every way. Part of him was a real, living, breathing man, yet, at this moment he felt like a murderous monster.

If only his father hadn't sensed Chloe's presence first? Maybe, if he had been paying attention he could have prevented her tragic fate. He grunted inwardly with disgust. It probably wouldn't have mattered. A fresh blood source so close to the village and gold mine meant she didn't stand a chance regardless of who found her first.

Mateo pictured the way she looked at the pizza place just a few nights ago. Her long brown hair tumbled over one shoulder in a teasing style and her brilliant blue eyes looked at him and his brothers with an enticing glint. She was full of life and promise. A sick feeling twisted Mateo's gut into a knot.

Now, the beautiful young woman named Chloe Webster sat in the back of the big cave with the other real ones who served as human blood sources for the mature vampires of the clan; her blue eyes void of their once shimmering sparkle, unseeing, and staring off into the blackness.

"Tell me what happened?" Mateo asked as he sat down next to Dawn on her beige tweed couch and pulled her into his embrace. Her body caved into his. Occasional shudders from her recent crying bout still shook through her.

"I think Chloe is missing because of me," she finally said in a shaky voice. "If anything has happened to her," she sniffed loudly before adding, "It's my fault."

"That's not true," he retorted in a forceful tone. He drew in a heavy sigh and began to stroke her hair gently. "For whatever reason Chloe went up to the Superstitions, she did it all on her own. You had nothing to do with it."

Her head shook from side to side in a weak motion. She didn't move away from his tight hold as she began to speak in a voice barely loud enough for him to hear. "There's something I need to tell you. You're probably going to think I'm crazy when I'm done."

"I would never think that. I love you. You can tell me anything." There was a heavy feeling pressing against his heart as he held his breath and waited for her to speak again.

"I had a really vivid dream. Like all my dreams, or nightmares, I've had lately." She exhaled a sharp breath.

Mateo rested his cheek against the top of her head. "Another erotic one?" he asked in a confused voice.

"No," she replied quickly. "It wasn't quite as realistic as those had been, thank goodness. This one was about the Lost Dutchman's Gold Mine."

A frown drew his brows together. An unknown dread gripped him in its tight rein. "Okay? What does this have to do with Chloe?" He heard Dawn suck in another deep breath.

"Generations of her family have been hunting for the gold mine. They were all certain the clues left by that old miner, Jacob Waltz, would lead them to the location."

"There have been many people who believed, or still do believe the gold mine exists, but it's just a legend, nothing more," he replied as more uneasiness crept through him.

She nodded her head slightly. "But suppose it really did exist and the clues Waltz left had been interpreted wrong all this time?" She pulled away from him and looked up at him. Tears that hadn't fallen were still cradled in the lower lids of her tortured gaze. Moisture from the ones that had already escaped glistened on the tips of her long brown eye lashes.

"What if someone—like me—had a dream, or call it a vision or whatever, that revealed the correct way to decipher the old man's clues?"

Mateo shook his head in bewilderment as a creeping sense of building panic inched through him. His carefully planned façade was beginning to crumble around him. If Dawn guessed—or dreamed—about what was really in that hidden gold mine, their time here in her world could be over.

"Sunday afternoon I had a dream about the clues Chloe revealed to me when we were camping and hunting for the gold mine that first weekend. This one was pretty realistic, too. Not in the way the sensual dreams were, but I dreamt I was actually standing on the mountain looking directly into a huge cave that contained rich veins of gold ore. I knew I had found the Lost Dutchman's Gold Mine. Well, in my dream, I knew, anyway."

He cleared his throat nervously. "But, Dawn, it was only a dream."

"Yes, I know," she agreed, and glanced off into the distance as if she was remembering every tiny aspect of her dream. "When I told Chloe about it, I think she thought the new details revealed in my dream were really significant. She tried to act all nonchalant, but I know she was dying to go check them out. I figured she would want to go back up there next weekend. I never imagined she would take off alone Sunday night." Dawn's eyes filled with new tears that spilled down her cheeks. "I just hope nothing happened to her because my crazy dre—"

"No, don't even think it," he cut in. "She is obviously an experienced gold seeker and hiker. She had to know going up to the Superstitions alone to hunt for clues you saw in a dream was foolish."

"But I—"

"No," he interrupted her again as he placed his fingertips against her trembling lips. "I'm not going to let you blame yourself for something you had nothing to do with."

She shook her head and opened her mouth to speak again in spite of the way his fingers were pressed against her lips, but he didn't give her a chance.

"Believe me. You didn't have anything to do with this. What happened to Chloe is not your fault." His hand moved away from her lips and his fingertips brushed lightly against the tears streaming down the side of her face.

She continued to stare into his dark gaze. He lowered his hand away from her cheek and cupped her chin. If only his loving touch could take away her guilt and pain. His bite could make her forget, he thought fleetingly.

The unexpected thought caused a raging thirst to rise in his throat. The yearning for her sweet tasting blood filled his senses. His mouth drew into a tight line as he tried to concentrate on what she was saying. He fought the beast inside him with every fiber of his being even though he was afraid it was going to win out sooner or later.

"We don't really know wh-what happened to her, yet," she said quietly. "Maybe, she just slipped and fell and is hurt, but she'll be okay once they find her."

He forced himself to nod in agreement. He slowly opened his mouth to speak. The thirsty fiend settled further down the back of his throat for the moment. "That's possible." His strength was growing…he was beginning to feel like his human self was gaining control.

A puny smile rested on his lips as he added, "Maybe she found the gold mine and ran off with all her new-found wealth so she wouldn't have to share it with anyone." He swallowed the bitter tasting bile in his mouth. Indeed, Chloe had found the Lost Dutchman's Gold Mine she had been looking for all her life. She was there now, sitting among all the riches, but she would never be leaving.

A frail smile barely curved Dawn's lips. "Yeah, maybe she really did find it? She knows those mountains so well, and she would never go unprepared. It could be possible she's up there somewhere mining all that gold right now, and..." Her voice trailed off and the feeble smile faded. She shrugged her hunched shoulders as if her words were too unrealistic to even say out loud.

He pulled her close against him. He couldn't bear the look of utter despair in her tear-laden gaze again. "I'm taking you to my place tonight. My condo is close by, and I think it will be good for you to get away from here for a while."

"But I cooked dinner," she mumbled.

"And it smells delicious. We'll take it to my place." He spent last night pretending to be in Tuscan so he could think about how to handle the Chloe situation when he saw Dawn again. He had also been getting the condo he rented ready, with the hopes she would go there with him tonight. It would be tricky to be at the condo with her only at nighttime, but he was determined to create as many beautiful memories there as was 'humanly' possible, because once they made their eternal home at the top of the Superstitions, those would be the last reminiscences they would have of being together here in her world.

Chapter Fourteen

"Your condo is so beautiful," Dawn said in a meek tone as she stood in the foyer and glanced around at the elegant surroundings. Her gaze rose to the tall glass windows that ran from the ground floor all the way past the balcony of the second story. "Working for the Apache Tribal Council must be a very lucrative profession."

"Thanks," Mateo mumbled without commenting on his fake career. He couldn't take credit for any of the furnishings or décor because everything was here when he rented the place. But whoever picked out the overstuffed brown leather couches, huge pale beige Flokati shag rugs, and expensive southwestern-themed artwork that hung on the walls, had a very discriminating eye.

He motioned for her to follow him into the kitchen, where high-end granite counter-tops in sandstone shades formed an L-shaped work area and a large free-standing island in the center of the room. After placing the pan of lasagna on the island, he turned toward her and asked, "Are you hungry?"

"I don't think I could keep anything down," she said with a sigh. "But you should eat." A weak smile curved her lips as she added, "I promise it's good. Lasagna is my specialty."

He thought about joking with her that he knew of

something else that was her specialty and it didn't have anything to do with lasagna, but he didn't want her to think he had forgotten about her missing friend. "I'll eat in a little bit. I'd rather just hold you in my arms right now."

Some of the tension seemed to ease from Dawn's tired expression as she nodded her head in agreement. "I'd prefer that, too." She reached out toward him and he wasted no time in wrapping his larger hand around her smaller one.

He led her into the living room where soft lights from strategically placed wrought iron wall sconces cast a romantic golden glow throughout the area. He had purposely placed personal items around the condo to make it look as if he really did live here. On the glass and iron coffee table a half-filled glass of water sat on top of a sandstone coaster.

One of his white western shirts was draped over the back of the tan suede recliner that sat in the corner of the room, and a pair of his barely-worn hiking boots on the rug in the front foyer. As he carefully arranged these normal-type belongings around the entire condo the previous night, he pretended he really did live here like a regular person. Like a real one.

He imagined what it would be like to wake up in the morning with the sunlight shining through the massive glass windows, and with her still cuddled in his arms in the big bed in the upstairs bedroom. He pictured them drinking coffee and preparing breakfast together in the cozy kitchen, or spending an entire day sprawled out on the comfy leather couch in the living room reading, watching television, making love, like any typical couple. Of course, his dreams of living a 'real' life with her were as crazy as Dawn thought her dreams were.

She sunk into the deep cushions of the couch and leaned against Mateo. He wrapped his arms around her waist and pulled her as close as possible. As always, he wanted to make love to her tonight, but he wondered if he was strong enough to make love to her without biting her now that it was becoming nearly impossible to be in her presence and not want to drink more of her blood?

He clamped his teeth together tightly in grim determination as his mouth and throat burned with the memory of her warm tempting blood. Maybe they shouldn't be intimate tonight.

"Mateo?" she said after a few quiet moments. "There's something I want to ask you. It's really important and would mean everything to me."

"Anything. I would do anything for you, my love." His voice sounded hoarse and filled with apprehension even to his own ears.

She twisted around and looked directly into his eyes. "You and your brothers know those mountains, probably as well as Chloe does, since all of you grew up in this area. Anton and Rafael told us they hiked around and looked for the gold mine all the time that first night we met them. Will you and your brothers please help search for Chloe?"

He stared back at her, unable to speak for a minute. She trusted him unconditionally. He could see it flashing like neon lights from her expression. She was putting all her faith and love into the one person who was going to eventually destroy the human life she was now living.

He felt a deep ache in his chest. But the lies just kept falling from his mouth. "Of course. We'll go up first thing in the morning to help search for her."

"I'll go with you."

"No, that's probably not a good idea," he retorted. "I mean, if it turns out badly, I don't want you there." He heard her gasp as she realized what he was insinuating. Her expression grew even grimmer as she nodded her head in agreement.

He felt as if a knife had plunged into his heart. There was a way he could spare her the pain of worrying or mourning Chloe, he reminded himself. He should just complete the mating process right now, but he was too selfish. He didn't want to give up his own desires to live here in her world for a while longer.

"Will you do something else for me, too?"

"Yes, of course. I would do anything for you if it's in my power to do it." He held his breath waiting for her request.

"Please make me feel safe again. Take me to bed, hold me close, and never let me go."

Her words were barely more than a whisper, but her unspoken meaning echoed through his ears loud and clear. Somehow, he would have to find the strength to make love to her without biting her again, because he needed her as much as she needed him right now.

Not wanting to waste one more precious second of their time together, he pulled her up from the couch and swept her up into his arms. A spiral staircase of heavy black iron curved its way up to the upper floor. He carried her up the stairs as she pressed her body into his and rained wet kisses on his neck.

By the time they entered the large bedroom she had

pulled his hair free of the ponytail that corralled the heavy mass at the back of his head. He loved how she obviously enjoyed immersing her hands in his long hair. The sensuous way she raked her slender fingers through the strands made his cock rise against the material of his jeans every time she engaged in this simple act.

He placed her on the floor at the edge of the king-sized bed. This room was also lit with a romantic glow from more of the wall sconces, but here they hosted a dimmer light more suited for a bedroom. He began to pull her lilac T-shirt over her head. She wore a simple beige bra underneath and he reached behind her back and unsnapped the enclosure with his first attempt and pulled it away from her body. She remained unmoving, gazing up at him with a look of absolute rapture on her face as if she couldn't believe he was real.

His love for her was so powerful and complete, yet edged with the nagging sense of guilt and uncertainty. There were moments—like now—when it really did seem as if she was already under his complete vampire spell, because it didn't seem possible this beautiful mortal woman could love him as deeply as he loved her.

His cock strained harder—painfully—against the fabric of his jeans. He reached out and cupped each flawless breast in the palms of his hands. She closed her eyes; her head tilted to the side and rebellious strands of her light blonde hair fell partially over her face and past her shoulder. The long wispy ends of her pale tresses trailed loosely over her upper arm and past her elbow resembling a cascade of delicate pastel silk threads.

A soft moan escaped from her slightly parted lips

as his nimble fingers gently massaged her erect nipples. He felt the breath catch in the center of his chest. Would she still thrill to his touch like this after the mating process was completed or was this magnificent display of passion only an emotion she could enjoy in her present human state?

His hands began to tremble against the silken softness of her skin as they held her breasts tenderly. Short breaths escaped from her parted lips, but her eyes remained closed. The feathery tips of her long lashes fluttered softly above the tops of her cheekbones for a second before they parted and her hazel eyes looked up at him.

As he met her gaze Mateo was reminded once again of the rich color of the brown sand that blanketed the desert floor and the brilliance of the green cactus native to this area. She was born to be his woman in every way.

How he adored and loved this woman—more than he ever imagined could be possible. He loved her in a way he was sure no other immortal man ever loved their eternal mate. He loved her so much he wished he could find a way to save her from her preordained destiny.

"I love you so much, Mateo," she whispered. Her arms rose and encircled his neck as her hands became lost in his thick hair. She pressed her half-naked body against him and pulled herself up until her lips were pressed against his mouth in a demanding kiss.

His arms enslaved her waist holding her as close as was humanly possible while his tongue invaded her mouth. His throat constricted with another fierce need he was barely able to control this time. He pulled back and pressed his lips tightly together.

The alluring taste inside her mouth made him want to savor all of her, and for a moment he worried he would lose control. The taste of her tempting blood was the only thing that would satisfy this diabolical urge coursing through his mind and body. He knew his human nature had to gain full control over his macabre craving fast, or tonight really would be their last night in her world...and the last time he would know what it was like to be her mortal lover.

Without opening her eyes, a soft moan was Dawn's only response to his abrupt departure from their fevered kiss. He focused on her soft lips and tried not to think of the taste of her sweet succulent blood. Maybe— hopefully—once he was making love to her, his voracious hunger for her blood could be satisfied in a different way.

But this growing famine was still demanding more than just her body; this unnatural craving sought much more and it was growing stronger than anything he experienced up to this point in his hundred years of existence. To his horror, he realized it might even be stronger than his love for her, even though he couldn't comprehend how this could be possible.

He reached out and anxiously began to push her jeans from her hips. Her eyes opened, surprised at his sudden urgency. But she complied with his quest and kicked her pants away from her feet. Still blissfully unaware of his strange behavior, she began to anxiously undo the black buttons running down his shirt of the same color. She didn't hesitate when she reached the waistband of his jeans, unfastening the snaps and shoving the pants down to a point where he could easily step out of them. Without the barrier of their clothes, they came together with a wild hunger.

Mateo clasped hold of her firm buttocks and pulled her to him. Her long legs wrapped around his hips while they were standing upright. Overcome with his sexual and immortal needs, he plunged backward onto the bed with her sculpted intimately against him. They bounced slightly in the middle of the thick mattress. He heard a soft gasp escape from her as he rolled over and pinned her beneath his body.

Pulling her slender legs up over his shoulders, she was an open invitation he could not resist a second longer, and his cock didn't need any guidance to penetrate her inviting pussy. He sank into her and heard her whimper softly as he pushed into her as far as her body would allow. He thrust deeper. If she protested, he didn't hear her.

Over and over his hips moved up and down, claiming her inside and out. She clung to him with impassioned desperation, while trying to prolong the release that would propel her into the unknown. Her hips—her entire body—were propelling up and down with each of his frantic movements. Their sweating skin was fused tightly together.

His body had never felt so consumed with predatory needs in the couple of times they made love before. His cock couldn't seem to burrow deep enough inside her and it felt as if it was filled with searing lava. When the volcano inside him did finally erupt, he wasn't sure he could remain in control of the evil he could still sense lurking so close in the back of his throat.

From the center of his very core he felt something

feral was pounding out of control and about to explode from inside his body. His mind and heart were fighting equally as hard to remain in control of the human side of him as his body was battling to control his primal urges.

The building sensation inside him reached epic proportions and he could not hold back the surge of fiery fluid that spilled into her as his body convulsed and plummeted back to reality. He felt Dawn's body go limp beneath him.

Sometime during the almost violent act of making love, the inner battle with his monstrous alter-ego emerged, and in the mist of the earth-shattering climax, Mateo had become vaguely aware of his mouth against her neck. There had been no rational thought or moment of hesitation as his teeth clamped down. Thick warmth flooded his mouth and washed down his throat as the euphoric sweetness of her blood overpowered every one of his senses in the most powerful feeling of satisfaction he could ever imagine.

After his animalistic orgasm everything was clouded with a mixture of horror, confusion, and the strong carnal urges still controlling his mind and body. He wanted to protect her from the revulsion of what he had just done to her. Yet, he still wanted to make hard impetus love to her again and again; he wanted to sink his sharp teeth in her soft enticing skin once more, and drink all her sweet nectar until there was nothing left.

But a slow dawning of what he was truly capable of doing to her began to grip hold of the human side of his rampant emotions. Shame, disgust, and a strangling fear stripped him of all the previous thoughts of his uncontrollable demonic needs. His tentative gaze lowered to look at her, although he was terrified of what he would see.

Dawn's orgasm had been as sensuous and overpowering as the one he experienced. He felt her on that highest summit with him, gripping him like he was all that anchored her to this earth, writhing in pleasure beneath him and crying out his name in abandonment until this last final second when he had done the unthinkable. Now, she was lying unmoving, her arms and legs limp against the mattress, staring up at him with the most hideous wide-eyed look of horror in her brown and green gaze that he had ever seen. His heart arrested in his chest.

Ever since the first time he had seen this elegant and romantic bedroom, he had been envisioning her long shiny blonde hair spread out across the navy blue velvet pillows and her beautiful pale-skinned body reclining on the matching comforter that covered this king-sized bed. Looking down at her now, he only noticed how deathly pale she looked against the rich dark coloring of the quilt.

Her fair skin should radiate with a satisfied glow from making love. Instead, fright drained all color from her face, except for several thin trails of deep red blood draining from the crescent moon shape of his bite, trailing down the side of her neck, and disappearing into the thick material of the velvet bed covering. Her beautiful hazel eyes, so recently overflowing with love and trust, were now wide with fright and disbelief.

He couldn't take a breath. His heart refused to start beating again. He recalled something he read a very long time ago. How ironic this strange memory should pop into his head now.

Dhampyres can go long periods without drinking human blood but fighting the urge when it could them can drive them into a wild frenzy. They can lose control when they are not expecting it. It can be so consuming they could even kill someone they love.

Why didn't he remember this significant bit of information sooner? Probably, because when he read it many years ago, it didn't have any real meaning to him. That had been long before he discovered the powerful love he was capable of feeling for his human mate. Unfortunately, his inhuman need for her blood was proving to be even more dominant.

It was the strange sound of her voice that finally brought his tortured mind out of its indecisive trance. Her tone suggested she had already resigned herself to the truth she suspected, but tried to deny until this moment.

"It was you," she murmured. "You really were the one in my dreams, only they weren't dreams, were they? And the-the night I went to the mountain to meet you. I thought I was sleep walking, or maybe, just losing my mind." Her eyes closed for an instant as if she was trying to remember—or forget—every small detail. Her lashes fluttered and parted again; her unwavering stare held his gaze prisoner.

"Then, I met you at the pizza place. You seemed so familiar—even your scent—I think I knew it even then. I just couldn't allow myself to accept it. It was easier to believe I was losing my mind." She swallowed hard and he saw fresh droplets of blood ooze from the bite wound in her neck.

He held his breath as his mouth and throat constricted with revolting yearnings once again. His lips clamped together as tight as he could hold them, while his gut twisted and flip-flopped in his stomach.

As much as he loved this woman; as much as he desired to be here with her in her human world, and as much as he wanted to protect her from her eternal fate for as long as possible; at this moment, he had never wanted anything more than he wanted to drink those tiny drops of blood from her soft neck.

If he gave into this overpowering craving again, he knew there would be no stopping.

Chapter Fifteen

The strange unnatural calm in Dawn's mind and body felt nothing short of weird and unreal. She was in the most defenseless position a woman could be in at this moment; naked, flat on her back, impaled by Mateo's body as intimately as possible, and she wasn't even sure if he was real or merely a figment of her obviously diminishing sanity. Shock was the only way to describe what she was feeling.

"What are you?" she asked in voice that sounded so oddly calm to her own ears. She should be trying to run as fast and far away from him as she could go, or at the very least, fearing for her life. Maybe she wasn't deathly afraid because perhaps Mateo Two Moons—her perfect man in every way—didn't even exist.

His eyes were black as coals as he stared down at her, and an unreadable expression held his face motionless.

"What are you?" she repeated in the voice she still didn't recognize as her own.

His mouth barely moved as he whispered, "Dhampyre."

"Wha—What?" Irritation was edging into her voice. "What the hell is that?" All at once she realized the excruciating pain in her neck. She reached up to cautiously touch the fresh blood pooling along the ridges of the teeth marks. Her shaking hand pulled back slowly as she stared at the red stain on her fingertips.

Her confused gaze rose again. An expression of pain and dread contorted Mateo's handsome face and his eyes were misted with unshed tears.

"Dawn, I'm so sorry," he said a hoarse voice. "I-I just lost control."

Her fingers shook more visibly as she glanced at the deep red smears along her fingertips. She could barely speak as she choked out the words again, "What are you really?"

"I was born a dhamp—half-human, half-vampire. My mother was human when I was conceived, and my father is a-a vampire."

He closed his eyes as if he couldn't bear witnessing the mortified look of disbelief on her face.

She wished she could close her mind to this lunacy as easily as he just blocked out the sight of her.

"There is no such thing," she stated in a low and surprisingly controlled voice.

He lifted his hips carefully, releasing his intimate hold on her, and rolled to her side. In spite of everything, the absence of him molded into her body felt as if a part of her was missing. She was cold and empty without his touch, yet at the same time, so thoroughly confused.

The expressive black eyes of the man she loved more than life were watching her again from within the perfectly handsome face she had memorized, and those lips she yearned to kiss every moment of each passing day were saying the most insane things. Was he really trying to tell her he was part...vampire?

"Mateo." She turned on her side and stared back at him. The pain in her neck reminded her that whatever was happening here was not natural, but she wasn't ready to believe the outlandish lie he told her. "This, whatever this kinky biting fetish is you have going on here, well, it's definitely weird, but it's something we can work on toge—"

"I know you are just trying to find a rational explanation, because what I'm telling you must sound so impossible," he cut in. He reached out and gently placed his hand against the side of her face. "I wish there was an answer that didn't include exposing you to horrors you never could have imagined exist. Most of all, I just wish I never had to hurt you in any way."

She could only stare at his beautiful tortured face. Did he seriously think she would believe the nonsense he was telling her? If she did, shouldn't she be pulling away from him in repulsion and horror? Begging for her life? Anything other than just lying here beside him with his warm loving hand against her cheek?

He was still her Mateo Two Moons, her perfect forever love. She reached up and placed her own hand over where his touched lightly on her face. His skin was smooth and hot, still sweaty from their recent love-making. He felt like what he was...just a man. Her man. A touch of a smile curved her lips.

"Vampires or d-dhamp—whatever you said, they don't exist. You are the man I love and want to spend the rest of my life with, and I refuse to believe anything else."

He pulled her into his arms and kissed the top of her head. She felt engulfed in love with his soothing gestures. There was no way she could believe what he said.

Vampires were cold pale creatures with long fangs

protruding from their mouths; they bit people in the neck and drained them of all their blood until they were nothing but hollow corpses. Vampires slept in coffins during the day and lived in castles in Romania or…what the hell was she even thinking?

Vampires did not exist.

"Do you want to take a bath," he suggested after a few minutes of silence. "It might help to calm you and we can talk while we soak."

His worried voice intruded into Dawn's conflicting thoughts of rationality and insanity and fictitious horror stories. *Yes please*, she thought as she nodded her head. *Let's do something normal like take a bath. But no more talking. Let's stop talking and thinking about crazy things that don't exist.*

She realized they were really perfect together…they were both certifiably insane.

She let him pick her up from the bed and cradle her in his arms as he carried her into the big master en suite. An over-sized oval tub sat in one corner of the room. He stood her on the brown tiled floor as he turned on the water. Dawn took his hand as he helped her step over the side. She sank down gratefully as hot water poured into the tub and over her numb body.

He climbed in behind her and she leaned back against him as soon as he sat down. This felt so perfectly normal. This was something an ordinary man would do with his woman after making mad passionate, somewhat deviant, love to her.

The biting thing—well, that was another story. Guess it was too good to be true that he could be perfect in every way. There were probably sex therapists to help him overcome that kinkiness. She would discuss this awkward issue with him tomorrow. Between Chloe's disappearance and now all this, she was too tired to think straight tonight.

When their bodies were immersed in deep water that teetered almost to the top of the tub, he turned the water off and wrapped both his arms tightly around her waist. She sighed and closed her eyes. Maybe she only dreamt all that insane stuff he told her about being a half-human, half-vampirey thing.

"We have to talk about it. Ignoring it won't change the facts," Mateo whispered in her ear.

She exhaled a heavy sigh. Okay, *Cowboy up, Cupcake*. Her neck throbbed as a reminder this madness was real. She swallowed tentatively, but thankfully, did not feel any more blood flowing down her neck.

"So, you really expect me to believe you are Dracula?" She retorted in a snarky tone as she shook her head slightly. "Dracula who drives a big truck instead of using your bat wings?" She tried to add a chuckle, because she was trying hard to make a joke. When she glanced back at him, she realized it wasn't working. Her attempt to laugh sounded grossly forced. A scowl was his only response.

"If I had followed the customs of my clan, the Blood Clan, you never would have found out the truth about me. The first night you came up to the Superstitions, and I came to you during the night in your sleeping bag, you would have been powerless to resist me. I would have completed our mating ritual and taken you with me. Your disappearance would never have been explained. From that moment on you would be living with me in my hidden village at the top of the Superstitions. You're only purpose would be to be my mate, to make love to me, care for my needs, and have my children so our bloodline could carry on."

His words echoed through her mind. The frigid storm racing through her body froze her to the core. Now, she was beginning to get scared. Not even the hot water could heat her as her body began to shake vehemently. Mateo's arms tightened around her.

"I'm sorry I had to say it so bluntly, but you refused to listen to the truth."

"I still don't believe you," she replied in a voice shaking as ferociously as her body. She choked down the heavy sludge in the back of her throat with a loud gulp.

"We live in the r-real world, Mateo. I love you, but this is getting seriously strange and freaky. I-I just don't understand why you would want to scare me like this? Do you belong to some underground vampire club or blood-sucking cult or something?"

"In my world we refer to humans—like you—as real ones," he continued as if he hadn't heard anything she asked him. "And, yes, you do live in the real world, my love. But I and the others like me, sleep in caves during the daylight hours. Only when the night begins to fall are we allowed to venture out into your world."

Her head was pounding as his words reached her ears. Now that he mentioned it, she never had seen him in the daytime. But they'd only known one another less than a week, so it hadn't seemed a big deal. The truth was she really knew nothing outside of the few hours they spent together—mostly making crazy uncontrollable love. Everything else about him was a complete mystery to her.

The one thing she did know was she loved him in

an all-consuming unexplainable way, and she had ever since the very first instant when their gazes met at the crowded pizza place last week.

"If I was to believe you, and I'm not saying I do, but—" She exhaled a trembling breath before continuing, "If I should entertain the idea of dhamp—"

"Dhampyres."

She swallowed loudly again. It was an intimidating sounding word. "Dhampyres," she repeated in a quiet voice. She cleared her throat. "Okay, for argument's sake, let's just say they do exist and they live in a secret village up on the Superstitions. It's so secret it has never been found even with all the people who hike around those mountains looking for gold and stuff. But these-these dhampyres can leave this secret place and steal women away from campsites or whatever and make them their love slaves?"

She shook her head as the absurdity of those words fell from her mouth.

He remained silent, so she continued. "If you are telling me the truth, and you are one of these so-called dhampyres, and you do live in this secret place with this Blood Clan—" She shook her head again in disbelief. "Then how is it possible you are here with me now, in this real place, doing things like—what did you call me—like real ones?"

Dawn twisted around in the water and looked at him. His ebony brows were knitted closely together and a deep frown held his lips captive. She could see her own pained reflection in his raven gaze.

"Or is the real truth that I have lost my mind and the past week and a half since I first went camping on the Superstitions never really happened at all? If this is the case, I should be institutionalized as soon as possible."

Mateo pulled her around in the tub until she was facing him. She sat on his thighs and her legs wrapped around his waist. It would feel so natural to make love again right now. But instead of being taken back to a place of sexual fantasy, they had to face the reality of something horrific and unbelievable.

"It's real, my love," he finally said. "It's all unbelievably real, and I realize how hard it is for you to comprehend. In time, you will know and understand everything. And I promise I will do everything in my power to make it all as painless as possible. I know you are confused."

"I know you are confused. Your mind cannot grasp what is happening. It's only your body responding to me at this time, because there is no way to resist fate. It was probably wrong of me to bring you here tonight since I'm not ready to take you to the mountaintop to become my mate, yet. But I just can't stay away from you now that I've seen you and held you in my arms. I promise you, I will find a way to come to you in your world before we both must fulfill the destiny set in motion since time first began. You must trust me, Udaya."

The words the faceless stranger had said to her the night she went to the Superstitions alone in a trance-like state came flooding back. They had not made any sense that night, and as crazy as it was, now they were starting to have some meaning.

"Wow," she whispered. Her eyes widened as the rest of his words came back to her in vivid recollection.

"I've been waiting for you my entire life."

"My grandmother and my mother told me about you when I was a child nearly a hundred years ago."

"I remember it all now."

"You are remembering things that happened on the mountain?" he asked in a worried tone.

She felt as if every ounce of courage drained out of her body. She was helpless to block the horrendous images lurking at the edges of her mind of ancient undead creatures living among the frightening—and nearby—peaks of the Superstitions. But if she allowed these images total access, she might really fall into the black chasm of insanity.

She wished she was back in Colorado right now, living her once calm boring life; dating losers or visiting the Sluts R Us Club when she got horny, and just being an average twenty-six-year-old.

But then she never would have met Mateo Two Moons.

His dangerously handsome face swam before her eyes when she tried to focus her gaze on him. He was just watching her, patiently waiting for her latest psychotic episode to pass. All the insane words he had spoken to her during those times on the Superstitions kept gushing through the barriers of her weakened mind.

"My destiny?" she asked nervously.

"Yes," he answered. "Since the day of my birth over a hundred years ago, and since the day of your birth over twenty-six years ago, we have been destined to meet, destined have dhampyre children together, and destined to spend all eternity together."

Mateo's voice, the voice she thought was so deep and sexy, had just spoken the most irrational words she'd ever heard. Did he honestly expect her to even begin to process any of this madness? It was just all too much.

Her head began to shake from side to side. "No. Not true. I refuse to believe you," she yelled as she pushed herself away from him. She jumped up and sprang over the side of the tub, splashing water everywhere on the floor with her sudden action.

Her feet had barely landed on the tiled floor when the entire room began to spin before her eyes. Everything around her began to go black.

****

Dawn tried to force her eyes open. They stung. Her body hurt. The fierce pounding in her head invoked a fleeting memory from spring break in Fort Lauderdale, Florida, during college days she only wanted to forget. She moaned out loud. When she finally pried her eye lids apart, the bright sun shining through the tall windows made her eyes burn. She squeezed her eyes shut again.

Damn.

She was still in Mateo's condo. If she was at her small cozy apartment, safe in her own little bed, she might be able to pretend everything that happened last night had only been another crazy dream, or make that, another crazy nightmare.

No such luck.

She placed her hands over her eyes and slowly let her lids separate again, allowing only slivers of daylight to peak between her fingers until she could bear the full force of the blinding glare. When she was finally able to focus on her surroundings, she immediately glanced around for Mateo.

She was alone—and naked—in the big velvet covered bed, in the middle of the fancy bedroom, in this big luxurious condo. It all seemed surreal. A quick scan of the room revealed the faded jeans and lilac tee she had been wearing last night laying on a plush blue loveseat along the back wall.

Last night…

Mateo's words began to filter back into her reluctant mind much too fast. *Vampire. Dham—whatever. Half-human. A hundred years. Children. Blood Clan. Eternal mate...*

She sat up in the bed in an abrupt motion. The room spun before her eyes and the uneasiness in her stomach threatened to make her puke. She closed her eyes again until the spinning in her head stopped and the churning in her stomach calmed down. The throbbing in her bitten neck, however, only increased as she reopened her eyes slowly and firmly repeated this was not really happening.

A noise from downstairs made her entire body stiffen. Was Mateo down there? Well, that had to be proof she dreamed all this nonsense, except for the abnormal biting, of course. The pulsating pain emitting from her neck proved that part was real. But if he really was down there cooking her breakfast this morning, like an ordinary boyfriend, then he could hardly be sleeping in the caves up on the Superstitions like he told her last night.

Today she would definitely make an appointment to see a psychiatrist, for both of them. What time was it anyway? Where was her cell? Damn. She left it with her purse downstairs last night. She scanned the room for a clock. Red digital numbers on the corner of the huge flat screen TV hanging above the rock fireplace along one of the bedroom walls flashed 8:13 a.m.

Oh no, not again. She was going to get fired from her teaching job, and it was going to be all Mateo Two Moon's fault.

Since her head and body were not feeling very sturdy right now, Dawn slid her legs over the side of the bed slowly and stood up cautiously on wobbly legs. She held the edge of the bed for a couple minutes until her head stopped spinning enough for her to walk without feeling as if she would pass out.

As she made her way over to where her clothes were laid out on the chaise, she was reminded of feeling almost this exact same way the day she thought she had the flu or had been bitten by a poisonous spider or bug after going camping with Chloe. Somehow, this had to be Mateo's fault.

"Shoes?" she whispered glancing around at the floor. Now she remembered. The black flip-flops she had been wearing were downstairs by the couch where she kicked them off last night while she and Mateo had been talking about Chloe.

Chloe.

The horrific thought of Chloe's disappearance crowded into her head with all the other outlandish thoughts she didn't want to think about. *Oh please, let Chloe be back home safe and sound this morning.* But even as she tried to force that happy ending in among all the other not so happy thoughts spiraling through her mind, Dawn knew it was not going to turn out that way.

If she allowed herself to believe all the bizarre stuff he told her last night, then she would also know the Superstitions were filled with unspeakable dangers, and they were far worse than the mere rumors of evil specters or ghosts anyone ever mentioned in the history books or ancient legends.

Chapter Sixteen

"Mateo?" Dawn called out as she cautiously made her way down the curved iron staircase. She stopped to rub her aching eyes, and clutched the railing again before continuing her descent to the lower floor. She seriously felt like one of the living dead right now. Ugh, probably not a good comparison considering the things he told her last night.

This condo had felt seductive and glamorous when they first arrived yesterday evening, but today it seemed far too bright with all the scorching sunlight flooding through the massive floor to ceiling windows that rimmed the front entry way and living room. This morning, however, everything was different than last night.

"Ma—" She halted at the bottom of the stairs when a stranger appeared from the kitchen. "What-Who are you?" she gasped. Her already queasy insides did a frantic lurch in her stomach.

The dark-skinned man smiled nervously at her. His straight shoulder length black hair was combed back behind his ears. He ran his fingertips around his ears as if to make sure the coarse strands were still in place.

"I am Billy Torres." He walked with a hesitant gait toward her and extended his hand as he approached. "Mateo has asked me to stay with you until he returns tonight."

Dawn shuffled back away from the short stocky man who was way too close for comfort. She clutched the bottom of the stair rail for support. "Where is Mateo?" She glanced toward the front door. There was no way she could get to the door without getting past this man, even if she was feeling strong enough to make a run for it.

His smile faded slightly and he lowered his hand back down to his side. "He said you knew everything. Well, he told me you knew everything about him, anyway."

If Mateo wasn't here, was he up there? She pushed the image of him lying Dracula-like in a wooden coffin in some sinister cave up on the Superstitions out of her mind. She tried to focus on what the man was saying to her.

"I am a member of the Clan Society."

"Clan Society?"

He shrugged his rounded shoulders. His blue and red plaid shirt looked a size too small on his hefty frame.

"It is the greatest honor in the Apache tribe to be chosen to help care for the Blood Clan. We make sure their existence is never threatened and all their needs are met."

This sounded way too real now. *Their existence?* "Am I being held captive here?" she asked in a meek voice.

His face contorted in surprise. "Oh no. Mateo was just worried about leaving you alone because you were so sick last night. I hope you are feeling better this morning."

Dawn stared at him, trying desperately to

remember everything that conspired between her and Mateo last night. She wrapped her arms around her midsection and leaned against the stair railing. She couldn't control the shivering in her body, or stop the notion in her resistant mind that all the horrible crazy things Mateo told her last night might really be true.

Vampires or half-vampires called damp-something? How did a once ordinary, well-educated school teacher allow herself to accept something so incredibly ridiculous?

"Miss Malone? I think you should probably sit down. You don't look so good right now."

She looked into the dark eyes of Billy Torres who stood only inches in front of her. He was barely as tall as she so their gazes were also level when they met. She gave her head a weak nod and tentatively took his outstretched hand. His skin was rough and calloused on the palm of his hand. He seemed like just a normal man, but then, so had Mateo Two Moons before last night.

****

Sitting at table in the brightly decorated yellow and blue alcove at the back of the expensive kitchen, Dawn stared out at the lush treed park adjacent to the condo complex. It was an odd green oasis in this land of mostly sand and cactus. A young mother with short spiky red hair was pushing a blonde child of approximately two years old in an infant swing on the wooden set in the play area. The curly haired toddler was squealing with glee and stretching her chubby little legs straight out in front of her as the swing flew through the air.

Mateo's words haunted her. *She was destined to*

have his children. His immortal half-vampire children? Half-breed had an entirely new meaning now. The sip of coffee she had just taken turned to acid in her mouth.

She was reminded of the not-so-insignificant fact they had never used protection from the first time they made love. The possible repercussions of those actions made a sick feeling settle in the pit of her stomach. She choked back the urge to throw up again. *Oh God.*

She started doing the calculations in her mind. What if it happened the first time they made love? Her period was due in just a few days. From past conversations with friends, she knew some pregnancy tests claimed to determine if a woman has been impregnated only seventy-two hours after conception. It had been five days since the first time she and Mateo were intimate. She needed to get one of those pregnancy tests soon. She absently touched the flesh-colored band aid Billy Torres had given her to cover the bite on her neck.

She tore her gaze away from the window. The happy sight of the mother and little girl doing regular-type things was a direct contradiction to everything in her life right now. Dawn glanced around the kitchen, surprised to see her body guard was not close by.

Until now, he had not left her side all morning, except for when she used the restroom. Billy Torres was not really like some hulking guard, though.

She glanced at her cell phone. It wasn't like she couldn't call someone for help. She could call 911 if she wanted to and tell them what? *Help…I've been seduced by Dracula.* A wry chuckle escaped from her lips.

Billy told her he called the school before she woke

up this morning to tell them she was ill again and would not be in the rest of the week. Apparently, whoever he talked to at the school believed him, and didn't even question why some random man would call in sick for her, because she checked her phone several times and there were no new voice messages or texts from anyone. She could be lying dead in her apartment right now, or be the mindless sex slave to some blood sucking half-vampire thing, and no one would even be the wiser. *Wow.*

Dawn rose from the chair where she had been sitting at the kitchen table and took a couple steps toward the large island in the center of the room. A bowl of shiny apples, pears and bananas sat on the counter, along with a huge glass vase of beautiful fresh-cut flowers in assorted sizes and autumn colors of orange, red and golden hues.

When she snooped in the fancy stainless steel refrigerator earlier this morning, she was surprised to see it stocked full with food. She even noticed a case of her favorite beer sitting on one of the shelves. A poignant memory of the romantic night she watched the moon come up with Mateo at the lake floated through her mind. She felt that swooning sensation again. How could she still yearn so desperately for his touch—for his love—and be so frightened of what he claimed to be at the same time?

When she had been upstairs earlier, she noticed an assortment of personal hygiene items for women filled the master bathroom cabinets and in the master closet were hangers with several articles of women's clothes. They were all brand new and still had tags on them, and all appeared to be her size and style. Obviously, this elaborate effort to make this condo feel like a real home was all for her benefit, because Mateo didn't even live here. If she were to believe him, he lived in some hidden village at the top of the Superstitions and slept in a cave like a bat during the daytime.

One thing for certain, she wasn't going to just sit here all day and do nothing now she was feeling decent again. She stepped cautiously toward the edge of the kitchen counter to peek into the living room. The layout of the condo was an open design concept, so there were no walls separating the two areas. Billy Torres was sitting in one of the suede recliners reading the local daily newspaper. Could it have some news about Chloe?

He glanced up as Dawn walked toward the couch. "You're looking much better, Miss Malone."

She forced a smile. In spite of the reason this man was here, he was not unpleasant to be around. She actually found herself liking him. "Dawn. Please call me Dawn." As with the previous times she'd felt sick, they were short-lived illnesses, and she was fairly certain now the nausea had something to do with the blood sucking thing. But she was too overwhelmed with everything else right now to dwell on that issue.

"Mind if I read that when you're done with it?" She motioned toward the paper in Billy's grasp.

He grinned and held the paper out to her. "I'm done."

She took the paper, noting the relieved expression on his face. Earlier she drilled him relentlessly about the things Mateo told her last night. But he was obviously a loyal and staunch member of the so-called Clan Society, and while remaining polite and respectful, he had not divulged one single secret about the vampire clan he was so honored to serve.

She sunk into the plush leather couch and scanned the front page. Nothing was written here about Chloe. Maybe that was good news. She flipped the paper open to the second page and the heavy sense of dread settled back down in the pit of her stomach.

Missing Woman feared dead

Chloe Webster, 27, of Apache Junction, AZ, has been missing since Sunday night in the Superstition Mountains. Local search parties, including the Maricopa County and Pinal County Search and Rescue Agencies and members from the White Mountain Indian Reservation have conducted extensive searches on well-known hiking trails and camping sites in the recreational areas, as well as in the mountain ranges of the Superstitions. Webster's vehicle was found Monday morning at a trailhead in the Superstition Wilderness Area.

That's it? Dawn raged inwardly. Nothing about how Chloe had been an experienced hiker in that area? Nothing about how she had been searching for the Lost Dutchman's Gold Mine for her entire life? Nothing about how many people had gone missing in those mountains throughout the course of history? Nothing about the vampire half-breeds who live in the secret caves somewhere up there on those daunting mountains, and who might have sucked Chloe's body dry of all her blood or turned her into a baby-making sex slave?

Her heart thudded frantically against her ribcage. Is that what happened to Chloe and to all those other hikers and gold seekers who just disappeared into thin air on the Superstition Mountains? The legends she read about the evil spirits rumored to guard the hidden treasure came gushing back into her thoughts. She was beginning to understand how the legends had come to be, but perhaps the rumored ghosts or demons were actually vampires or dhampyres...like Mateo Two Moons and his brothers?

"Are you okay, Miss Mal—Dawn?" Billy asked.

His voice forced her back to reality. She was unaware she was crushing the newspaper into a tight wad in her fisted hand. She turned to look at him, but her vision was filled with images of her friend's blood-drained body lying somewhere among the secret caves at the Blood Clan's hidden lair.

"Maybe you should rest for a while," he added. "You are as white as a sheet again."

She nodded and raised her shaking hand up to wipe the sweat away from her brow. "What time will Mateo be back? I really need to talk to him."

He glanced up at the clock on the wall shaped like a huge Native American drum. It was just a few minutes past noon. "He should be here shortly after sunset."

"Of course," she mumbled. Vampires can't be out in the sunlight. How stupid of her. "I'm not feeling so hot again. I think I'm going to lie down for a while, maybe try to take a nap." She tossed the wadded up newspaper down on the coffee table and headed up the curved staircase without looking at Billy Torres again. She had at least seven hours before Mateo got here.

Once in the bedroom, she raced around the room, weighing her limited options. French doors opened onto small balcony outside of the loft bedroom. There were no stairs leading from the balcony to the ground, and the drop down had to be at least twenty feet. She drew in a deep breath and surveyed the ground below. Could she land that jump without breaking both her legs? Doubtful.

The sound of footsteps coming up the stairs caused her nerves to shatter. She ran to the bed and plopped down on the mattress. Rolling onto her side she curled her body into a ball, closed her eyes, and tried to take deep even breaths as if she were asleep. The razor edges of her anxiety were making it difficult to breathe at all. Why was she freaking out like this? Billy said she wasn't a prisoner here.

Maybe she should just tell him she had errands to run. That would be a natural thing to do, right? She could just say she needed to pick up something for dinner; check her mail; drop off some dry cleaning; find out if she was pregnant with a half-breed vampire, you know, typical stuff like that.

She realized she was holding her breath and if she exhaled now he would know she was faking sleep. Whether or not she was being held here against her will, she couldn't ignore the panic making her insides quake.

She had her back to the doorway, so she had no way of knowing how long Billy stood there. But he was obviously making sure she really was taking a nap. Maybe it wasn't something so threatening. He might just be checking to make sure she was okay. Regardless of why he had come up here, Dawn just wanted him to leave.

She forced herself to lie still as she slowly let the pent up breath escape from her parted lips. Finally, after what seemed an incredibly long time, she mustered up enough courage to slowly roll back over and check to see if he was still there. She was alone in the quiet bedroom, but she hadn't heard him going back down the stairs. Was he lurking somewhere close by?

Cowboy up, Cupcake. That goofy phrase had always meant so much to her, mostly because Jeremy said it to her so many times throughout the years, even though he was usually making fun of her when he said those three silly words.

How she wished she could call her brother right now and ask for his help or advice or just to hear his voice. The yearning to talk to him and let his calm logic reassure her everything would be okay was so desperate it made her heart hurt, yet she knew it couldn't happen regardless of how much she wanted it.

Jeremy had a way of getting her to talk about everything and anything, and she sure couldn't tell him about the bizarre things going on with her the past week and a half. Nope…no way. She could not call Jeremy until all this lunacy was behind her. His other favorite quote, '*If you're not livin' on the edge, your takin' up space*', didn't even begin to compare with what was going on in her life right now.

However, she was not going to accomplish anything until she could calm down and at least try to act like a rational person, in a totally irrational situation, and that was not going to be easy. She sat up precariously and waited for a few minutes before she scooted to the edge of the bed. Billy was nowhere to be seen. She tip-toed to the closet and peeked inside again. There were even shoes in her size. There wasn't time to analyze how Mateo knew all this stuff about her. She grabbed the white running shoes and yanked the size tag off the side. Although, she was certain there would be some socks in of one the bureau drawers, there was no time to look. Her bare feet slipped easily into the shoes. She quickly laced them up.

Fortunately, she now had her cell phone in the back pocket of her jeans, but her purse was still downstairs on the table in the foyer by the front door. She really couldn't leave here without that purse, because it contained her wallet and the keys to her truck. She took a huge deep breath. Her neck began to ache where Mateo had bitten her. It reminded her of why she needed to leave here now. She forced her feet to step forward.

The landing at the top of the stairs was visible from most of the lower floor. She had never felt more defenseless and exposed in her entire life. She wasn't even sure why she was so afraid right now. Billy sure didn't seem like a dangerous man. But she couldn't forget he had taken a vow to protect the Blood Clan, which probably meant he would stop at nothing to fulfill that promise. *Wow.* She was really starting to sound like she believed this outrageous stuff.

There were no sounds coming from anywhere upstairs or downstairs. Dawn stepped down one stair. Still nothing. She inched down a couple more steps. Her heart was wreaking havoc in her chest. Billy might hear it pounding because it sounded like roaring thunder to her ears. One more step then another and another.

Now, she was standing at the bottom of the stairs, and thankfully, still no sign of her bodyguard. Her arms were stiff and her hands were clutched into fists so tight her nails were digging into her palms. She was only several feet from the front door. Her black leather purse was lying there on the long narrow table with the tiled top in southwestern colors of blue and coral. It was just a few more steps away.

She froze as her hand reached out to grab her purse. A phone was ringing. *No.* Her nerves splintered into a million pieces as her body erupted in a cold sweat.

"Hey. I was just going to call you."

It took a moment before she realized it hadn't been her phone ringing. Because, of course, she hadn't thought to turn her cell off before she began her daring escape. Billy must be sitting at the little alcove in the kitchen. It was one of the few places not visible from the front entry. He was talking to whoever called him and he didn't seem to be aware of her presence.

She grabbed her purse and reached out to the door knob on the front door. Her hand was sweating and shaking so profusely she was surprised she was able to turn the knob. The brown wood door opened with ease, and thankfully, with very little noise. She took a shaky step though the threshold.

She was outside, and Billy was still talking on his phone, but her ears were too filled with the deafening sound of her thrashing heartbeat to hear what he was saying. Carefully, she pulled the door shut.

There wasn't time to think; she just started running blindly down the walkway, past the little playground where she had seen the young spiky haired mom swinging her baby girl, past people who were walking on the sidewalk, some of them walking dogs, or others driving down the streets in cars; all blissfully unaware of the unspeakable horrors that slept in the caves up on the nearby mountains.

She ran until she saw her little truck parked in front of her apartment, and until she was sure her lungs were going to burst. She didn't stop running until she was sitting in the cab. Then she just started driving as blindly as she had been running. Sunset would be here all too soon.

Chapter Seventeen

Leaving Arizona...

Dawn pulled over and stared at the sign along the side of the deserted highway. It was illuminated only by the headlights of her truck. She knew she would soon be seeing a sign that would say, *'Entering Colorado',* just a few yards farther down the road. The sun had gone down several hours ago and due to her decision to avoid the freeway it was taking longer to get to Colorado. If someone was looking for her, they would probably assume she would be on the interstate.

Someone? Mateo.

Just allowing his name to float through her mind caused such an ache in her breast she was sure her heart would cease to beat. How could she miss someone—something—that was not even real? But she couldn't deny all the real feelings consuming her now.

As she had driven frantically out of Apache Junction and away from Mateo earlier today, she had been tormented with indecision almost as engulfing as her relentless fear. Everything that happened since the first time she went to the Superstitions with Chloe still seemed too outrageous to accept. But there were so many other things to consider that she couldn't ignore.

The unbelievable events in the past few days made her wonder if it really could be possible all the spooky legends and scary fairy tales and myths from ancient times were based on real monsters, or dare she think it—real vampires? Maybe pretending they were just the figment of someone's wild imagination was the only way for real ones to deal with the overwhelming horror of learning the truth.

She stared at the Leaving Arizona sign until it became a hazy blur in the rays of her headlights. Beyond it was endless darkness as if nothing else existed for her when she crossed that line.

Leaving Arizona. Leaving Mateo. Loving Mateo.

The pain in her breast burned hotter, expanding through her belly and extremities, up through the top of her head, until her entire being was raging with anguish too great for her to bear. She leaned over the steering wheel and let the persecuting sobs rack through her body. There was no stopping the glaring realization she wanted to go back to Mateo as desperately as she wanted to run as far away from him as possible. Neither option seemed plausible.

Crying was easy. She had done it for hours now. Making the decision to turn around and go back to Apache Junction was proving much harder. Had she continued to drive through the night, she would almost be back to her hometown in the western mountains of Colorado. But instead, she parked here for half of the night blubbering incoherently about not being able to live without Mateo, and wanting to be more than an incubator for vampire babies in caves somewhere up on the Superstitions forever.

Forever—was a *very* long time.

In the end, she realized she couldn't leave without knowing what really happened to Chloe, or most of all, without knowing if there was a way to be with Mateo without becoming a sex slave—slash—baby maker. She couldn't run from the way she felt about him no matter what her future entailed. The overwhelming love and deep desire she felt for this man—this dhampyre or vampire—was her entire life now. She had to be with him, and she had already been away from him for too long.

Exhausted from crying and thinking about unthinkable things for so long, Dawn remained hunched over her steering wheel as she tried to find the energy to drive back to Apache Junction. She didn't notice the big dark truck that pulled up behind hers, or the man who walked up to her pickup, until he had opened her door and the overhead light broke through the blackness in the cab. Instinctively she threw her hands over her eyes to block the unexpected glare. Deep terror clutched her in its grip at the thought of being attacked by thugs on the side of the road.

Then his perfect face filled her vision and her world. The tremendous anxiety and cold empty feeling inside of her was replaced with love and relief in less than an instant.

"Mateo," she choked through a lingering sob. "How did you find me?"

He shrugged his shoulders and shook his head in a slow motion. "I felt your tears. They led me to you." He reached out and tenderly cupped his hand under her chin. "I will always find you, Udaya. You are my destiny and I am yours."

Another sob shook through her body. "I love you so much. But I don't want to be under your spell, living in a cave with no purpose other than to have abnormal babies."

Mateo's eyes closed for an instant. He drew in a sharp breath. "I don't want that either. That's why I came up with this crazy scheme to be with you in your world. I was hoping it would buy us some time so I could try to figure out another alternative. But it's backfired on me." He shrugged again and his shoulders hunched over.

A long strand of hair escaped from his ponytail and trailed along the side of his face down past his chest. Dawn's fingers yearned to smooth the errant strand away from his cheek. Just the thought of touching him induced a profound yearning inside of her that shook visibly through her entire body.

"I realize now that I really blew it," he continued. "This might have worked, for a while longer at least, if I had been able to resist biting you and starting the mating process. I just wanted you so badly, in every way, I lost all control. You will never know how sorry I truly am."

"I'm trying so hard, but I don't understand all of this, Mateo.

"I will tell you everything, but right now, we need to get back to Apache Junction before the sun comes up."

There it was again—stabbing her smack in the middle of her heart and demolishing her fragile dreams once more. Cold hard reality. A dozen questions filled her mind about his immortal existence, but there wasn't time for talking, because he would burn in Hell if the sunlight touched his immortal skin, right? *Damn.*

Her body suddenly felt as wasted as her mind right now, and she wondered how she was ever going to find the strength to drive back to Apache Junction.

"Billy will drive your truck back," he stated as if he could read her thoughts. "You're riding with me."

She hadn't noticed Billy Torres until now, but there he was, standing right behind Mateo. It was hard to tell in the dim light whether he was pissed at her for sneaking away from him, or if he just felt bad at being such an inept bodyguard. Mateo pulled her gently from her truck. She glanced at Billy as they walked past him.

"I'm sorry," she mumbled. He nodded his head but didn't speak as he climbed into the driver seat of her truck.

Mateo remained silent when they settled into the cab of his much larger vehicle. The engine roared to life just as Joseph Red Feather's mystical guitar music flowed through the air. For a moment, she was transported back to the night they shared their first romantic date. It had been just days since that perfect night, but so much had happened in such a short time, it felt more like a lifetime ago.

"Mateo, I—"

"Dawn, I—"

They both fell silent. He reached across the truck console and picked up her cold hand. A jolt of excitement, combined with the sharp edges of her nagging anxiety, raced through her body. Her hand shook. He squeezed tighter. She didn't pull away.

"You told me the last time your hand was shaking this much you were seriously turned on. I don't suppose I could be so lucky this time?" He gave a quick chuckle. "I could just pull on over to the side of the road right now." His attempt at humor failed when she didn't respond. More silence followed.

"Why did you stop?" he finally asked. "You could

have been to your old home in Colorado by now."

She shrugged and glanced at the spot on her thigh where their hands were entwined. His touch was so overpowering. She hated how she didn't want him to turn loose of her ever again. She was already his love slave. Why would she even try to fight against it any longer? "You still would have found me, right?"

"Yes."

"It's that destiny thing, right?" Her hand convulsed in his tight embrace as another tremor shook through her body.

"Yes."

She opened her mouth and blew out the rush of breath she couldn't force down into her lungs. "Is there any way—I mean—can we still try to find a way to be together like-like a real couple, like real ones? There has to be another option besides going to live in those caves forever."

She tightened her fingers around his hand this time, adding, "I'm really scared, Mateo."

Mateo turned toward her. "I know. I am too," he said quietly. "I didn't expect it to be so hard. I thought I could pretend to be a real one with no major consequences. I envisioned we could be like a real couple, for a while, anyway." His shoulders gave a heavy shrug. "We'd date and have fun. Fall in love in the natural human way, make love, all at night, of course. I wanted us to have a real love story." He shook his head as a deep sigh echoed out of his mouth.

"I wanted you so desperately though, and in more than just in emotional and sexual ways. There is a hunger so much stronger than I ever imagined driving my vampire instincts when I'm around you. I couldn't stop myself from biting your neck or your wrist almost every time we've been together." He swallowed hard before adding in a tense voice, "I have never experienced anything as potent as the lure of your blood. It's a temptation I'm too weak to resist."

Dawn tried to force back the panic bubbling in her breast. This biting thing was so hard to accept without freaking out again. "If-if you hadn't bitten me, I never would have known what you really are. At least, not until you were actually ready to take me to your village to live as your mate, right?"

"Well, yes. Maybe? But I'm not sure. I really don't have any explanation for what happened. All the male vampires from my clan have always drunk blood from the neck, the wrist, then from the thigh of their mates the first time they came to them on the mountain. After that, they are mated forever. No one from my clan has ever tried to do what I've done with you."

Her thoughts returned to the first night when she and Chloe had been camping in the Superstitions. She remembered the strangling fear she felt. But now she didn't know what to feel. If he followed the customs of his clan, she wouldn't be sitting here right now. This was a hard and terrifying realization for her to acknowledge with all the other thoughts spinning through her head.

"Is it my fault Chloe is dead?" As the words fell from her mouth she thought it felt as if the temperature in the cab of the truck plummeted to sub-zero.

Mateo stared straight ahead. "She is not dead."

"Oh, thank God," she gasped as she turned toward him. "She's safe then?" He still didn't turn to look at her. His jaw was set in a firm line. His eyes remained focused on the road. Her relief waned.

"No."

The inside of her mouth felt as if it had just turned to dust. A razor-edged pain ripped at her breast again. Not dead. Not safe. Did she want to know what that meant? "Do you know where she is? Is she still on the mountain?"

His head nodded barely enough for her to notice.

"Is-is s-she—has she been chosen to ma-mate—"

"No," Mateo cut in without further explanation.

A train wreck of emotions crashed through her heart and mind. She stifled the cry in the back of her throat. Chloe was still alive. That was the most important thing. "Is there something we can do to help her?"

"She cannot be helped," he stated in a flat tone. He offered no further explanation.

His silence was as harsh as any words he could have spoken about Chloe's fate. If Chloe was on the mountain with Mateo's clan, and it was not for the purpose of mating, what other motive would a clan of vampires have for taking her captive?

The black sense of doom that seeped into Dawn's consciousness made her wish there was a secluded corner where she could curl up right now. She could not allow herself to think about the other possible reasons Chloe would be in the vampire village. There already too much insanity for her mind to absorb, and learning what was really happening to Chloe might break the last little grip of reality she was so desperately clinging to at this moment. She would ask Mateo to tell her all there was to know about Chloe, but she would wait until she felt strong enough to handle the entire truth.

"So, what's going to happen to me now?" she asked in a feeble voice after a long pause.

He glanced at her this time. A poignant smile curved his lips. "I suppose that's up to you."

"I-I didn't think I had a choice, especially after I pulled this stupid trick tonight."

"Only Billy knows what happened today. He is honor-bound to obey me. He won't tell anyone else." He leaned closer. "I love you so much, Dawn. I still want to be here with you, in your world, for as long as possible. But eventually, we will both have to fulfill our destinies, and once I take you to the mountain, to my village, you will never leave."

His gaze held hers for a moment before he was forced to turn back to watch the road, but his words held her prisoner.

Never leave.

She uncurled her fingers from his and clasped them together in her lap. His hand rested on her thigh for a few minutes longer, but eventually he pulled away and wrapped both hands around the steering wheel.

They drove in silence for the rest of the long way back. Dawn's mind was making disconnected decisions, yet deciding nothing. She tried to imagine how she would say goodbye to her beloved parents and to her brother and sister-in-law before she went to the mountain with Mateo for eternity. It was too painful to even imagine.

She wondered how far away she could get if she left first thing in the morning, maybe took a plane to another country? Would she ever be able to get far enough away so he couldn't feel her tears? Probably not.

Did she really want to try to leave him again? *No.* It was useless to waste energy thinking about anything other than how she would learn to accept her fate, because she knew she was going to be with Mateo forever. It was, after all, her destiny.

She would wait to talk to Mateo more about the future until tonight. There would not be much time once they got back to town this morning, because it wouldn't be long before the sun would be coming up.

"Do you want to go to the condo or to your apartment," he asked as the Apache Junction City Limit sign came into view. His voice sounded tired, strained.

Dawn's own fatigue was about to engulf her and she could barely function. Her eyes burned from lack of sleep. Her head felt like her brain had exploded from too much thinking. There was still a dull ache in her neck. If only she could snuggle in Mateo's strong embrace and sleep the day away. She wished, when they woke up, everything would just be normal, and all that happened the past few days would be just one more bad dream. Except, she didn't have dreams. She had real nightmares.

"My place," she managed to say with what small amount of energy she had left. It would still feel semi-normal there, or so she hoped.

He didn't react. He merely turned in the direction that would lead back to her little apartment.

She noticed he glanced in the rear-view mirror again. He had done this several times, and she assumed he was checking to see if Billy was still following them in her truck. She didn't have the strength to look back herself. But as Mateo pulled up to her apartment, she saw her white pickup pull up beside them.

When she grabbed for the door handle, Mateo jumped out of the truck and came around to her side. The engine was still running. She climbed down from the passenger seat without waiting for his help, but he was standing so close she staggered up against him once she was on the ground. She wasn't sure if her legs could support her much longer. He didn't give her a chance to try to make it to her front door on her own. He wrapped his arm around her waist and let her lean against him as they walked to her apartment door. If not for all the craziness in the past twenty-four hours, this would have felt so perfect.

As she reached into her purse to find her keys, he reached down and slid his hand under her chin. Tilting her face up so she was forced to look at him, he stared deeply into her eyes. Dawn was too tired to resist, even if she wanted to.

"I'm not going to give up in my quest to find a way for us to live here in your world for as long as possible. But you must also know I have gone completely against the customs of my clan, and I don't know if I can hold off the inevitable indefinitely."

His eyes were holding her gaze captive, and his voice sounded so filled with love and torment. Until this moment, she hadn't realized he was suffering every bit as much as she was about their future.

"My love for you has no boundaries, Udaya. I would give my life to protect you."

Her head nodded slowly. "I know," she whispered.

Mateo's hand lingered a moment longer under her chin. He looked expectant, waiting, hoping she would say something else. Words she wanted to say teetered on her arid tongue. He released his hold on her chin. His eyes had a strange shimmer as if tears were waiting to fall. He turned and walked slowly back down the sidewalk to where his truck was still idling.

She remained rooted to the spot, watching him walk away. Her heart followed, but her feet refused to let her run after him. She opened her mouth to call out to him. Words failed her. Mateo climbed into his truck where Billy Torres waited for him. They pulled away, disappearing around the corner at the end of the street.

"I love you, too, Mateo Two Moons, forever," she called out, finally finding her lost voice. The faint glow of the rising sun appeared in the sky overhead. A new day was dawning.

Chapter Eighteen

Thursday was pretty much of a wasted day. Dawn had fallen into a deep black sleep the minute her head hit the pillow after Mateo left her. She hadn't even bothered to remove her clothes. Only the tennis shoes she had taken from the condo were kicked off by the front door. The instant her eyes opened, though, all the madness of the past few days washed over her and any rest that might have dimmed the pain was gone.

She glanced at the clock on her bedside table. Three-thirty in the afternoon. Approximately four hours until sunset. Four hours until she saw Mateo again. Four hours to make the final decisions about how she would say goodbye to her loved ones and tie up the loose ends of her human life, just in case there was no way to prolong that destiny thing Mateo kept talking about and he ended up taking her up to the Superstitions tonight.

Never leave...she couldn't get those two menacing words out of her mind.

The time had come for her to do whatever it took to conquer her irrational fear and let it happen. But just how was she going to do that? The idea of walking away from her entire life and everyone else she loved and cared about was too painful to think about, even if she could no longer avoid it.

At least, her neck felt better today. It didn't hurt or

ache when she touched her fingers against the spot where the band aid still covered Mateo's bite. There were no signs of the nausea she experienced yesterday morning at the condo, either. It was becoming more and more obvious the sickness she randomly felt was definitely induced by Mateo biting her, because it was always after those frightening episodes when she was so queasy and dizzy.

Since she was feeling good right now, she'd better start figuring out what she had to do before she left to be with Mateo forever. But she had no idea how to even begin planning for the end of her life as a real one. Damn, that sounded so crazy.

Once in the shower, letting the water run extra hot over her body, she was finally able to begin to formulate a vague plan for today, at least. The first thing she wanted to do was get on her laptop and look up everything she could find about vampires, dhampyres, and their offspring, even though she realized there would only be legends and myths about these immortal beings because they weren't supposed to exist in real life. Right?

Then, she would stop by the store and buy a pregnancy test. Not even scolding hot water could warm her frosty body up when she thought about the pregnancy issue. She touched her abdomen tentatively; still as firm and flat as ever, of course. What if there was a teeny dhampyre or whatever already growing in there?

Oh God.

Would she even have a chance to know it, love it, and be able to watch it grow up if she were already under his immortal spell as his eternal mate? It? A dhampyre? No. Just a baby. Her baby. And Mateo's baby.

A whole new barrage of questions filled her overcrowded thoughts as she tried to fathom the idea of bearing his children. Just the entire idea of having any baby was scary enough, but having a half-human, half-vampire one was mind-boggling.

She quickly grabbed a clean pair of faded blue jeans, a loose fitting pink tunic top, and slipped a pair of pink flip-flops on her feet. They matched the petal pink nail polish she painted her toenails last Friday night when she and Chloe went to the pizza place to get a bite to eat and a couple beers for what they thought would just be a typical start to another regular weekend.

The night she met Mateo Two Moons. The night her world changed forever. Nothing would ever be the same again, especially if she was already carrying his baby.

A sense of panic gripped her insides and twisted them into a heavy knot in the pit of her stomach. The research could wait. First, she had to get a pregnancy test before she could concentrate on anything else. As she grabbed her purse and rushed out of her apartment toward her truck, she was struck by the heat of the late Arizona afternoon. It must be one hundred degrees today, but she was shaking as if she was in the Arctic.

Dawn noticed the interior of her truck smelled faintly like Billy Torres. Not an unpleasant odor, just a manly smell of soap and sweat. She guessed it could be expected since he had been in her truck most of the night driving back from the Colorado/Arizona border. Still, he smelled nothing like Mateo, whose musky cologne made her knees feel weak even now as she recalled his sexy scent.

Mateo Two Moons once again invaded her body and soul. He told her last night his love for her had no boundaries, and she knew her love for him had no limitations, either. Still, the idea of already being pregnant with his baby was almost more than she could handle, particularly when she was still trying to come to terms with all the other unbelievable factors involving their future.

As she pulled into the pharmacy parking lot, she was trying her hardest to convince herself there was no use agonizing about this pregnancy thing, yet. She just needed to know for sure she wasn't so she could concentrate on all the other things she had to worry about. Luckily, she wasn't worried about seeing anyone she knew because she was certain she would be incapable of acting like a sane person right now.

Fifteen minutes later she was back in her truck with a bright red bag sitting in the passenger seat. A loud relieved sigh escaped from her. She had skulked up and down the aisles of the feminine needs department so guiltily she was surprised a security guard hadn't followed her out of the store to see if she shoplifted something.

She glanced over at the little unassuming bag that was so important to her right now. There were two pregnancy tests in the bag because the box said taking a second test was advisable for accurate results.

Just as she was rushing up the walkway to her apartment her cell began to ring. She nearly threw the bag and its contents all over the sidewalk. It was her mom. She didn't answer. There was no way she could talk to her right now. Since she didn't leave a message,

Dawn assumed she wasn't calling about anything urgent. She would return the call when things got back to normal.

Oh wait. Dawn chuckled in a sarcastic tone as she reminded herself once again of how her life would never be normal again.

There was absolutely nothing glamorous about peeing on a stick. Ugh. She read the directions several times since this was, thankfully, the first time she ever had the need to do one of these nerve-wrecking tests. Of course, she had never been this irresponsible before, either. Oh, and she had never made love to, or been bitten by, a vampire until the past week, either.

So many firsts lately.

As she counted down the ten minutes until the test was finished, she stood in front of the mirror above the bathroom sink. She gingerly pulled away the skin-covered band aid covering the bite on her neck and tossed it in the trash.

With a tentative glance, she tilted her head to the side and looked into the mirror to examine the wound that was healing fairly quickly from the looks of it. The slight indentations resembled a half-moon shape as if Mateo had bitten her with all his front teeth—just like the one she had on her wrist.

No fangs? Nothing about Mateo Two Moons was typical, not even his vampire bite, she determined with an aggravated huff.

She drew in a deep sigh and reached out to retrieve the narrow plastic stick from the bathroom counter. *Please, no pink line, no pink line.*

Her breath clogged her throat and prevented her from taking a breath as she forced herself to focus on the narrow area that contained the results. The breath she was holding escaped in one huge hissing exhale. No pink line! Whew!

Thank you, God. She continued to stare at the little white and blue stick in her shaking hand as she let her extreme relief calm the thrashing in her breast. She had been prepared for the very worst, and now, she was shocked to discover it turned out in her favor, for a change.

There was no need to take the test again. She would have taken a second test if this first one had been positive, but she decided not to push her luck. Okay, maybe that was not so responsible, but she couldn't go through another torturous ten minutes. She had to research things that weren't supposed to exist.

In folklore, a dhampyre is the result of a human mating with a vampire. The word originated in the Albanian language where dham means 'teeth' and pire means 'to drink'. The powers dhampyres possess are the same as vampires, but they do not have all the typical weaknesses associated with vampires.

Dawn stared at her laptop screen. *To drink with teeth.* To drink human blood from necks, wrists, and thighs with teeth? It still didn't match what Mateo told her.

There were other encyclopedia sites with even less information. And all the book sites listed dozens of romantic fiction and horror stories about dhampyres, but what she needed to find had nothing to do with fantasies. She was living the real-life horror story. From what little she already knew of Mateo's Blood Clan, dhampyres, their customs, vampirism, and their offspring, she was not sure how much romance was involved once three major parts of her body were sucked on by her dhampyre/vampire lover.

All that was left for Mateo to bite was her thigh, and the thought of being bitten there was not something she was ready to remotely think about, yet. The little hairs along the back of her neck were standing on end with that fleeting thought.

There were, however, lots of Internet sites and blogs about so-called real vampires, which claimed legions of undead blood suckers truly did exist all over the world. Nothing came close to describing the type of existence Mateo told her about concerning the secret caves where his clan slept during the day, or the Clan Society who protected their secrets, and most importantly, eternal mates and the dhampyre children born of a human mother and a vampire father.

She glanced out the window and realized it was nearly dark. Mateo would be here soon. She turned off her computer. An odd mixture of building excitement over seeing him again churned in her breast, along with the ever-present apprehension she couldn't escape now that she knew what he really was, and the important role she would play in his future once he took her up to the mountain.

She shook her head and gave a resigned sigh. When did she start to believe all this craziness? She kept recalling his words from last night.

I don't know how long I can hold off the inevitable. Never leave.

Dawn clenched her teeth tightly to keep them from clattering together. How could she just go willing with him when it meant giving up her entire life? How could she not go with him if it meant not being with him forever? It was a hopeless situation.

She grabbed a sweatshirt as the night shadows settled into complete darkness, and went out to sit in the white plastic lawn chair on the little stoop outside her front door. She enjoyed sitting here in the evenings to watch the sun go down. But tonight, she was focused on something more important. From here, she would be able to see Mateo as soon as he drove down her street.

The thumbnail slice of the new moon rose in the velvet black of the sky, and soon afterward, hundreds of tiny stars began to sprinkle the vast expanse overhead. The beauty of the night was lost to her as she stared at the street—anxiously waiting—for the big black truck that never came as the hours passed.

As the early morning signaled the start of another new day, she was slumped down dozing in the chair. A couple, obviously coming home after the closing of some bar or club, woke her up around four with their drunken giggles and loud voices. They staggered past her to an apartment a couple doors away without acknowledging her presence.

She stretched out her cramped body and pushed up from the hard chair once the couple disappeared into the other apartment. She raised her arms over her head and stretched again. Every inch of her body ached from the long hours she sat, and slept, in the uncomfortable chair. A huge yawn escaped her mouth. She wrapped her arms around herself to ward off the coolness from the early morning temperature.

Where the hell was Mateo? How odd he hadn't come to see her last night? Could he really work for the Indian Bureau? Was he out of town on business again? Why wouldn't he at least call? She refused to think about anything serious happening to prevent him from coming to see her. But it seemed inconceivable he wouldn't have come to see her—or at least call—after everything that happened between them in the past few days. They had so much more to talk about.

Her fatigued mind was filled with so many thoughts and unanswered questions, but right now wasn't the time to dwell on them if she had any hope of getting a little more rest.

She changed into a pair of gray knit shorts and a white tee before pulling back the bed covers and sinking into the mattress on her bed. She was going to go to work today in spite of the fact Billy Torres told the school she would be out all week due to illness. It was already Friday, and she had things to tidy up in her classroom before the weekend, just in case she didn't make it back there next week…or ever again.

With that sordid thought in her mind, she was determined to get a couple hours of quality sleep if she had any hopes of making it through a hectic day at school. Plus, her body desperately needed the comfort of her bed after the long hours she spent scrunched up in the chair outside her door. What a stupid waste of time that had been.

As she drifted off to sleep, her last thoughts were of how she was a complete dumbass to wait outside all night for Mateo. He apparently had better things to do than worry about her. She could be long gone again—to somewhere on the other side of the world this time. For all he knew, she could actually be pregnant with his half-breed child, but did he care?

Apparently not.

Whatever, Mateo Two Moons, hope you had more

fun than I did last night, she told herself in a pissy inner voice as she fell into another deep dreamless sleep.

****

How was this possible? She slept until noon. Until recently she never needed an alarm to wake her in the mornings. Her body's internal clock always woke her in plenty of time to get to work. Those days were over obviously. So much for going to work again today. Her foul mood focused on one person.

Mateo Two Moons was to blame for everything crappy in her life lately. But for some really amazing things, too, she reminded herself as tingling hotness spread through her body. She groaned, and rolled over taking the pillow with her and clamping it down tightly over the back of her head. It didn't block out the fact she was still seriously pissed at him for not coming to see her last night. Not even a call? Just where the hell was he anyway?

She gave a disgusted grunt and rolled onto her back. Angrily, she kicked the blankets away from her feet and sat up. There was no use lying here whining about not seeing him last night. He would surely be here tonight, and she had plenty of things to do until then.

Showered, with her long blonde hair pulled up on top of her head in a messy bun, and snacking on a tuna sandwich, Dawn made an impulsive decision to go to Mateo's condo. It was probably no more than five minutes away if she drove there, but it sure seemed considerably farther when she escaped on foot from Billy Torres the day before yesterday. She still felt a little bad about that episode. Billy was merely Mateo's wing man. Hopefully, he wasn't in trouble with Mateo because of her attempted escape. Besides, here she was, and it had all been for nothing, anyway.

Still munching on her sandwich, she grabbed her purse and headed out the front door. She climbed into her pickup and drove toward the condo where Mateo told her the nightmarish things she was still having a hard time accepting. Driving to the lavish condo complex today felt really strange for some reason.

Daytime was beginning to seem strange. All that mattered now was nighttime when she would see Mateo…hopefully.

She parked on a side street. For some unknown reason, she felt it was best if it wasn't obvious she was here. As she walked through the empty little playground the negative pregnancy test popped into her mind. Of course, she reminded herself, the instructions included with the test recommended she take a second test to be sure.

She shoved the infant swing defiantly as she passed where the cute little blonde girl played. Maybe she should just take that second test when she got home— just to have it settled once and for all. And there would not be a next time unless they used protection, she told herself firmly. Even dhampyre babies should be planned.

There would be a next time, right? Where was he last night, anyway?

Her feet felt a bit reluctant walking up to the front door. She was recalling the sheer terror she felt when she charged out of here barely forty-eight hours ago. She was convinced she was running for her life. What a waste of time and emotion. Mateo was her destiny and she would never try to leave him again.

Just standing here at his front door, even though she knew he really didn't live here, made a longing ache inch its way through her body and settle heavily in her heart. She wanted more time with him...here and not in some ominous world on top of the mountain. There just had to be a way to make this work, didn't there?

The door was locked. She knocked, just in case. No one answered, of course. On the off chance there was a key hidden somewhere, she picked up the corner of the rubber scrolled welcome mat on the stoop in front of the door.

"Ha!" she said when she spotted the long silver key on the cement under the mat. Good thing she wasn't here to rob the joint. She unlocked the door and replaced the key back under the mat before entering the empty condo. Standing in the foyer she relived the last time she had been here. It was almost the same time of day, only then she was sneaking out instead of sneaking in. The condo was filled with the afternoon sunlight streaming through the tall windows. But today it was deathly quiet.

She walked into the kitchen. The flowers in the glass vase on the island were wilting and the fruit in the bowl was not looking much better. A sense of sadness crept over her. Mateo had gone to such great lengths to make this place welcoming and comfortable. But she had not appreciated any of it. Did he really think she would just be able to accept everything he told her without freaking out just a little bit? Or...a lot?

She wandered to the large curved stairway and stared up at the second floor. As she walked slowly up the stairs she imagined what it would be like to live in this beautiful place with Mateo; to live here like a regular couple. Like real ones. She would teach school and come home to him every night. They would do all the things regular couples did in the evenings, then go to bed, make love, take showers together, or long romantic bubble baths. After sleeping wrapped in one another's arms, they would wake up, make love again before having breakfast together and heading off to work.

A wistful smile curved her lips as she stood in the doorway and looked at the king-sized bed with the elegant navy blue velvet spread. She wanted a regular life so much with Mateo. But that sort of life was the fantasy.

She walked to the huge closet and pulled back the mirrored door. His shirts and pants were still hanging there along with the new garments obviously meant for her to wear when she was here. There was something so normal about seeing 'her' clothes and his clothes hanging together. She reached out and removed the white silk shirt she recognized as the one Mateo had worn on their first date. Holding it up to her face she drew in a deep whiff and closed her eyes as a faint trace of his manly cologne and natural musky scent filled her senses.

"Oh, Mateo," she said as she rubbed the silken material against her cheek. "Why does this have to be so hard? And so damn scary?"

With a sigh, she replaced the shirt on its hanger and put it back in the closet. She slid the door shut and turned away. Maybe, somehow, a miracle would happen and they could still figure out a way to make this work without going to the caves on the top of the

Superstitions for the rest of forever.

It was late in the afternoon when she returned to her apartment. She stopped by the public library and checked out some older books about vampires and the Lost Dutchman's Gold Mine she had seen referenced online when doing research yesterday. There might be something in them that would tell her more than she found online. It just didn't seem possible clans of vampires, or dhampyres, could exist for centuries in the Superstitions without someone—somewhere—knowing something about them.

Hours later, she switched on the lamp sitting on the end table beside her couch as the last of light began to fade outside her windows. Her eyes felt heavy and tired. She had been reading through the library books and still was not able to find anything about half-breed vampires or legends of the Lost Dutchman's Gold Mine that could relate to the things Mateo told her about his clan. Only the references to the gold mine being guarded by evil spirits and supernatural demons made Dawn wonder once again if they really could have something to do with vampires instead.

She put the books on the corner of her oval coffee table and stretched her arms over her head. It was completely dark outside. Mateo should have been here by now. She grabbed the TV switcher and began to scan the guide on the screen to see what was on tonight.

It sure wasn't the first Friday night she had spent alone. So, why was she feeling like she was going to die if he didn't call or come to see her? *Call him*, an inner voice suggested. Um? *No.* He knew where she was; she had no idea where he was, and she was too stubborn to give him the satisfaction of knowing she was dying to see him. She pushed the channel button on her switcher.

Dracula's Bride was just coming on. She chuckled out loud when the title popped up in the TV guide on her screen. She'd pass on that one tonight. She pushed the off button on the switcher. Concentrating on a movie was going to be impossible, anyway.

Mateo really wasn't going to blow her off two nights in a row, was he? Why would he do that? Was he testing her? Waiting to see if she would come running up to the Superstitions again to see him? Well, he'd be waiting until Hell froze over.

Wasn't she supposed to be his destiny; his end-all-forever-everything? Did vampires change their minds about possessing an eternal mate? Maybe he decided she was more trouble than she was worth and he was out looking for a new forever-everything.

Bite me, Mateo Two Moons. Oh wait, you already did...several times. A cynical snicker escaped from her mouth.

Joseph Red Feather's guitar chords began to sing from her cell phone. The breath stopped short in her throat. She grabbed the phone from the coffee table. "Hello," she said in a squeaky tone of voice.

"Hello, beautiful," Mateo's deep voice echoed. There was a pause. "Are you okay?"

"Great," she lied as her head filled with the words she would really like to say to him...*I'm seriously pissed you didn't call or come to see me last night. Eternal mate here, remember? And where are you tonight, damn it?*

"How are you?" she asked curtly.

"I'm good." There were a few seconds of silence

before he spoke again. "I was wondering if you would like to have dinner with me tomorrow night."

Her heart felt as if it had just sprouted wings and was fluttering around in her breast. All her previous anger disappeared before the first flutter. "A d-d-dinner? Date?"

"Yes, a date for dinner." He chuckled. "And dress up. We're going into Phoenix, okay?"

Breath...speak...be sane, she instructed herself. "Okay. After the sun goes down?" *Really? What time should I be ready?* Now, that would have been the usual response. Of course, the question was extra stupid because he couldn't come out of his cave until the sun went down, anyway.

Another chuckle came from Mateo's end of the receiver. "Yes, after the sun goes down. See you then. Oh, and Dawn?"

"Yes?"

"I love you."

"I love you," Dawn answered softly. She held the phone to her ear for a moment after he hung up. A formal dinner date. In Phoenix. With Mateo Two Moons. It sounded perfect. Just perfect.

Chapter Nineteen

Forcing himself to stay away from Dawn was more difficult than Mateo imagined it would be. He had every intention of being with her last night and again tonight, but things were not going so good in his village.

The previous evening, when he had awoken from his daylight slumber, he learned Rafael's mate, Lydia, had gone into labor with their latest dhampyre. His grandmother and mother, as well as Anton's mate, had been attending the birth as was the custom of his clan. For the first time in their history, something had gone horribly wrong.

As he returned from the bottom of the mountain where he had gone to get cell service so he could call Dawn to make their dinner date, he saw his grandmother waiting for him. Her poignant smile tugged at his heart. He forced a weak grin when he walked up to take her out-stretched hand.

"We are ready to begin," she said in a soft tone, motioning for him to accompany her. She was wearing her best ceremonial dress made of soft cream colored deer skin. It was knee length with long fringe hanging almost to her ankles. The same trim edged the shoulders and cascaded over her arms. The intricate beading decorating the upper body of the ancient dress was exquisite and fragile. This gown was worn for the most special of occasions, and today, one of the saddest. Her long thick black hair hung in two braids over her shoulders and was adorned with eagle feathers. She was beautiful and regal. As always, Mateo filled with pride and awe knowing she was his grandmother.

As they entered the sacred circle where they would perform the primitive curing ceremony, he saw his own parents standing beside the pit where a massive fire roared. They both wore their finest ceremonial gowns, and were as impressive looking as his grandmother.

He drew in a heavy breath and smoothed down the front of his heavy leather ceremonial shirt. In traditional Apache fashion, it was decorated with striped raccoon tails and brightly colored ribbons. In his hundred years, he had only worn this shirt and the matching leather leggings a dozen or so times before. Those times had been happy occasions when Anton and Rafael each brought their mates to the village and when each of their children had been born. Wearing them now felt so uncomfortable.

He watched his grandfather walk up to the fire pit as another strong sense of pride washed through him. Drago was without a doubt the most extraordinary man he had seen or known. He, too, wore his best ceremonial shirt and leggings, but he also wore an elaborate headdress made of eagle feathers and porcupine quills.

Mateo's mother motioned for him to come to stand beside her as the ceremony was about to get underway. Tonight, they would pray to the Gaan, the Apache reference to spirits of the mountain, for guidance. Then, they would ask the Apache God, Usen, to take the spirit of Rafael and Lydia's stillborn dhampyre son to the

Apache afterlife. Although these ancient ceremonies were traditionally conducted when someone passed away in the Apache tribe, they had never been performed by Drago's Clan before now.

Lastly, they would perform the curing ceremony to hopefully rid the Clan of whatever curse had been put on them to bring this tragedy upon their village. Always before, dhampyre children were born strong and healthy; their fragile human genes were infused with the nearly indestructible genes of the century old vampires who sired them.

The previous night, however, after an especially long and grueling labor, Lydia had given birth to a boy who was beautiful and flawless in appearance. But he never took a breath regardless how hard the women attending the birth tried to revive him. The remains of the tiny infant were now wrapped in a blue and tan woven blanket and laying on a rock altar built beside the fire pit.

Mateo stared at the tiny lifeless bundle through the flickering flames of the fires. The death of this dhampyre was the most tragic thing to ever happen in their village, and it left the entire clan in a state of disbelief and shock. His grandfather instructed members of the Clan Society on the Apache Reservation to get in touch with other society members from Blood Clans in different parts of the world to see if any of them experienced such an unexpected tragedy, or if any of them had heard of a stillborn birth in all of the Blood Clan's history.

Late last night, Drago called a meeting of his entire clan so they could discuss different theories as to why this misfortune might have occurred. They wondered if a new and unheard of virus could be affecting the Clan, either from the blood supplies they drank from or the tainted environment itself.

In the three centuries he lived, the senior vampire had seen so many changes already. He talked about the human blood sources they needed for survival and how he was concerned they were now contaminated with synthetic food supplies and numerous diseases. He worried the air they breathed was filled with putrid fumes and toxic wastes that drifted up from the world of the real ones. Nothing was pure in this world anymore, he warned.

Drago even suggested perhaps some of the venomous infections of the real ones, like cancer, were somehow infiltrating the strong immune systems of the Blood Clan. If this was true, their entire existence could be threatened. Once again, he contemplated if the time had come to cut all ties with the modern world and live in total seclusion as the clans in olden times had done.

As Mateo had listened to his grandfather speak the previous evening, he realized the changes he felt were imminent for his clan could be the exact opposite of what he was hoping for. He envisioned they would soon find ways to live among the world of the real ones without living in dread of extinction.

But his grandfather was constantly suggesting they become even more reclusive than they were now. In spite of how much Mateo loved and respected his wise grandfather, he knew if Drago ordered them to stay on the mountain and never go down to the world of the real ones again, he would have a difficult decision to make.

His heart ached now as he watched Rafael

approaching the fire pit, holding his sobbing wife against his side. Lydia's face was pressed into her mate's chest and her body shook with inconsolable sorrow. She wore a white shawl over her black hair and a loose-fitting buckskin dress. Rafael was decked out in his ceremonial suit like the rest of the clan. They stopped next to the alter that held the lifeless body of their newborn son.

Anton and Nita appeared next, leading all the dhampyre children of the clan. Their six children walked beside Anton. The oldest, one of three sons, Chaz, was fourteen years old and Mateo was surprised to see the boy recently cut his long dark hair short in a choppy style like many of the real ones in his age group. Mateo could not remember any of the males in their clan ever cutting their hair.

A faint smile curved Mateo's mouth as Chaz walked past him. He was a tall handsome boy and carried himself in a dignified way that suggested he was older than he really was. In Blood Clan years, fourteen was still considered barely more than an infant for a male since Chaz would not become a fully mature vampire for another eighty-six years.

Chaz's mother, Nita, carried Lydia and Rafael's three-year-old son on her hip, and their ten-year-old twin daughters walked beside her. All three children resembled their Canadian-born mother more than they did their vampire father. Right now, they all focused their full attention on the rock altar where their baby brother lay silent and cold.

With the entire clan gathered around the fire pit, Drago began the ceremonies with ancient Apache and Spanish prayers, a combination of his original Mexican

Blood Clan and those of his Apache mate, Raven. They danced one of the Apache dances of her ancestors, and when the praying and dancing were done, they consumed blood drawn from the human sources held in the caves.

There were three real ones in the cave at this time. Typically, there was only one blood source kept in the cave at a time since the full grown male vampires needed only a small amount from a real one every few days to suppress their thirst for blood. Raven and Rosa, who were also immortals now, drank a minimal amount of blood and usually not as much their male mates. But when a dhampyre child was about to be born, Drago would request the Clan Society to bring an extra real one to the mountaintop. Blood from the additional human would be used for the special ceremonies they conducted in the few days preceding the impending birth.

In spite of the fact the Clan was educated from the books and teachings of the world of real ones, Drago and Raven still adhered to the outdated beliefs that preparing special potions from blood to be drunk by everyone in the clan, even the children, would help ensure the birth of a male child. Human blood would also be massaged into skin on the belly of the mother once she went into labor.

Regardless of Mateo's past attempts to talk to his grandfather about the complete contradiction to scientific fact that a female or male child was determined from the genes of the father's sperm at conception, Drago still believed the sex of a dhampyre child was not established until the final moments before they entered the world, and the outcome was greatly influenced by the special ceremonies conducted and blood potions consumed by the clan in the days preceding the birth. The elder vampire could be open-minded about many things involving the world of the real ones, but he refused to consider any other possibilities when it came to the birth of the dhampyre children.

Mateo shifted his weight from one foot to the other in a nervous motion as the gourd of blood began to circulate among the clan. Chloe Webster's blood was not needed for the birthing ceremonies. But her relentless curiosity and determination to find the Lost Dutchman's Gold Mine led her to the location of the village hidden at the entrance to the legendary gold mine. As with all the others in the past who wandered too close, she could not be allowed to discover the secrets of the gold mine without paying the ultimate price.

Even the crazy old miner, Jacob Waltz, had not climbed high enough to follow his own clues. The smaller vein of gold he discovered was in caves lower down the mountain. He mined out that limited source long before his death in 1891.

The Blood Clan left him alone for two reasons, the main one was because most of the people he told about his gold mine thought he was crazy; and also, because the zealous gold seekers who did believe his wild tales of endless veins of gold sometimes got a little too close to the secluded caves, which provided an extra bonus of human blood to the clan.

"Drink, my son."

Mateo snapped out of his deep concentration about the past and the present, and how it would affect the future of the clan. He reached out and took the antiquated gourd flask from his mother and tipped it to his mouth. The blood was lukewarm and thick going down his throat. It satisfied his primal need, but since tasting the indescribably sweet blood of his eternal mate, the life source of any other human was not so tempting right now.

Udaya. His Dawn. Her name and her beautiful image floated through his mind. He couldn't wait to be with her.

Mateo's hands shook slightly as he handed the blood-filled gourd to Anton. He did not know which of the human blood sources provided this drink for the ceremony, but the thought it could belong to Chloe Webster made it a bitter taste to swallow. He wondered if Chloe would still be alive when he finally brought Dawn up here to the village.

The homeless alcoholics who usually provided them with blood did not last more than a couple weeks before their emancipated diseased bodies gave out from lack of blood. But a young healthy source like Chloe could last several weeks or longer, and as much as he hated to acknowledge it he knew the time was drawing near when he would be forced to bring Dawn here.

He glanced around at his solemn family. They all looked like they belonged in a different century. Tonight, even the youngest children wore the ceremonial outfits crafted hundreds of years ago, most likely by his grandmother's family when Drago had first come here to claim Raven as his mate.

Right now, Mateo also looked entirely different than when he left the mountain to visit the world below. In addition to his centuries old tanned buckskin outfit and knee high moccasins, his hair was hanging in two long braids over each of his shoulders. There were red streaks of human blood drawn across the sides of his face. He was the epitome of a savage vampire in every way.

Tomorrow night he would dress in his trendy clothes and drive his shiny new truck to town, where he would pretend to be just a regular man, a real one, for the short time he would spend with Dawn.

As he stared into the fire pit where the fiery fingers of the crackling orange flames were reaching toward the ebony sky overhead, he felt a sinister omen lurking in the shadows. At this moment, he realized just how drastically different his vampire world was from the world below the Superstitions. Was there really any way to combine the mysteries of his vampire clan and Dawn's human world without incurring tragic consequences?

The ceremony finished with the heartbreaking burning of the tiny body in the roaring fire pit. Lydia's tormented wailing drowned out all other sounds. Mateo looked up at the unusually cloudy sky. The barely more than a fingernail moon peeking from the shadows of the clouds curved in a menacing and unnatural looking shape. He lowered his gaze just as Rafael and Lydia were walking past him.

His brother leaned toward him and hissed through gritted teeth, "This is your fault. Because of you wanting to change the way we have done things since the beginning of time, our Clan is now cursed."

He stared at Rafael in stunned silence, before he reached out and touched his brother's arm. "I'm sorry, my brother. I don't understand why you would think I caused this?" Rafael pulled his arm away without answering. His cold unyielding expression bespoke his innermost feelings.

A current of icy wind whipped through Mateo as he watched the remainder of his family began to move away from the fire and the last remains of the burning child. He glanced around to see if anyone heard his brother's harsh words, but it appeared no one else was aware of the accusation Rafael hurled at him.

There was no basis for his brother's allegation. But he had to find a way to prove it wasn't true—to his brother and to himself, because if he was the reason this tiny dhampyre male was now no more than a pile of smoking ash, he would never forgive himself.

Chapter Twenty

Dawn had wanted to wear this dress for ages and it just never seemed appropriate for even the dressiest of after-school functions or any of her previous dates. Her sister-in-law, Teresa, Jeremy's new wife, had given this unique dress to her because it was too tight on her figure, which was slightly fuller than Dawn's slender body. The dress was an exquisite vintage mini from the sixties; a sleeveless black silk sheath with an intricate black lace overlay covering the entire—skimpy— length. But from where the length ended at upper mid-thigh, delicate threads of fringe fell from the hemline of the dress and swirled in a teasing motion around her lower thighs whenever she moved.

She even had the perfect CFM's—come-fuck-me shoes—to wear with this sexy dress. Four-inch stiletto sandals with the thinnest of straps traipsed over the tops of her feet, and delicate t-straps wrapped around her ankles, all in tiny shimmering rhinestones. She had bought them to wear with this dress, so this was the first time she was getting to wear them, as well.

Leaning toward the mirror, Dawn slipped the wires of her long dangling rhinestone earrings into her ear piercings and stood back to survey the day long effort of looking as beautiful as possible for Mateo Two Moons. Her glossy red lips parted with a satisfied smile. It was worth splurging today at the beauty shop.

Her updo was messy perfection with long tendrils of blonde hair tumbling down her back, and framing her face. Tiny rhinestones were sprinkled among the swirls of hair and sparkled when she moved her head in the slightest bit. Afterward, she asked for the works, and had a manicure and pedicure. Now, her toenails and fingernails were a shiny red that matched her lips.

She was ready to go way too early. As she glanced at the clock on her nightstand, the extra pregnancy test she hadn't taken yet caught her eye. Maybe tomorrow she would make time for the second, and totally unnecessary, test. Oh, and she would remind Mateo they needed to use protection tonight. Her knees grew weak as everything between her legs began to tighten with the thought of what they would undoubtedly be doing before this night was over. Everything except the biting thing, she hoped.

She needed a drink.

A glass of red wine didn't do much to calm her nerves, but it did help pass the time. It seemed impossible that only a week had passed since her first date with Mateo. Tomorrow would mark a week since Chloe disappeared, too. Dawn took another huge swig of wine. How could she even think about going out and enjoying herself when Chloe was...what?

The local newspaper today said search parties were still looking. She thought about the disturbing words Mateo said when she pushed him for an answer. *Alive, but not safe.* A sharp shudder raced down her spine. Alive—that was all that mattered.

She heard the roar of his big truck pulling up outside as she drained the last drop of wine from the glass. The sun had been down for only a short time. He must have driven like a maniac to get here. She grabbed her small black beaded evening bag and headed to the door the instant she heard the light knock. When she pulled the door open, she was fairly certain she experienced that swooning thing again.

Damn. Wasn't there a law against a man looking this gorgeous?

Mateo's mouth curved in a half smirk, half sex smile that made one side of his full lips turn up just slightly more than the other as his hungry gaze raked up and down her body with brazen and obvious lust. "Udaya, you are so beautiful," he said in a husky voice. "I've missed you so much."

"So are you, and so have I," she murmured in a desperate-sounding voice that once again sounded alien to her ears. It had only been two days since she'd seen him, but it felt like two years. She let her own gaze admire the magnificent man who stood in her doorway.

His long luxurious hair was loose tonight; the shiny raven locks were tucked behind his ears. Her fingers curled into tight fists at the sides of her body in an effort to resist the urge to reach up and immerse them in those beautiful thick strands.

He was wearing a sharply tailored black suit jacket over a black dress shirt with the top couple buttons undone. A narrow white, gray and black diagonally striped tie was loosely knotted below the open collar of his shirt in a manner suggesting it was ready to be pulled from around his neck at any moment.

Her fingers uncurled for an instant, yearning to loosen that teasing tie the rest of the way and pull it in a slow, leisurely motion from around his neck. She gulped and pulled her fingers back into her palms. Her red nails dug into her skin.

His shirt was loosely tucked into the waistband of black jeans that caressed his hips and thighs just enough to define the strong form of his lean muscled legs. A shiny silver oval buckle adorned his black tooled belt and peeked out from between his jacket.

Dawn's fickle hands now wanted to undo that belt, pull it slowly—or maybe really quickly—from his belt loops, drop it to the ground, and begin unfastening his jeans.

Hot didn't even begin to describe the way this man looked tonight.

As she was seducing him with her zealous thoughts, he emitted a low whistle and grabbed her hand and began to twirl her around. She felt the fringe on the hem floating over her thighs. It was a total turn on to know he was staring at the way the long strands were lapping teasingly against her bare skin.

"This is one hell of a sexy look you have going on here, Miss Malone. You are giving a whole new meaning to fringe." He cocked one brow, adding, "And my people do know our fringe." His eyes moved down to her towering rhinestone sandals and back up to the top of her rhinestone adorned head. "I might have to cancel our dinner reservations because I'm not sure I want to share you with anyone else tonight."

He shook his head and sighed. "I suppose anticipation is part of the fun, though." His voice was filled with innuendo. The provocative expression on his face bespoke his inner most thoughts as his eyes narrowed and misted with desire.

Her insides began to quake. "We don't have to go out tonight," she managed to gasp.

A heavy sigh escaped him as he leveled his shimmering gaze on her face. "That is way too tempting, but tonight is kind of special because Joseph Red Feather is playing at a club in Phoenix and I've made reservations for the concert and dinner." His handsome face drew into a conflicted frown. "But—"

She reached out and put her finger against his lips. "We have the entire night ahead of us and I would love to see Joseph Red Feather. We might skip dinner, though."

He hesitated for an instant before his lips curved into a smile behind her red polished fingertip. "I definitely don't need food when I'm with you, but I was pretty excited to know Joseph Red Feather was playing locally again so I could take you to hear him."

She smiled and without hesitation leaned forward, rose up on the toes of her stilettos slightly—with this added height she was not that much shorter than him—and placed her glossy red lips against his mouth.

The instant their lips touched, his mouth pressed hard against hers as he shoved her against the wall just inside the doorway. The sound of the front door slamming shut behind him was as loud as roaring thunder but neither of them noticed.

His hands encircled her waist as his hips pressed against her body. She felt his cock straining through the front of his jeans as it swelled into her abdomen. Her legs turned to pulp. The beaded evening bag made a slight crackling sound when it landed on the floor at their feet. The crotch of her lacy black G-string, and all areas of skin surrounding it, became soaked with her uncontrollable desire for this dangerously sexy vampire.

Savory kisses devoured her lips, while his hands ran down her hips and under her fringed hem. He slid the dress up the short distance to her waist and let one of his hands find the thin thread of elastic on the side of her panties. With one yank, the delicate strap broke. He pulled the panties from her body and tossed them to the floor.

Then, in a much gentler motion, he pushed her legs apart with one hand and let two fingers of the same hand find the soft folds of her clit. His fingertips rubbed between the silken creases causing her to grow so wet she felt a rush of heat soar through her face. But there was not time to dwell on embarrassment because his fingers slipped inside of her and began to work themselves in and out, around and around. Her body squirmed and writhed with the witchery being created by his long fingers.

"Oh God, Mateo," she cried out as she was seduced to the point of panting delirium.

Her hands shook as she slid them from around his neck where they had naturally entangled themselves in his long hair and down to the shining buckle right above the huge hard ridge pushing against the strain of his jeans. The buckle fell away with her first attempt, and so did the snap at the top of his jeans. As her impatient fingers tugged his zipper down, his anxious cock popped out from the tight confines of the denim pants.

She shoved his pants to his thighs as he hitched one of her legs up on his bare hip. For a moment, she massaged his rock-hard cock. It felt hot to her touch and the tip was swollen to the point it felt as if the skin was strained to the breaking point. Dawn's pussy clenched with anticipation to have him inside of her.

With exact precision, she positioned the inflated head to where his fingers had just been working their glorious magic. He grasped her buttocks and effortlessly held her up as he drove deeper inside her. His eagerness was apparent as he moved with the reckless abandonment this impetuous sexual act induced.

Although he tried to hold her tighter against his body to protect her from hammering against the wall as much as possible, his efforts were in vain as they both clung to one another and crashed back and forth against the hard barrier in their throes of lust, abandoned cravings, and most of all, forever love.

An ecstatic cry escaped from her lips as their bodies continued to mesh together, and the magnitude of their thrusts continued to grow. The fringe on her dress was swaying wildly against her bare buttocks. It was slapping against his hands where he held onto her hips.

Oh yes, he was so right...fringe had a whole new meaning now.

The excitement of this spontaneous act of raw desire drove her to the brink of madness. Intense pleasure built. It was uncontrollable and encompassed every one of her senses. She knew he was reaching the same level of frenzied climax by the increased force of his movements.

Mateo exhaled a loud breath and she felt the gust of air ruffle through the long strands of the hair that tumbled down the sides of her neck. Her orgasm had come a few seconds before his, so she remained anchored to him and unmoving until he had a moment to regain his composure. A soft chuckle reached her ears. His words began haltingly and breathless.

"I—think—we—better—not—stay—away from one another for so long next time." He chortled again. "Damn, woman. You make me lose all sense of control, and until you, my entire life was about nothing but control."

She kissed the side of his head where his thick hair tumbled loosely over his ear now. "You say that like it's a bad thing."

He moaned in defeat, then pulled back from her and planted another wet kiss on her mouth. But he didn't allow his lips to linger as if afraid he wouldn't be able to restrain himself again. "I hope your neighbors in the adjoining apartment aren't home," he said with a smirk.

Her neighbors were the last thing on her mind right now, Dawn thought as a sly smirk curved her lips. Nothing was going to take away from the excitement of the mad love they just made right here in the entryway to her apartment. Every time she walked into this room from this moment on, she was certain she was going to giggle and blush and get turned on all over again.

He chuckled at her reaction, then sighed deeply as if he didn't want to end this erotic experience. He clasped his hands around her waist and raised her body up slightly until their most intimate parts separated. There was an embarrassing suction sound, and a warm surge of bodily fluids flowed down the insides of her thighs. A hot blush flooded her face.

"I-I should probably—" She motioned toward the door leading to her bedroom and bathroom with a tilting motion of her head.

He nodded in agreement, smiled a bit seductively, and turned loose of her. As she walked precariously away she noticed he was bending down to pull up the pooled wad of denim material from around his ankles. A satisfied smile parted her lips. *Hot damn*. That was some wild and kinky action. And she loved it. Maybe next time maybe he could tie her up. She had some fringe he could use.

****

The drive into Phoenix felt nothing short of incredible. Rock tunes blasted from the truck stereo. Mateo had made a special CD just for her with an assortment of rock songs. They were both giddy as they were lost and enthralled in the excitement of being together again; not talking about the inevitable, and most definitely basking in the glow of their recent act of primitive up-against-the-wall-love-making.

The bright city lights of Phoenix swallowed them as he drove down the crowded streets. Dawn rarely came here, so she was enjoying a different pace from the more laid-back atmosphere in the smaller community of Apache Junction. As usual, he seemed to know exactly where he was going and before long they pulled into the parking lot of a towering hotel franchise. A flashing marquee announced the performance of Joseph Red Feather in the rooftop lounge.

Mateo held her close against his side as they entered the elegant hotel lobby. She noticed several women glance their direction, their discriminating gazes checking her man out from head to toe, then appraising her with cool reserve. With her blonde hair and fair skin in contrast to his darker Native American coloring, Dawn thought they must look striking together, especially dressed as sharply as they were tonight.

She also wondered if they both looked as radiant as she was feeling at this moment. Was it obvious that just a short time ago they were engaging in an unrestrained sexual escapade? Maybe it was flashing across their faces as brightly as the marquee outside, because she couldn't wipe the silly grin off her face, and when she glanced at him, he wore a secretive smile on his lips, too.

Heavy gold doors slid open as they waited for the elevator. She felt his hand rest protectively in the middle of her back as they entered the small enclosure and stepped to the back wall as several other people crowded in with them. He leaned over and whispered in her ear, "Did you put your panties back on?"

Dawn stifled a cough and glanced sideways at the middle-aged woman standing beside her. A fire flamed through her face when the woman met her gaze and grinned. She leaned toward him and placed her evening bag over her mouth as she whispered back, "You ripped them off me, remember?" She gave him a coy wink and smiled smugly when she saw his mouth gape open. *Ha! That will teach him.* Of course, she had put on a new pair of panties before they left her apartment. It served him right, though. Now, he was standing here in this crowded elevator imaging she was as bare-assed as he was.

Oh, why did she have to think of that? Now, she was imagining how it felt a short time ago to undo his jeans and hold his hard cock in her hands, right before he crushed her up against the wall and put it—*stop it.*

She could feel the perspiration popping out all over

her face as her fresh pair of panties grew wet once again. Thankfully, the doors of the elevator parted and everyone began piling into the large foyer on the rooftop lounge. She stumbled forward with Mateo guiding her by the arm. She chanced a look at him. The mischievous smirk on his handsome face was infuriating.

Once they stood in line to enter the lounge area, she tried to focus on something besides the lascivious activities she had planned for Mateo when they got home tonight. Home? With Mateo. That sounded so perfect. But she and Mateo would never have a real home together. No downer thoughts on this special night, she told herself in a firm inner voice.

From inside the lounge she could already hear music. She reached out and grabbed his hand, entwining her fingers with his. He graced her with the familiar smile that seemed to radiate from the white brilliance of his teeth to the shimmering raven gaze of his eyes.

As they were ushered into the elegant restaurant and lounge on the rooftop of this high-rise hotel, Dawn gasped at the sight before her. The entire room was encased in sky high windows, which gave the illusion of being out in the open. The tables, railings, and everything in between were lit with twinkling white lights. Beyond the windows, the entire city of Phoenix was spread out on the sprawling desert floor. Millions of lights from the buildings below seemed to be an extension of the lights from this room.

The amazing visual took her breath away, and combined with the mystical rifts of Joseph Red Feather's guitar, she felt as if she had crossed into another fantasy world. This was a common occurrence since Mateo Two Moons entered her life.

He pulled her chair out for her when they were directed to their table by a young waitress who appeared to be of a Native American descent. She couldn't keep her flirty gaze off Mateo as she placed drink and food menus on the white tablecloth. Dawn noticed he seemed completely oblivious to the girl's open drooling and focused his attention toward the musician on the stage at the opposite end of the room.

"Joseph's great, isn't he," he said as he reached across the table and grabbed her hand.

"Most definitely," she agreed. She loved the sound of the Apache musician's music, but she loved watching her sexy Apache vampire even more. By the look of excitement on his face, it was so apparent how much he enjoyed being here, and hearing his favorite musician in person. The flickering of the white lights seemed to mirror the sparkle in his eyes. He glanced at her and their gazes caressed one another as he squeezed her hand gently. A soft smile curved his full lips. Her love for this immortal man consumed every inch of her soul and physical body.

The bottle of expensive champagne they drank was perfect. The filet mignon they ordered for dinner was perfect. Mateo was perfect—as always. Joseph Red Feather was perfect. Right now, everything in Dawn's world seemed just perfect again.

When there was a break in the music, she excused herself from the table to freshen up her makeup and to make sure her hair was still holding its carefully styled just-got-laid-look she paid so much money to achieve. Once in the ladies' room, she stood before the mirror and stared at her glowing image.

It had been hours since their enthusiastic tryst against the wall in her apartment, but she was still radiating a special glow only an act of such intense sexual activity could inspire. A smile claimed her kiss swollen lips as she thought about the amazing man who waited for her in the next room.

The vampire?

The unbelievable and secret world he claimed to exist in when he was away from her could not be as awful as it seemed if he was a part of it. But she was not going to think about any of that stuff tonight, she reminded herself.

The music was beginning again as Joseph Red Feather started his last music set of the evening. Grabbing her evening bag, she headed out of the ladies' room. She had only taken a couple of steps, though, when the breath stopped short in her chest and her feet ceased to move.

Mateo was walking toward her. Like a sleek dark panther, he moved through the crowd on the dance floor. His long hair had slipped out from behind one of his ears, partially covering his eye on that side of his face, and tumbling provocatively over one of his broad shoulders. Wearing all black, and in this dim lighting, his raven hair seemed to blend into his black jacket and shirt, making it appear as if his thick tresses had no ending.

She reminded herself to breathe.

As he drew nearer, she could see the suggestive glint in his dark gaze. His thoughts were as transparent as the glass enclosure surrounding this rooftop establishment. Was he going to seduce her right here?

Right now? She could only hope.

He was still several steps away, but his burning gaze was reaching out and touching her entire body intimately. His eyes moved over her with slow persuasion, before coming to rest on her trembling lips, which were parted with the panting breaths she was now taking.

If he kissed her right now, she was sure she would be the one who would lose control this time, and they might have a repeat performance of the one they had earlier tonight in her apartment—right here in the middle of the dance floor.

She drew in a ragged breath and unconsciously held it at the back of her throat for a moment before exhaling it in one sharp gust.

A slightly crooked smile curved his full lips as he held his hand out toward her. Her legs felt unsteady and weak on her sky-high stilettos.

"May I have this dance, Miss Malone?" he asked in a deep husky tone.

Swoon. Swoon. Swoon.

She stared at him with wide eyes. She couldn't speak, so she merely nodded her head and reached out to take his hand. As their fingers entwined, Dawn was sure fireworks just went off overhead. He pulled her into his arms and they moved into the throng of other couples dancing to the slow romantic music. But she didn't notice anyone other than the immortal man who held her in his loving embrace.

Her head rested in the crook of his neck and she breathed in the musky scent of his intoxicating cologne. One of his arms encircled her waist, holding her as close to him as possible. Their other hands were clasped together against their sides as they swayed to the haunting music wafting among the twinkling lights encircling the dance floor.

If it could be in her power she would never allow this enchanting night to end. She knew without a doubt this was where she had always been destined to be—in his arms now and always.

As the music gently faded away, Mateo bent her backward with a graceful dip and leaned down over her. Time was suspended in this amorous moment as his mouth descended on her lips and claimed them with a tender kiss. It was more enchanting than a dream. And this was a dreamland Dawn wished she could stay in forever.

Chapter Twenty-One

"Your place or mine?" Mateo asked as they passed the Apache Junction City Limits sign.

Dawn drew in a heavy sigh. The new Joseph Red Feather CD Mateo purchased from the musician's stash of merchandise on a table in the hotel lobby played softly from the truck stereo. As always, when they were in his truck, their hands were entwined.

"I love the condo. It's so beautiful, but I hate being there when you're not."

"I'll be there with you until right before sunrise."

She nodded slightly. "But then I wake up and you're gone. My imagination and emotions go crazy. I'm either scared shitless or I'm so desperate to see you. I can't stand it."

"I prefer the second choice," he said, chuckling. His voice grew more serious. "I'm sorry you are so afraid. I hope you know I didn't expect things to turn out this way."

She squeezed his hand tighter. "I know, but there is so much I still don't understand." Endless questions just started falling from her mouth and she couldn't stop them.

"Will I still know who I am when you take me to the mountain? Will I ever see my parents or my brother and sister-in-law again? Will I remember any of them? What about my teaching career? Will everyone just think I'm dead? And what about those babies you say we are going to have? Will I be able to love them and watch them grow once I'm fully under your vampire control? Most of all, will I still feel this intense desire and overwhelming love for you I am feeling right this very second?"

Mateo turned to stare at her. He untangled his hand from hers and put both his hands on the steering wheel as he slowed the truck down and pulled over to the side of the road. He turned in his seat and reached out both hands, placing one on each side of her face.

"Udaya—Dawn, I'm so sorry I didn't tell you everything before. I've left you alone with all your fears and questions, and that was so wrong of me."

Her head tilted to the side and she closed her eyes for an instant as she let his hands cradle her face. When he was touching her like this, it was so easy to pretend he was just the human man she loved with all her heart and soul, and they were just a normal couple in love. She opened her eyes and met his troubled gaze. "I don't want to just be an empty, mindless shell of a woman whose only purpose is to have half-breed babies until I get too old to be useful anymore."

He gently pushed one of the long strands of blonde hair away from her cheek and smoothed it behind her ear. "Your beautiful inner soul will never die, and you will still be the loving passionate woman you are now. You will remember your family with fond memories. But you will have no desire to see them again. Once I complete the mating process, you will not want to be anywhere but on the mountain with me and our children when we have them. Your life will be devoted to the Clan and you will live forever. As I've told you before, this is your fate and nothing can prevent it from happening."

Dawn was helpless to stop the shudder that shook through her body. "I will never die? I would become like you? A dham-vamp-pire?"

He shook his head as a slight smile touched his mouth. "A vampire. Remember, a dhampyre is half-human and half-vampire, like our children will be. But I will not turn you into a vampire for a very long time, not until—" He shook his head again, adding, "This is not the place for us to have this talk. I'll take you home then I will explain everything." He hands slid away from Dawn's face as his attention returned to driving.

A thick permeating silence settled inside the cab of the truck as they drove the rest of the way to Dawn's apartment.

She slumped in the seat as her mind spun with the bits of information he had already given to her. She wouldn't be completely mindless apparently, and she would remember her human life here, but she would never see her family again; never stand before a room full of eager young students to teach again; probably never experience another romantic night dancing to live music; never...

But to not be with Mateo Two Moons forever? Well, she already determined that was never going to be an option, either.

Her door opened and he was lifting her out of the truck. She had taken her high-heeled sandals off after they left the hotel; they dangled from her hand, the rhinestone straps shimmering in the pale moonlight. He carried her to the apartment and let her lean down so she could unlock the door with the key she had taken from her evening bag.

He didn't put her down until they were in her bedroom. As he placed her on the mattress so she was leaning on the pillows against the headboard, she tossed her shoes and purse on the floor beside the bed. He kicked his boots off and removed his black blazer before sitting down next to her on the bed. She watched him turn to switch on the small lamp sitting on her bed side table. Her overpowering love for this vampire made her entire being ache as she observed every small gesture he made and as she cherished each moment they spent together.

Mateo's hand seemed to freeze in mid-air after he turned on the light. His gaze was glued to the nightstand. She looked to the spot he was staring at. *Damn it!* She left the extra pregnancy test laying there.

"Dawn?" he gasped without looking away from the box.

"I'm not," she retorted. "I took a test yesterday and it was negative. The directions say you should do it twice to be sure, but I never got around to it."

"But—" He stopped and looked down at her. "Why did you even take one? I mean, what made you think you might be pregnant already?"

"My paranoia," she replied with a shrug and a shake of her head. "I know it's probably way too soon to tell. But I'm not, so no worries." She felt a heated blush flare up her cheeks. Why the hell had she left that stupid box laying there?

He settled back against the pillow and was silent for a moment before pulling her into his arms. "We may be running out of time, you know."

Her breath trembled slightly when she drew in a

heavy sigh. "I thought we had eternity?"

He kissed the top of her head. "We do in my world. But recently something happened in my village that might change things in the future for our kind."

The tone of his voice sounded different. She sensed whatever happened was bad—really bad.

"I don't think I want to hear this," she said in a meek tone.

His long pause made her certain she didn't want to hear whatever he was about to tell her.

"Rafael's mate, Lydia, gave birth to a stillborn dhampyre two nights ago." His voice was barely more than a whisper.

"What? Rafael had a dham—I prefer to just think of them as children, okay?" Her mind could not comprehend the words he had spoken. She thought about Mateo's two handsome brothers, Rafael and Anton, whom she met on the mountain when she had been camping with Chloe, and again the night they met at the pizza place. It never occurred to her they would have women or mates, as Mateo called them, and children of their own.

"As you know, I'm the youngest of my brothers. Anton is the oldest. He and his mate, Nita, have six dhamp—children; three girls and three boys. Rafael and Lydia have twin girls and a three-year-old boy. The baby who died was also a boy." He drew in a heavy sigh and rested his cheek on the top of Dawn's head. "This is the first child my clan has ever lost. He is the first to be stillborn in the history of all of the Blood Clans as far as we know."

"My God, Mateo, I'm so sorry." She snuggled closer to him. The life Mateo and his clan lived in those secluded mountains was so much more involved than she imagined. "What do you think happened?"

He shrugged. "It's beyond comprehension. We have always believed when we mate with real ones—humans—the combination of our blood with our mate's blood creates a strong healthy child. That was always the way it was before this happened. The males are the strongest of all because we become full vampires as we mature, and we must carry on our bloodline. But even the female dhampyres born to the clan, who live common human lives are free of illnesses or disease until they grow old and die, usually of natural causes, because they have the strength of their father's blood in their veins. After the mating process is completed, I will share a small portion of my blood with you occasionally. It will keep you healthy and strong while you are still a mortal."

The core of her existence hardened to stone as she tried to absorb all he was telling her. She swallowed hard and her throat constricted with the idea of drinking Mateo's blood. Her stomach did an unexpected twist. How much more would she be able to accept without freaking out again? She pulled back slightly and looked up at him. His own pain was apparent in his expression.

"So, the girls do not become vampires as they age?" she asked, trying to concentrate on little bits of information at a time. "Only the boys? And they are normal when they are young but grow up and become vampires?" She placed her hand up to her forehead and closed her eyes for a moment as she tried to absorb this new knowledge.

"Yes, my sisters were all born around hundred years ago, like my brothers and me. They lived in the village on top of the Superstitions until they were young women, then they moved down to the Apache village with the real ones. They married real ones and had children that were also human. They grew old in the typical way until they died of old age."

She stared, wide-eyed, at him. "I can't even begin to wrap my mind around the idea you are more than a hundred years old." She rubbed at her temples as they throbbed unmercifully. "You and your brothers, you look like you're in your twenties. Are all the men in your clan like that?"

"I'm so sorry to be causing you all this pain. I'll get you some aspirin for your headache."

She shook her head. "No, I'm fine. I just need answers right now."

His frown drew his thick brows together as he nodded in agreement. "Yes, all the men stop aging in appearance around twenty-five years. This is also when we start to drink human blood, although we still eat food. We do not become mature vampires until we are a hundred years old. It is around this time our mates will come to us."

She pulled completely away from him now. "Wow," she whispered as his words sunk in—drink human blood—that was the really scary part. "And you're not just talking about drinking the blood from your mates, are you?"

"No," he said quietly.

The thoughts in her head were too horrible to speak out loud. Even though he had already done it to her, the idea of Mateo biting someone else and drinking their blood like the blood suckers in the horror movies was more than she could deal with. Her mind spun with more images of the pale undead creatures she had seen in the books she had been studying the past couple of days.

But she had only to look at him to see he was not like the monsters in books and movies. She tried to clear her mind of the upsetting images and focus on learning all the facts she could so she could try to understand what Mateo truly was. Yet, the numbing terror controlling her mind at this moment was stuck with another horrifying thought.

Someday, he said she would become a vampire, and that would mean she would need to drink human blood. This was too unbelievable to comprehend. She moaned out loud.

"Dawn?" he asked in a worried tone. "You know I could just end this agony you are going through right now if you wanted me to? I can't bear seeing you like this. It's going to happen sooner rather than later, anyway, and once you are my mate in every way, and living in my world, you will not have any more worries."

She looked at him in disbelief. "A baby just died. How can you say there is nothing to worry about in your world?"

He exhaled sharply. "You're right. But as I told you before, this has never happened in all the history of the Blood Clans. We can only hope it will never happen again."

"So, why now? What changed that would cause a baby to die for the first time?"

His voice sounded tortured when he answered, "I wish I knew. We have no answers. Only heartbreak and disbelief rules my clan right now. We have reached out for help in finding answers, and hopefully, once we hear back from other Blood Clans we will know more. If it's happening to other newborns in different parts of the world we might be able to figure it out. Some of the other clans have doctors in their Clan Societies. They might be able to do tests or something. If it's only happened in our clan, to Rafael and Lydia's baby, I don't know if we will ever find out what happened. Their child has already been cremated."

Silence engulfed the bedroom. Other Blood Clans? How was it possible for vampires and dhampyres to exist in all parts of the world for centuries without being discovered? Dawn could ask questions all night about the things Mateo had just told her, and she did want to know everything. But there was time for those questions and right now she could only envision one thing...Her fate was going to happen sooner rather than later.

When it was time for it to happen, she would not fight against it, because she knew she wanted to be with Mateo always. At this moment, though, maybe they should just concentrate on the time they had left to spend here in her world before their destinies led them to his world.

She pulled up to her knees beside him and straddled his lap with her legs. Her fringed mini dress was hiked up around her waist, but she didn't care. As she placed her hands on each side of his handsome face, she saw the look of surprise filter through his eyes. Gazing into the shimmering depths of those twinkling eyes was as alluring as peeking through Alice's looking glass in Wonderland. She didn't know what she would find, but she knew she had to step through to the other side if it meant being with this vampire forever.

"Kiss me," she commanded in a breathy tone.

One thick brow lifted slightly over his eye for an instant. As her intention became clear to him, his gaze glowed with eagerness and his long ebony lashes closed half way as he leaned forward to obey her order. She slid her hands up into his hair and leaned into him to meet his lips with her own. They touched lightly at first. His lips were gentle, almost timid as they came together. Pulling her closer, his arms wrapped around her waist as his kiss intensified. She grabbed handfuls of his hair in her tightening grasp and rose from his lap to push her body hard against his.

Bending over him, she continued to kiss him with forcefulness as their lips devoured one another. His hands were up under her dress, clutching the thin straps of her panties for the second time tonight. "You know you want to rip them off again," she murmured as she pulled her lips from his mouth for an instant.

One swift motion and her only other pair of black lace G-strings were shreds. She didn't even have time to give them a second thought. As he pulled them from between her legs, he asked in a sly tone, "Like this?"

Her pussy throbbed and grew wet. She sat back down on his lap, wanting him to feel how hot he made her. His cock was hard and pressing against the material of his black jeans. The ridge of it swelled into the area between her legs, making everything below her waist contract and quiver.

She released the tight hold she had on his hair and grabbed his loosely knotted tie. Her eyelashes narrowed as she smirked.

"I've wanted to do this all evening," she said in a

suggestive tone as she leaned back slightly.

Her nimble fingers slipped the loose knot in his tie apart. The tip of his tongue dampened his parted lips. A soft moan escaped from her own mouth as her desire for him raged out of control.

"What else have you wanted to do to me?" A slight tremor in his voice hinted at his anticipation as he looked up at her with eyes hooded in growing desire.

She stopped short of letting the tie slide completely away from his neck as she grasped it close to his throat and used it to pull herself up to him roughly. Her lips hovered just over his, brushing lightly for an instant as she answered, "Everything."

His breath flooded her mouth as he answered, "I will be your sex slave tonight, my love. Anything you desire…it's yours."

He was making her so wet it could get embarrassing if she wasn't so seriously turned on right now. She leaned back and cast him a provocative smile as she cocked a brow in the suggestive manner he had done early. "Take your clothes off," she ordered with authority. He swallowed hard enough she could see the Adam's apple in his throat expand for an instant.

"Um? You need to—" His head tilted to the side as he motioned for her to move.

"Oh yeah." She groaned inwardly. Now, the really awkward part was about to happen. She rose to her knees and swung one leg over his thighs so he was free to get up. The wet spot soaking the front of his pants was a glaring tribute to how much she wanted him. Her only consolation was her womanly juices saturated the area over his swollen cock, and it was about to rip itself out of his pants. It was more than obvious he was every bit as turned on right now as she was.

She reclined on the bed as Mateo rose to his feet and stood in an awkward pose as if he wasn't sure what to do next. She was reveling in this new-found power over him.

"You are my sex slave, remember?" Dawn said as she stretched her legs out and crossed her ankles in a modest gesture. She smoothed the ruffled fringe on the hem of her dress down over her bare thighs. "I want you naked. Then, I want you—" She let her gaze travel slowly down over his body as she added, "Inside of me."

Mateo stared at her as if he were looking at her for the first time. For a moment, Dawn wondered if she was taking this dominatrix thing a bit too far. A nervous fluttering in her stomach caused a quivering frown to tug at the corners of her lips. She started to say, 'Just kidding', when a wicked smirk curved his mouth. His eyes narrowed and his gaze raked over her body with unrestrained longings that made her feel as naked as she had just commanded him to be. Excited anticipation shook through her body.

He began to undo the little black buttons running down the front of his black dress shirt. His fingers moved slowly, pushing every button through each of the button holes with deliberate intention. His piercing gaze never left her face.

It took all her willpower to remain calm and still on the mattress. She wanted to jump up and rip that shirt off his body, especially as his hard, muscled, six-pack peeked out from between the material of the shirt when he finally had all the buttons undone. She swallowed hard, and waved her hand through the air in an impatient motion for him to continue.

A teasing smirk curled Mateo's lips. "I like it when you are bossy. What other surprises do you have in store for me?"

Dawn gulped heavier this time. She was acting like she knew what she was doing, but the truth was she had never been quite this adventurous in the bedroom before. His impulsive actions earlier this evening inspired her to be a little naughtier than usual and right now her body was alive with eagerness, and her mind was on overdrive with wanton thoughts. Otherwise, she was just winging the rest of this dominate stuff.

"You'll never find out if you keep wasting time," she taunted, hoping she sounded more confident than she was feeling.

His thick eye brows rose slightly. He obeyed. The black shirt slipped from his shoulders, sliding down his muscled arms and disappearing to the floor beside the bed. Dawn let her gaze linger on his well-defined shoulder muscles and firm pecks. She remembered the first time she had seen those finely-toned muscles move under his white western shirt the night they met at the pizzeria; the night she had fallen in love with him.

She was jolted back to the present when, with a slow brush of his fingertips, Mateo pushed the long strands of his hair back from his forehead in a sensual motion. Giving his head a slight toss, he sent the rest of the heavy mass swirling over those broad shoulders. The floodgates broke between Dawn's legs. Her hands curled into tight fists in her lap.

He was so incredibly hot. And he belonged to her for eternity. She was going to be nothing more than a smoldering pile of soaking wet ash at his feet long before eternity got here.

Since it was obvious he was enjoying torturing her to the brink of madness, she attempted to keep from writhing all over the mattress in delirious rapture. She reminded herself this might be the one and only time he would be her love slave if their fates had anything to do with it. But, oh God, if he didn't get those damn pants off soon, she might have to rip them off with her teeth.

He sighed as if he was in no hurry and casually undid the clasp on his belt. The silver buckle dangled at the side of his bulging erection for a moment before he reached down and slowly pulled the belt from the loops on his jeans. Her gaze honed in on his washboard stomach and the way a tiny bit of hair trailed down from his bellybutton to places still barely concealed by his low hanging jeans. She couldn't stop the impatient moan that escaped from her dry mouth.

With the belt still dangling from his palm, Mateo held the leather strap up. He grabbed an end in each hand and pulled it taut. It made a loud cracking sound. One cocked brow and a lopsided smirk transformed his expression into one of mischievous intentions as he asked, "Will we be needing this, Miss Malone?"

Dawn gasped. His innuendo was clear. She shook her head from side to side in a negative motion. This joking around was fun, but she wasn't sure how far she wanted to go with this roguish game. She was open to trying new things, but the idea of being whipped with his belt did not sound like much fun.

A smirk reclaimed his lips. He tossed the belt aside, then unsnapped his jeans and slid the zipper down with one swift motion. Hooking his thumbs in a belt loop on each side of his slender hips, he began to pull the pants down past his muscled thighs. He kicked them away from his feet and stood tall with his arms held out slightly from his body presenting her with a full-frontal view.

She made a discreet attempt to clear her throat. To her ears, it sounded more as if a frog was croaking. He didn't seem to notice or care. As this flawless man stood before her, she reveled in the realization that he was hers—her man—her dangerous vampire. His impressive cock stood out proudly below his masculine v-shaped abdomen, which was lean and taut. His legs were long, sinewy, with well-defined thigh and calf muscles.

Yes, he truly was perfect.

"Well?" Mateo asked as her lustful gaze held him captive. "Don't you think you are the one who's a bit overdressed now?"

His voice snapped Dawn out of her drooling trance. She glanced down at her lacy fringe-trimmed dress and realized that as excited as she had been to wear this dress earlier tonight, she was way more anxious to get out of it now. She grinned impishly and scooted to the edge of the bed, sliding off so she was standing right in front of him. This game wasn't quite over, yet.

"Take it off," she said forcefully, "And don't waste any more time, understand?"

"Loud and clear," he retorted as he leaned over and grabbed the fringed hem of the vintage dress and pulled it effortlessly over her up-stretched arms. Since her second pair of panties for the night were already long gone, and he didn't wait for her to order him to remove her black lace push up bra, in barely more than a blink of an eye she was as naked as he was. A fevered flush rippled through her body and made a light sheen of perspiration break out on her skin. This was delicious torture.

"Wasn't I supposed to be inside you now? That was an order, wasn't it?" He glanced down at himself, adding, "And it appears I'm standing at attention."

"Oh, babe, I do think you're getting the hang of this," she muttered as he grasped her bare buttocks and fell onto the mattress with her landing on top of him. She giggled as they thudded against the bed and bounced together. But when she glanced up, she noticed a strange expression filter through Mateo's face.

"What?" she asked in a tentative tone.

"I would like to try something, but I don't know if I'm strong enough to do it without hurting you."

She drew in a deep sigh. "Okay? Does it have to do with that biting thing?"

A chuckle escaped Mateo. He reached up and pulled one of the little rhinestone hair pins from her blonde curls. A long tendril of hair swirled down along the side of her cheek. His lips parted slightly as he exhaled a passion-laden sigh.

She could feel his cock pressing hard and full against her bare thigh. The inferno inside of her was raging again. He could just slip so easily inside of her right now, and she was so ready. But obviously, he had something else in mind. Should she be scared? She didn't have time to ask as he unexpectedly rolled her back over, pinning her beneath his hard body. The sudden movement made her squeal.

Now, his swollen cock was throbbing against her stomach. The heat it radiated against her already fevered skin was sweet agony and only increased her curiosity and desire. She immersed her fingers in the profusion of his long hair as it fell over his shoulders and covered her bare skin with its lush strands. Her red nails raked through the heavy locks, down along the back of his neck and dug slightly into the hard muscles rippling at the top of his shoulders.

He began sliding his body down the length of hers in a slow, sensuous decline. His mouth trailing hot kisses along the side of her neck, on each of her breasts, making her nipples hard the moment his lips encircled their eager knobs. His lips continued lower, lightly nipping and kissing down to her waist. When his wet tongue darted into her belly button on his sweet descent, she squirmed with delicious anticipation.

His mouth rained more kisses and teasing bites over her taut stomach. He gently kissed the downy blonde curls covering the tip of her pelvic bone. Her pussy tightened with the expectation of how those taunting lips were about to take her to a whole new level of sexual euphoria.

He gently spread Dawn's legs as his head slipped between her thighs. The fleeting thought of how close he was to the spot in her thigh that concealed the large blood artery he so desperately wanted to bite passed through her delirious mind, but she was too far gone to care.

Her hands slid downward with him, still entangled in his long hair. When the tip of his tongue flicked along the sensitive edge of her clit, her fingernails unconsciously clawed into his scalp. Her body buckled up against his face of its own accord. She felt his hands grasp the sides of her waist to hold her down on the mattress. If this was what he meant about hurting her, oh God, he could hurt her anytime he wanted to because it was hurting so damn good.

His tongue worked its way into the concave of her pussy and flicked in and out, lapping around in teasing swirling motions. Her juices overflowed as he tasted the succulent nectar of her womanly core. He drove her to the brink of a frenzied orgasm, then produced a phenomenal climax that sent her washing over the edge with nothing more than his extraordinary tongue.

When he finally rose from in between her shaking thighs, she was certain she couldn't handle another mind-blowing event like the one that just occurred. She was wrong.

The sweet indulgence of his tongue had only been a precursor to the rest of his plan to make her *his* love slave...tonight and forever. And to think she actually thought she was being the dominate one earlier this evening.

Her body gave no resistance as he rolled her back over to the top position. His hands were still clasped around her waist and he effortlessly impaled her on his cock, which was still standing straight up. She was reeling from his tongue porn, but as she sank down letting him slide deep inside and fill her completely, she was elevated to an entirely new level of pleasure. She grasped onto his hips and gazed down to meet his shimmering black gaze. His expression was so filled with awe and love as their gazes locked she knew without a doubt she was the most cherished woman in the world.

They began to move together, his hips rising up and her hips driving down to match each of his movements. She arched back as his hands cupped her breasts and kneaded them gently in his palms. She held on to his muscled hips, unaware of how deeply her nails were digging into his skin. Their hunger for one another seemed to have no limits and his energy was boundless. But Dawn matched his endurance until they both lay breathless, exhausted and fulfilled in more ways than their mortal and immortal bodies ever imagined.

After tonight, she truly understood the meaning of the phrase, 'Rode hard and put away wet'.

****

With her head resting on his muscled chest and her fingers splayed out on his chiseled stomach, she stared at the way her shimmering red nails complimented the golden bronze of his satiny skin. They were just a perfect match in every way.

She was finally feeling she could talk coherently after their most passionate night so far, and she had to ask a couple more questions before she knew he had to leave her.

"Why were you worried about hurting me earlier? Was it because your mouth was so close to the artery in my thigh?"

His fingertips were gently traipsing along her cheekbones and her jaw line as if he was a blind man and was trying to memorize the features of her face with his touch. He sighed heavily. "It has been difficult—excruciating—for me to be around you without wanting to drink your blood. Ever since the first time I bit your neck and tasted the indescribable sweetness of your blood I have fought the greatest battle of my life just to remain in control when I'm with you."

His arm slid down to encircle her body when he

felt her shudder. "I didn't know if I was strong enough to taste more of you without losing what little constraint I had, especially since I was so close—" He wrapped both of his arms around her shivering body.

"So, you were worried about biting me down there," she murmured. It was not a question; just a statement. It was terrifying, and even a little sad, for her to realize every time they were together it was a grueling test of his strength to keep from sucking more of her blood. But it was also an amazing testament to just how much he loved her.

"My entire existence now is about loving you and protecting you, Udaya, even though I have chosen to take a different path to begin our eternal life together than the one charted since the beginning of my vampire clan. I don't know where this new course will lead us, but I know as long as we are together we will be able to overcome all the obstacles thrown in our way."

"I trust you," Dawn whispered. "You are my entire existence now, too. I will follow you anywhere— whenever you are ready to lead me there."

She heard him exhale softly against the side of her head. As scary as it all was, she no longer had any doubts loving this immortal man with every fiber of her being and spending eternity with him had always been where she was bound since the beginning of her own life, too.

They held each other in the quiet dark of her small bedroom for a while longer. She knew he would be leaving and there was one more thing she had to know before he left her this morning, although she knew the answer was going to be hard to hear.

"Will you please tell me where Chloe is?" she

asked in a quiet tone that seemed to shatter the peaceful atmosphere.

A moment passed before he answered, but it felt more like eons. "She is at the gold mine."

"The-the Lost Dutchman's Gold Mine?"

"Yes. It exists and my family has guarded it for over two centuries."

"Oh, my God," she whispered as her mind spun with all the stories, legends, and wild imaginings about the Lost Dutchman's Gold Mine. It was real. Chloe believed and searched for that treasure until the day she—what?

"Chloe is still alive, though?" Her raspy voice asked.

He cleared his throat before speaking again. "Unfortunately, my father was the first one to sense her presence. Like others before her who got too close to our encampment and to the cave which contains the rich veins of gold, she could not be allowed to discover all the secrets of our hidden world."

Dawn's body was numb as her mind tried to comprehend what he was saying. "But you said before that she wasn't d-dead." Another vicious tremor shot through her body. He held her tighter.

"Not yet," he said in a mournful tone. "She is still with the other blood sources, the real ones who provide the mature vampires of our clan with human blood. She is not in pain and does not have any idea what has happened to her. Her mind is gone. My father put her under his vampire spell and bit her before she even knew what was happening. He did not kill her. But eventually she will be drained of all her blood and her body will not be able to survive."

His voice was just a hoarse whisper when he added, "You will never know how sorry I am about your friend. But it's not your fault, and I won't allow you blame yourself. She was not going to give up until she found that gold mine and once she did find it her fate was sealed. It would have happened with or without you or any dream you might have had about it."

The heavy weight of guilt and the unbearable pain kept her from answering. The sensible part of her brain told her he was right about Chloe's relentless quest to find the gold mine, but there was nothing else rational about what he was saying.

She couldn't even begin to comprehend Chloe sitting mindlessly, partially drained of her blood, in a cave surrounded by the gold she had sought so desperately to find for her entire life. Dawn tried to push the horrific image out of her mind. Acknowledging Chloe's fate along with all that he had told her earlier tonight would be more than her fragile state could handle right now.

There were things too horrible for words concealed in those mountains, and now she was also aware of innocent children and their human mothers who dwelled among the destruction and terror. There was so much she still had to learn about the hidden world where she would be living for the rest of her life—and eternity, but could she deal with more? Hopefully, her love for Mateo would give her all the courage she would need. She told him she trusted him, so now she just had to prove to him, and herself, how much.

Chapter Twenty-Two

Sunday morning. Alone. Dawn felt a strange sensation flood through her chest, a tightening around her heart and hard lump in her throat. Tears were escaping from her eyes and she couldn't stop them. It had only been one week and two days—nine days—since Mateo Two Moons entered her life. Well, if she counted the first time she had seen him in her dreams, which she knew now really wasn't a dream, it had been two weeks and two days.

It was such a very short span of time, zilch when compared to eternity, since this vampire had invaded her entire world in every way. Nothing was, or ever would be, the same. She wiped angrily at the wayward tears wetting her cheeks and the pillow under her head. She hated waking up without him, but she hated the idea of him lying Dracula-like in some gloomy cave even more. Would it be better when she was lying there in that black hole next to him? She shuddered and pulled the sheet and bedspread up to her chin.

Her mind was a vortex spinning with all the information he had given her about his clan of vampires, dhampyres, and everything else last night. Worst of all, was the information he disclosed regarding Chloe's fate. A roaring furnace couldn't warm the icy blast that chilled her to the bone.

If only she could remember all the romantic and

beautiful memories from last night and forget about the rest of it.

The out-of-control sex in her front foyer was the prelude to an evening of enchantment and romance. Dancing with Mateo among the twinkling lights at the rooftop lounge to the soft guitar music of Joseph Red Feather would always be one of her most cherished memories. The sexual game they played afterward that led to an extra erotic love-making session, still made her body quiver with residual longings. An elated smile curved her lips.

Making love with Mateo was beyond anything she ever imagined. She hoped the intimate part of their lives would never change, but would it still be the same when they were together on the mountain for all eternity? She pushed those thoughts away. For a moment longer, only those perfect images from the previous night filled her mind, and the tears stopped. But she couldn't pretend forever that everything was as perfect as she wanted it to be.

The unwelcome image of Chloe clouded her happy thoughts once again. Dawn squeezed her lids shut and tried to block out the tragic picture Mateo described about her friend's fate at the top of the Superstitions. The tears returned heavier than before.

Although, she wished she could give Chloe's family some sort of closure, she knew it would probably be easier for everyone to believe she had fallen to her death somewhere in the high rugged peaks of the Superstitions like it was believed so many before her had done. If they only knew...

Dawn became aware of a new concern that rattled her to the core as a fierce determination claimed her.

No one could ever know the truth about the half breed dhampyre children, human mates, and centuries old vampires who lived at the Lost Dutchman's Gold Mine. Mateo and his entire family's existence would be threatened. She knew she would protect them with her life, because soon she would also be one of those hidden secrets.

Wiping away the last of her tears, she forced herself to get out of bed. As she glanced at the clock, she gave her head a disgusted shake. It was nearly noon.

"What have you done to me, Mr. Two Moons?" she said with sigh. Well, for one thing, he totally destroyed her internal clock. Tomorrow was Monday, so tonight she would have to remember to set the alarm for the next morning. She couldn't trust herself to wake up early enough to make it to school on time.

With all that happened over the past few days, she had almost forgotten she was still a school teacher. Just a very short time ago, teaching had been one of the most important things in her life. But the idea of being at school tomorrow with the students and the other teachers, who had no clue of all the unbelievable secrets Dawn now harbored, seemed completely foreign and so removed from her new life with her immortal lover.

Every day, every minute, since Mateo entered her world, it was getting harder and harder to function in a normal way. There was no denying she was his love slave in almost every way already, even without being under his vampire spell. Why did she even think she could pretend to live her regular life any longer?

Since she missed three days of teaching last week, however, she had to at least try to be responsible about her job for as long as she was still here. There were loose ends to tie up in her life before she became Mateo's mate. Besides, what if something happened and she ended up not being with him in his hidden village on the mountain for all eternity? Something unforeseen might happen and they would break up and she would still need her teaching job, right? She gave a loud snort. She was acting like she was still living in the real one's world. That world ceased to exist the first night she went up on the Superstitions and confronted her destiny.

His handsome face floated through her mind and the love she could not deny overflowed from her heart. She would live on the mountain with her dangerous and sexy vampire; she would have his dhampyre babies and do anything else he compelled her to do. He didn't need to bite her in the neck, wrist, or thigh to make any of those things happen. He was her eternal mate as much as she was his, and she would never be able to live without him.

Dawn sighed. It was seriously time to get up and do something ordinary, like laundry. *Ugh.* She glanced over and saw the extra pregnancy test on the bedside table. Maybe she should just get that over with once and for all. As she slipped into her blue robe and started to grab the pregnancy test her phone started ringing.

"Hi, Mom," she said cheerfully and with a sense of relief that she was diverted for the time being from the dreaded blue stick in the box.

"Hi. Finally. I've been worried about you. I haven't heard from you and you haven't picked up when I've called lately."

A brief sense of guilt overcame Dawn. Her mom

was awesome, but she worried way too much. "No need to worry. I've been busy, but everything is perfect. How are you and Dad?"

"We're perfect, too. So, what's been keeping you so busy?"

Her mom's curiosity was obvious. "I met someone, someone, umm, special."

"Really? How special?"

Dawn giggled. It felt silly talking about Mateo like he was just some regular guy she was dating. "Don't freak out, but he's, well, he's the one. I'm in love, big time."

She heard her mom gasp and she wished she was able to see her face right now.

Ever since Dawn's brother had gotten engaged a couple of years ago and married last spring, her mom had been more than a little anxious for Dawn to find someone to settle down with, too. She could only imagine how big her mom was grinning at this moment.

"Oh, my God. Seriously? Well, I need all the dirt on this guy. What's his name? What's he look like? When will I meet him?"

Dawn chuckled. "Well, his name is Mateo Two Moons. He's Native American, from the local Apache tribe. He's so amazing—just perfect in every way—and he's absolutely gorgeous."

"Wow. So, when are you bringing him to meet us? Thanksgiving maybe? I think Jeremy and Teresa are coming for Thanksgiving, too. I can't wait for all of us to be together. That would be perfect."

She closed her eyes for a moment, suddenly grateful her mom couldn't see the look on her face. *Yes, Mom, that would be perfect. But no, mom, we won't be coming at Thanksgiving or Christmas or ever. He's a vampire, you see, so he can't leave his cave in the daytime. Wow.*

"Soon, you'll meet him soon," she lied. A sick feeling made her stomach tighten. She had not lied to her mom since she was a teenager and told her those cigs in her backpack belonged to her friend. Her mom didn't believe that story back then, would she believe her now?

"Maybe we'll just plan a trip to Arizona soon. Your dad could use a vacation."

Dawn tried to keep the spectrum of emotions tearing her up inside from edging into her voice. What if this was the last time she would ever hear her mother speak? "That would be great. Hey, Mom, I need to get going. Sorry."

"Okay. But I need to hear more about this Mateo real soon."

"Okay, soon." She heard a slight tremor in her voice. "Hey, tell Dad hi for me. And, Mom, I really miss you guys."

"Aw, Honey, we really miss you, too."

"Love you, and Dad, too. Bye." She held her hand over the speaker on her phone in an attempt to block the sound of her choked sob.

"Bye, love you more."

She dropped the phone on the bed after she hung up, threw herself face down on the mattress and gave into the rush of tears she was unable to control. She couldn't bear the thought of what her family would go through when she did go up to the mountain with Mateo and was never seen again.

The heartbreaking memory of talking to Chloe's

dad after her disappearance came to Dawn's mind. Chloe believed she was going to find the Lost Dutchman's Gold Mine for her father when she went up to the Superstitions and met her horrible fate. Dawn would be going to meet her destiny knowing how much her family was going to suffer after she was gone. How could she do this to them?

Somehow, she needed to stop thinking about all this stuff before she passed out from all this useless crying. She refused to give up hope that somehow Mateo would be able to figure out a way for her to continue to live her life here as a real one, and still be his eternal mate.

Pushing herself from the bed, she grabbed the pregnancy test from the night stand and headed to the bathroom. She would get this nonsense out of the way, so she could concentrate on getting ready for school tomorrow. She had papers to grade from last week and needed to work on a lesson schedule for the coming week. For now, she had to keep functioning like she was still living her old life, no matter how hard that was going to be.

****

Dawn parked her truck in the same spot Chloe parked her SUV when they had come here to camp a little over two weeks ago. It was also where Chloe's vehicle had been found after her disappearance last week. The sun would be down soon. She double-checked to make sure the doors were locked. Hopefully, Mateo would get her frantic text messages as soon as he left his village tonight. If he didn't, and she was sitting here alone for too long, well…*Cowboy up, Cupcake.*

The desert could feel lethal and lonely at any time,

but at night the encompassing peril was strangling. She glanced around at the heavy darkness starting to blanket the view where, just moments ago, she had seen faded light. It was almost gone now and only foreboding black was settling over her truck inside and out.

She was having a hard time taking a full breath and the panic making her entire body quiver was ruthless. This sense of terror was even worse than the way she felt when she hiked up here with Chloe on that first night. Because now, she knew there really was something deadly and dangerous—immortal—hiding in the depths of the rugged mountain range.

Every sound made her breath clog deeper into her throat and chest. She kept imagining the horror Chloe must have endured when she had been out here alone the night she disappeared. But she hadn't known the extent of the real dangers awaiting her on this mountain. Dawn was very much aware of the risk she was taking. Sitting at home waiting for Mateo to come to her was not an option either. She desperately needed him now, and she would wait here forever if that was how long it took for him to find her.

Chapter Twenty-Three

Billy Torres did not even try to hide his relief to be leaving the secret encampment when Anton Two Moons escorted him back down to his truck at the base of the mountain. It was obvious how nervous it made him to be up on the Superstitions at night, even though his position as a Clan Society member insured his safety when he was there. One of Drago's grandsons always accompanied him up and down the mountain to make sure he didn't encounter any problems with wildlife or anything else that could cause him injury along the narrow rocky trails.

He only came to the village at night if he had something extremely important to talk to Drago about. Learning about other stillborn births in Blood Clans around the world was urgent enough for him to travel to the village late in the day, which meant he wouldn't be off the mountain until after the sun went down.

They had received news that several dhampyres had been born dead in four different clans in other parts of the world. One unfortunate clan in Alaska had two stillborn births just a couple weeks apart. All but one of the deceased infants had been cremated. Only a female child who was stillborn in Switzerland had been preserved. Her body was taken to a doctor who was the brother of a Clan Society member in Geneva and could be trusted to conduct tests on the dead infant without revealing any secrets regarding the child's parents.

A discreet autopsy revealed the baby's blood had been infected by a strange virus that invaded her body, most likely right before or during her birth. Although, the Swiss doctor didn't know what caused the infection, he hoped he would be able to develop an antidote from the blood he extracted. But it was going to take time and there could be more tragic deaths until he had it perfected. It wasn't the best news, but at the very least, it was some sort of an explanation.

After hearing Billy's news, Rafael apologized to Mateo for blaming him for the death of his son. For the first time since this tragedy happened, Mateo felt a renewed sense of hope for his clan, and a huge relief the bad feelings between him and his brother were gone.

Now, he had to get to his beautiful mate, because he couldn't wait to see her again. But before he could get out of the village, his grandfather approached him and detained him even further.

"It has been a while since you have been going down to meet with your mate in her world," Drago said as he motioned for his grandson to sit with him beside the fire.

Mateo nodded and reluctantly sat down cross-legged next to his grandfather. Dawn told him she would be waiting at the condo tonight and he had been dreaming of holding her in his arms on the big bed with the velvet bedspread since the second he opened his eyes at sunset this evening.

"Yes, Grandfather," he said trying not to sound irritated. "It is going much better than I hoped. My mate is—"

"It is time," Drago interrupted. "Time to bring her

here and end this nonsense."

He stared wordlessly at his grandfather. "I don't understand? Has something else happened?"

"Your mate has to come up here to the mountain as soon as possible. It is too risky for her and for all of us."

A heavy disappointment settled in Mateo's chest. He knew time was running out, but he kept hoping there would be a way to make his time in Dawn's world last a little longer.

"There is no immediate danger, Grandfather."

Drago drew in a heavy sigh and glanced toward the big cave which held the darkest secrets of the Clan. "Anton said the woman your father brought to the cave recently was a friend to your mate."

His grandfather's remark surprised him. He knew Anton had not disclosed this information with any thought of malice, but it certainly did not help in his quest to delay bringing Dawn up to the village.

"My mate has no idea what happened to her friend," he lied. "The woman my father brought here was a lifelong gold seeker. It is believed she fell to her death somewhere on the mountain while looking for the gold mine." He shrugged and hoped his nervousness was not apparent to his grandfather. "The same as all the others in the past."

For a moment, Drago was silent. A thoughtful frown held his face in a stoic expression. He reached down and played idly with the material of his white loincloth, the only article of clothing covering his muscled and youthful three-hundred-year-old body.

"There is big change in the air for our kind. I feel it in the wind that whispers along the tops of the highest ridges. The death of Rafael's child and all the other babies in different clans are proof we are not as invincible as we have always believed."

Mateo felt a numbing sensation grip his insides. "A change, Grandfather? What do you mean?"

A heavy sigh escaped from the older vampire. "I first felt it years ago, when you began to seek more knowledge of the real ones and their world below. Although our kind has always been somewhat curious of the real ones, you were the most insistent one, the one who always wanted more than to read the books and learn their languages and spend more than an occasional night among them." He smiled wistfully at his grandson. "But I knew you wouldn't be the last."

Confusion filled Mateo's mind. He shook his head and shrugged.

"Anton's eldest son," Drago continued, "He is very much like you. Maybe even more curious than you are."

"Chaz?" Mateo questioned. "What do you mean?"

"Yes, Chaz is full of inquisitiveness. He asked his father to allow him to spend more time with the real ones on the reservation and to explore the world below the mountain. Just like you did when you were his age, Grandson."

A grin touched Mateo's lips. He remembered the consuming desire to know more about the real ones when he was Chaz's age. "I would be happy to take him with me sometimes," he suggested. *But not tonight*, he thought as the image of his beautiful flaxen haired woman floated through his mind.

Drago nodded as if he already knew his youngest grandson would extend the offer to show his oldest great-grandson the world beyond the mountain. "I'll admit I have thought about denying Chaz's request. It worries me that one of you might accidentally reveal something to the real ones about our clan."

A sinking feeling worked its way through Mateo. To deny Chaz, or any of them, the right to leave and explore the world outside of this village would be incomprehensible. Yet, Drago was the leader of this clan, and his word would always be the final ruling. Although he fought an inner battle, wanting desperately to disagree with his grandfather, he was more afraid of saying something that would sway his grandfather to make a disastrous decision without further consideration.

"I know how you feel about this," the older vampire stated when Mateo remained silent. "You are true to the clan, and I know you respect my position. I also know you are going to be the one who leads us to the next evolution of our kind."

Mateo took a deep breath. "I only seek to make our world better for all of us."

Drago's head moved in agreement. "It is a fine line we tread, Grandson. You know I believe we have only survived this long by remaining hidden and not letting our secrets be known to anyone other than the Clan Society." He chuckled slightly, adding, "Chaz actually believes we can expose ourselves to the sunlight, even past the crucial twenty-five-year mark." He laughed and shook his head. "Who among the adult vampires here would want to risk testing his theory, and most likely, end up a pile of cinders on the ground?"

The breath stopped short in Mateo's chest. His mind exploded with all the possibilities he considered through the years, especially after reading how dhampyres supposedly did not have the same weakness as full bred vampires. But then, he always had to wonder how the authors of those theories had come to these conclusions, since real ones didn't know real vampires or dhampyres even existed.

He questioned why the books about so-called real vampires always assumed they had insatiable and uncontrollable urges to drink the blood of any human they could find. Unlike the Blood Clan, the imaginary vampires drank only blood; never eating food, drinking water, or needing any other sort of substance to survive.

The storybook vampires were supposed to have two retractable fangs which they used to pierce their victims in the neck and drain all the blood from their bodies. The Blood Clan had no such fangs, only teeth like real ones. Except for their mates, whom they bit during the mating process, when drinking from any other human blood source, they could either bite the person on any part of their body with all their front teeth, or they would drain blood from a vein and drink it from containers.

It was apparent virtually nothing was known about vampires. Maybe he and Chaz needed to discuss some of the theories they were both so curious about?

"I've wondered about such things, myself, Grandfather," he admitted. "Have you ever thought about why the vampires described in books are so drastically different from our clan?"

Drago stared thoughtfully at his grandson for a moment. His head slowly began to nod. "Yes. I have wondered about many things. But I remind myself there are so few of us—the males who would carry on our

Veronica Blake

bloodlines—if we were to test out any of these notions, and we ended up destroying ourselves, it could be disastrous. It is my responsibility to ensure this clan survives, so I have not been willing to risk losing even one of us to explore any of those speculations."

"I understand," Mateo agreed. He had never been brave enough to test out any of the concepts he thought about, either.

"So, we come back to the subject of your mate," he said. "I assume you have been intimate with her?"

Mateo's mouth gaped open. "Yes," he finally mumbled.

Drago seemed oblivious to his grandson's embarrassment. "She could be carrying a dhampyre already. It is imperative the process to make her your mate is completed so your woman, and hopefully, the male dhampyre she might carry, is made strong and healthy after the completion of the mating process."

He reached out and rested his hand on Mateo's forearm for a moment as he added, "She must be here under our protection. We have already lost a male dhampyre and who knows if the Swiss doctor will ever be able to find a cure. One thing is for certain, though, we cannot take any more unnecessary chances with the future of our clan."

Mateo could only nod his head in agreement. As much as he hated to give up on his dreams of spending more time in Dawn's world with her, his grandfather's words made sense. He couldn't bear the thought of anything happening to his mate or their future offspring.

The fleeting memory of the pregnancy test laying on her nightstand passed through his mind. She said she wasn't pregnant—yet. But it would happen. The Blood Clan believed their mates were chosen because they were fertile and could produce strong dhampyres, even though it sometimes took a woman many years to conceive and the births could be few and far between. Since the beginning of their kind, no barren woman had ever been chosen to be a mate. According to clan history, all this was preordained.

Mateo choked back the heaviness in his throat and glanced around at his surroundings. Night had completely engulfed the mountain and less than a half-moon was peeking out from in between the scattering of clouds.

His parents were cooking meat over a small fire pit at the entrance to the cave where they slept during the day. Rafael and Lydia's three children were playing close by, but there was no sign of their parents. After Billy Torres left and Rafael made peace with Mateo, Rafael and his mate retreated to their cave. Mateo was sure Billy's news about the other stillborn births affected them deeply and they needed some time alone to deal with their own grief.

Anton and Nita were having a dinner of venison stew with their six children. The entire family was sitting crossed legged around another small fire pit. All of them looked exactly like their ancestors looked centuries ago, except for Chaz, who appeared to have entered the modern age with his short haircut. Although he was bare-chested and wore no shoes on his feet, he was wearing a pair of denim jeans instead of the usual white loincloth the men and boys wore around the village. His full plate of food was sitting on a rock beside his feet. The teenager wore a headlamp around his head for light and held a book in his hand. All his concentration appeared to be focused on the words he was reading. Mateo smiled, remembering how he had been when he was young. How had he never noticed before now that Chaz was exactly like him?

He looked back at his grandfather. He hoped the time was right for him to ask this question again, and maybe this time he would receive an answer. "Grandfather? Why did you leave your original clan in Mexico and come here to find your mate, instead of waiting for her to come to you as has always been the custom of our clans?"

Drago's mouth opened then closed. He blinked and looked away from his grandson for a moment. The silence before he answered was dense and heavy in the air. "I have always known I would have to answer that question eventually." A poignant smile rested on his lips. "And I have thought many times how I was going to answer you. But there is only one story to tell." He shook his head and focused his intense gaze on Mateo. "My clan in Mexico was strong. We had many male dhampyres in our village. My great-grandfather was our leader, and he was a kind and powerful man. He protected us always."

Mateo grinned. "Like you." Drago returned his smile.

"Thank you." He stared off in the distance as his mind recalled the past. "I was just becoming a fully mature vampire—like you. I was very curious about the world of the real ones, too. Like you, and like Chaz."

He could only stare at his grandfather in stunned silence. Never had he suspected his grandfather ever wondered about anything other than protecting the secrets of the Blood Clan.

"I would leave my village, hidden deep in the Chirallcula Mountains and explore the villages of the real ones down below." He chuckled. "I was an impatient young vampire. I was anxious for my mate, your grandmother, to come to me." He touched his bare chest above his heart and added, "Though she was far away, I felt her presence and somehow I knew she would be coming from the Jicarilla Apache tribe that lived at the base of the Superstitions."

Drago glanced over at Raven. She was sitting by the fire with Anton and his family, but her gaze was focused on her mate as if she knew he was talking about her. Her mouth curved into a smile when she saw him look in her direction. His head nodded slightly as he smiled back. He looked away from her and settled his gaze back on his grandson.

"So, to answer your question. I don't know why I decided to go against our customs and come here to get my mate instead of waiting for her to come to me. There was just this moment of clarification, and I knew it was time for me to leave Mexico and come here to start my own clan." He glanced briefly at his mate again. "In my heart, I just knew."

Mateo continued to stare at his grandfather as he digested all this new and surprising information. He could only begin to imagine the turmoil his grandfather must have endured when he made the decision to leave his family and original clan over two centuries ago. Although, he had always admired his grandfather, at this moment he realized just how strong and wise the ancient vampire truly was. His respect and love for his grandfather filled his heart and overflowed.

He rose to his feet as his grandfather followed him. The two vampires embraced, and when they parted, their gazes met. In the glow of the firelight, Mateo saw the depth of love and understanding his grandfather also felt for him.

"Thank you, Grandfather," he said in an emotional tone. "Thank you for sharing your amazing story with me."

Drago stepped back as he nodded and smiled. "Go to your mate now. I know you will make the right decision."

Mateo glanced around the peaceful village and at the family he loved so much. A calm feeling settled over him. He had felt uncertainty about the future for so long now. Lately, he had mostly been worrying about forcing Dawn to give up her human life and live a life of obscurity as his eternal mate in the shadows of the rugged cliffs here on the Superstitions.

He desperately wanted to live in her world with her, because he always believed there was something more for his kind other than hiding in the caves and hoping they would not become extinct. Now, he was convinced there was so much more out there for his kind, more than he ever dreamed possible. He just knew it in his heart.

With a renewed sense of hope for the future, he began his descent down the mountain. He envisioned his beautiful blonde mate waiting for him in the luxurious condo in Apache Junction. They would spend the night making sensuous love in the big bed and he would cherish each and every moment they spent in one another's arms while they were there, because whether they were in her world or his, all that mattered is they were together.

A smile claimed his lips and a feeling of excitement rushed through his body. Udaya. His Dawn. He would love her forever.

Chapter Twenty-Four

Dawn remembered this sort of darkness. It was the most intense and engulfing blackness she ever experienced. The first night she camped on the mountain with Chloe she experienced this same feeling. It was as if the rest of the world was swallowed up by this overpowering nothingness.

She pulled the brim of her old straw cowboy hat down over her eyes and wrapped her arms tightly around her waist as she crunched down in the driver's seat as far as possible. Mateo could come down off the mountain at any location and the odds were slim it would be anywhere near where she was parked right now. This was the only route she knew, though, since this was the way she had come with Chloe—and on the night she had come up here on her own in that weird trance to meet Mateo.

With any luck, he would sense her presence here, and would know where to find her like he had on the night he found her parked along the side of the road at the Arizona border. He felt her tears that night when she foolishly thought she wanted to leave him. Hopefully, tonight he would feel her fear.

The stress of everything going on was making her stomach churn with nausea, and she squeezed her eyes shut as she forced down the threat of vomit hovering at the back of her throat. She placed her hand on the door handle in case she needed to make a quick exit to throw up.

Her thoughts kept returning to Chloe. She couldn't stand thinking of the way Mateo described how she was now. She only wanted to remember her as the beautiful vivacious young woman who had such a zest for life and had been such a wonderful friend to her in the short time they had known one another, as well as the love and devotion she felt toward her students and family. Dawn found it especially touching Chloe wanted to find the gold mine so her dad would know of its existence before he died.

Her stomach heaved again as she pulled her cowboy hat off her head and tossed it over on the passenger seat. With the back of her hand she wiped the heavy beads of sweat from her forehead. It was not helping. As scared as she was, she hated the idea of throwing up in her truck. She yanked the door open and was only able to stumble a few steps forward before the small amount of food she had eaten earlier today ejaculated out of her mouth. Her entire body began to shake uncontrollably.

Violent waves were thrashing around inside her stomach. She felt as if she might puke again, but she was too vulnerable out here. She took a couple of faltering steps backward toward her truck. It didn't matter if she did get sick in her truck, she couldn't stay out here in this threatening blackness for one minute longer. The shaking in her entire body was causing her teeth to chatter together like mini jackhammers and the rising panic was stripping away all her senses. Was this what it felt like for Chloe right before...

Dawn could not even cry out when she was

grabbed from behind. Her mouth was wide open, but her scream was frozen on her tongue and she couldn't emit a sound. Visions of handsome vampires who looked like her beloved Mateo but only wanted to drink her blood and stick her mindless body in a cave for future feedings, flooded her mind with a terror so great she couldn't even attempt to get away. In blind terror, she fell into his arms.

"Dawn. Are you alright?"

It took a moment for her to realize who was holding her until his worried voice finally penetrated through the horrors raging through her head. "Oh, thank God, Mateo," she cried as he turned her around to face him. She couldn't make out his features in the impenetrable darkness, but she didn't need to because she had his face memorized. "I was so scared you wouldn't be able to find me here."

Her arms moved around his neck of their own accord and she buried her face in his shoulder. She felt the softness of his cotton shirt against her cheek and smelled his intoxicating musky scent. All her fright disappeared into the encompassing black of the dessert night. She was where she was supposed to be...and she would never leave again.

Mateo held her tight until the shaking in her body began to calm down. "You are sick?" he asked in a worried tone.

"I was just so scared, and I started to think about Chloe and how you said she was now. I don't know if I'll be able to handle seeing her like that."

His kissed the top of her head as he continued to hold her close. "You won't have to see her, and I promise you, I'm going to do everything in my power to protect you from any more pain."

Dawn leaned against him, letting him support most of her weight as her legs continued to feel wobbly and weak. He was all the strength she needed, and as long as he was next to her, she knew she could face anything.

As much as she wanted to kiss him right now, she was too worried she would taste like vomit and he always tasted like a delectable mixture of tangy and sweet candy. She ran her tongue over her teeth and swallowed hard as she burrowed her face deeper into his muscled shoulder.

"I don't have cell reception in our village, but I received all your messages when I came down from the mountain. Why did you come here? It's so dangerous for you to be here at night for so many reasons."

She nodded her head, still overcome with the raging panic she felt before he arrived. It had been crazy for her to come here tonight; she realized that now. "I know. I should have waited at the condo like I said I would, but I…" She took a deep breath. "I'm ready."

"Ready?" He repeated.

"To go to the top of the mountain. I want you to make me your mate tonight." She said the words as quickly as possible before she lost her nerve.

He was silent for a few moments. "We received some news in our village. Billy Torres came up on the mountain tonight to tell us they learned from other clan society members in different parts of the world about other stillborn births among dhampyre babies."

The breath caught in her constricted throat. There were already so many confusing and scary thoughts spinning through her mind right now. She wasn't sure she could deal with his news about dead babies.

"My brother blamed me for the death of his son. He thought my attempt to change the traditions of our clan with you somehow cursed our village."

Placing the palm of her hand gently against the side of his face, she replied in a hoarse whisper, "I'm so sorry, Mateo. The last thing I want to do is cause problems between you and your family."

"But now that we have learned of five other babies who were stillborn in other clans, Rafael knows his grief was causing him to be irrational. We talked tonight before I left the village, and everything is good between us again."

"I'm so glad to hear you and your brother are okay. Do they know what happened to all of those poor babies?" She tried to keep her building anxiety from overtaking her frail grip on reality.

He shrugged and exhaled a heavy breath before relating Billy's story about the new virus that was affecting women of the clan and their unborn babies.

"That's horrible," Dawn gasped. "Is there a cure? How many more babies could be affected by this—this virus?"

A heavy shrug lifted his shoulders. "There is a Swiss doctor who believes he can develop an antidote from the tissue he extracted from the dead baby who was not cremated. But it will take time."

The uneasiness she felt about the things he was saying was settling into a queasy heaviness in her stomach again. There was nothing to do now except to face whatever the future held for them.

"I'm pregnant," she blurted out. "I took the second

test and it was positive." She drew in a shaky breath and continued. "So, I went to the store and bought two more tests and they were both positive." She barely took a breath as she rushed on, "I just can't spend every day waiting to see you only at night, then sometimes, you don't even come to see me. But most of all, I can't go on pretending to live a normal life anymore, especially now that I'm having your baby. I refuse to live another minute in my world if we can't be there together, regardless of what might happen to us, or to our baby. I just want to be with you forever. It's our destiny and we can't deny it any longer anyway, right?"

After taking a gulping breath she rushed on. "I will leave my truck here and there's a note in there saying I went looking for Chloe and if anything happens to me to tell my family I love them, and that way they will have some idea what happened to me. I mean, it's going to still be horrible for them, but—"

"Did you just say you are pregnant?" Mateo interrupted in a shocked tone. He leaned back and stared down at her.

"Yes," she mumbled. "Are you surprised it happened so soon?"

He chuckled and slightly puffed up his chest. "Well, no, not when you are as virile as I obviously am."

She rolled her eyes. "Whatever," she retorted. They were both silent for a few more seconds. "I'm still scared Mateo, so very scared."

He pulled her up against him again and rested his chin on the top of her head. "That makes two of us. But no matter what happens, please know I will never fail you, my love. You will be my mate in my world, and I will also be your man in your world."

"What do you mean? Don't you just suck the blood from my thigh and the party's over?" she asked in a confused voice.

A chortle escaped Mateo. "I had a bit more in mind for you, my beautiful Udaya."

Her mind was spinning. "Is it possible there is a way I wouldn't have to just be your baby-making sex slave?" she asked. "I—I would like to be more, I want to be everything to you, if that's possible."

He gently lifted her chin up with his fingertips, His vampire sight had no problem seeing her in the darkness, and he could tell her eyes were beginning to adjust to the lack of light as their gazes met. "There is a new world for our kind on the horizon. I won't give up until I find a way to blend my world with your world so maybe someday we will be able to walk in the sunlight together."

"I still don't understand," she answered, growing more bewildered, yet more hopeful, by the second.

"I don't understand it all yet, either, but I know there are many changes coming for the clans. We—you and I and our children—are going to be the ones to blaze new trails for our kind." He reached down and gently placed his hand against her abdomen adding, "Should this child be a male, it is my greatest wish he will be able to walk among the people in both our worlds, the Blood Clan and the real ones, without having to hide in the caves during the daylight."

She remembered something she read about dhampyres when she had been researching them. *They did not have all the weaknesses of full blooded vampires.* Could Mateo have discovered something that would make it possible for him to come out in the daytime? Is that what he was talking about? What would this mean to their future, and to the future of their children? Did she dare hope?

"Do you still trust me," he asked quietly.

"I trust you with my life." she answered. "I trust you with our baby's life."

"Then, are you truly ready to become my mate in every way?"

Dawn's heart thrashed wildly in her breast; her legs threatened to give out from under her, and her intestines knotted into a tight ball in her stomach. All coherent thoughts were lost to her mind now.

This was it. This was forever. And forever was a very long time.

"Yes, in every way," she whispered as she closed her eyes and pressed her body up against him again. His kiss stole her breath away as he picked her up in his arms and carried her to where his truck was parked at the edge of the reservation.

She did not look back, nor did she think of what lay ahead for them. When she told him she trusted him, she meant it with all her heart. Mateo Two Moons possessed her body, mind, and soul. When the first rays of the sun rose in the desert sky tomorrow morning, they would be together in every mortal and immortal way for all eternity.

Chapter Twenty-Five

Mateo watched his woman from the shade of the dense trees. He hoped someday soon he would be able to endure the sunlight for longer periods at a time. His tolerance to the rays of the sun was still weak, but he was growing stronger all the time and every day he was able to stay out a few minutes longer. To be standing here under nothing more than the shade of the tree branches during the daylight hours—without feeling like he was going to burn to a pile of ash—was more than he imagined would be possible.

The first few times he attempted to venture out into the sunlight, the pain had been excruciating. His skin felt like hot coals were igniting in each of his pores and he could barely last more than a minute or so without retreating into the safety of the cave to recover. But he refused to give up, and the pain gradually lessened. Now, there was only a slight burning sensation in the areas where his clothes didn't cover his skin, and he didn't feel that until he was in the direct sunlight for at least fifteen minutes or more.

The clan also believed being awake during the daytime was impossible, but he was sleeping less during the day and growing more tired at night time. Eventually, his sleeping habits should be the same as his mate's and they could sleep together through the night and be awake together all day—something they were both anxious to have happen as soon as possible. But until that time, a small cave nearby provided Mateo with a dark sanctuary for his daytime slumber while his body was still acclimating to his new schedule.

Once he completed all these miraculous transformations, he would share his accomplishments with other Blood Clan members. But now, every day was still an experiment. He was confident that ultimately his kind would be free to live openly among the real ones without worry of being detected.

It saddened him to think this was always a possibility. For centuries, the clans had dwelled in total seclusion when they could have lived a much fuller life. He understood, though, how hard it was to defy all the ancient superstitions and beliefs.

Overcoming his own tremendous fear of being destroyed when he challenged those antiquated myths was the hardest thing he had ever done. If he had been wrong, he wouldn't be here to spend eternity with his beautiful mate and their child.

A poignant smile curved Mateo's lips as he thought about how fortunate they were. His dream of having a real love story with his mate was reality and it was more amazing than he had ever imagined it could be.

Dawn cradled Yuma in her arms as she gazed out toward a beautiful array of wildflowers in vibrant shades of red, yellow, and purple dotting the lush green grasses of the mountain meadow. Yuma meant 'Son of the Chief' and since they had come to the San Juan Mountains in the Colorado high country, Mateo was now the chief of his own Blood Clan, so his first-born son had been aptly named.

Secluded in the thick forests of spruce, fir, aspen,

and towering lodge pole pines this peaceful new encampment was a secure haven for Mateo's little family. They had bought a large camper trailer to live in while they were in the process of building a sprawling log house on land they purchased. Dawn and Mateo's children would be raised in a real home with all the modern conveniences.

Eventually, even Dawn's family would be able to visit them. Right now, they still believed she was traveling abroad with her wealthy Native American lover. At first, convincing them she abruptly resigned from her teaching job and impulsively left the country had been a hard sell.

Mateo worried they would try to find her, but she called them on a regular basis until her parents, brother, and sister-in-law, finally began to believe her when she told them she was so much in love with her new man she didn't care about anything other than seeing the world with him at her side. He knew she hated lying to her family, but she understood it was necessary to protect everyone involved.

When he was fully able to present himself as a real one, they would inform Dawn's family they were back from their worldly travels, and they would also tell them Yuma had been born while they were out of the country. It was all pretty far-fetched and not an ideal plan by any stretch of the imagination. But it was still so much better than her original plan of letting them think she perished in the Superstitions while looking for her missing friend.

Mateo filled with pride as he gazed lovingly at his mate and their newborn son, although there was still a part of him having a hard time letting go of the overwhelming panic he felt as he had delivered Yuma five days earlier.

Every day, as Dawn's due date had grown nearer, he had been consumed with worry that this child could be afflicted with the unknown virus still attacking newborns in Blood Clans around the globe. A total of eight dhampyres had been stillborn to date.

Thankfully though, a couple of weeks ago, the doctor from Switzerland sent word out he discovered the stillbirths were being caused by a new and extremely rare form of bacterial infection related to something called a Group B Strep Infection—an infection some human women carry in their body without ever being aware of it, because it usually doesn't cause any symptoms.

In very rare cases, however, infected pregnant women can transmit the virus to their baby during delivery, which can cause stillbirths. For some unknown reason the women among the clans who did have this silent infection were transmitting the deadly strain of this disease to their newborns in recent months. The Swiss doctor felt there might never be an explanation as to why this was happening all of a sudden, but he was confident he perfected an antidote and this serum would soon be ready to use on all the human mates who were still in their childbearing years.

Dawn was due to give birth before the serum was ready and there had been no way of knowing if she carried this lethal infection in her body until she gave birth. It had been an unspoken terror they both lived with every minute of her pregnancy.

She had gone into labor mid-morning, and since Mateo was still learning how to exist for brief periods in the daylight, he had been asleep in the cave. By the time he had awoken late in the afternoon, she was terrified and gripped by contractions coming hard and fast.

When his brother's mates had been in labor at the encampment on the Superstitions, the women assisted one another. The men had no idea what went on in the birthing hut. But Dawn had only him to help her through her pain-ridden ordeal. He felt completely inadequate and helpless as she endured hours of intense labor before finally giving birth to a perfect—and healthy—male dhampyre in the early morning hours of the following day.

Mateo found it beyond comprehension how she had been able to endure such agonizing pain and even survive, let alone be able to be up and recuperating so quickly. He knew the agony he felt those first few times he went into the sunlight was nothing compared to the pain she suffered to bring their son into the world. She was even more extraordinary than he imagined and his love for her just kept expanding.

His smile widened. Motherhood definitely agreed with his beautiful mate. The sunlight was shining on her long blonde hair and the thick straight tresses resembled pale white satin flowing around her shoulders and past the middle of her back. Her smooth creamy complexion seemed to have acquired a radiant glow throughout her pregnancy and it hadn't faded even after Yuma's birth. A happy twinkle lit her hazel eyes with contentment ever since Mateo made her his mate on that fateful night in Arizona…the night he conducted his first of many experiments that would forever change the future of Blood Clans.

Since their custom was to drink the majority of blood from their mate's thigh until she passed out, he decided to try something less drastic. He had only drunk a small portion of the blood from the artery in Dawn's thigh—not enough to cause her to lose consciousness.

She had been reluctant at first, but he convinced her to drink a small amount of his blood that first night, too. Hopefully, she would benefit from his vampire strength and stay strong and healthy during her child-bearing years. Although she suffered through a few days of flu-like symptoms similar to the ones she endured when he had first bitten her neck and wrist in the beginning, after the sickness subsided, Dawn felt better than ever and had no problems during the rest of her pregnancy.

More importantly, and much to their relief, she still retained all her own thoughts and human desires. How this would affect her in the future was still very much in the trial stages, but they were prepared for whatever may come. If anything happened, and Mateo felt she was in any danger from illness or anything that afflicted real ones, he would complete the mating process at once to keep her safe. But until that day came or until the time when he would make her immortal, they planned to cherish every minute of this new life they were discovering together.

Today, she was wearing a pair of jeans and a plaid shirt in shades of lavender with a pair of white flip-flops on her feet. Mateo was also wearing jeans, boots, and a green T-shirt. His clan would not wear the outdated garments worn by his grandfather's clan. Since this property bordered National Forest land, it was inevitable real ones would occasionally stumble across their isolated home. When this happened, their clan would not appear to belong to a different century.

His grandfather gifted them with enough gold from the Lost Dutchman's Gold Mine to last them for centuries, and Mateo already compelled a Clan Society from the local Southern Ute tribe to see to the human-type needs of his small clan. With any luck, the need for a Clan Society might not be necessary in the future if he continued to find ways to live among the real ones without revealing their vampire nature.

Dawn glanced up and noticed him standing in the canopy of trees. Her instant smile warmed his heart. She began walking toward him; the small precious bundle in her arms concealed in a soft colorful woven yellow and white Indian blanket. As she entered the shaded area in the grove of trees, she pulled the blanket away from Yuma's miniature face so his intense gaze could stare up at his father. His golden skin tone was a lovely mixture of his father's bronzed hue and his mother's pale coloring, but his shock of thick hair was as ebony as his eyes.

Mateo gently rested one of his hands on the top of his son's downy head, and placed his other hand against his mate's soft cheek. "Udaya," his whispered. "There has never been a man more fortunate than I am, because I will be able to love you forever."

Dawn's misted gaze rose to lock with Mateo's raven one as she replied softly, "Forever is not long enough."

About the Author

Veronica has spent her entire life in Colorado enjoying outdoor activities such as hiking, dirt biking and camping. She considers herself a hopeless romantic and a seeker of endless adventure. Life, family, friends, and music are her inspirations.

Veronica is switching genres and working on a paranormal romance series. She's very excited about taking her writing career in a new direction and is thrilled to be a new author for The Wild Rose Press, Inc.

~*~

Visit Veronica at

http://veronicablake1423.wordpress.com

https://www.facebook.com/Veronica-Blake-Writer

~*~

To chat with Veronica Blake and other Wild Rose Press authors of erotic romance, join us at

www.groups.yahoo.com/group/thewilderroses.

Also Read

Melt in Your Mouth
By Skye Kohl

Mocha Magic Book One

http://a.co/0ChzBRG

After her parents are forced to sell their bakery due to the economy, Elizabeth Carpelli wants security, and that means a dependable man with a college education and a stable job. No matter that her degree in marketing is being wasted in a coffee shop. She wants it all. But then, with the help of her boss, and the most deliciously sensual chocolate, she discovers lust beyond her wildest dreams in a no-commitment arrangement with an uber-fit carpenter—a blue collar worker.

Having his heart ripped in two by a cheating fiancée, Hank Lehman wanders into Mocha Magic to drown his sorrows in a steamy black brew. When the sweet and sassy barista gives him an offer he can't refuse, chocolate body paint and a canvas of silky flesh with no strings attached, it may just help him forget his past and turn his future toward a more tasty adventure.

Thank you for purchasing this
publication of The Wild Rose Press, Inc.
If you enjoyed the story, we would appreciate
your letting others know by leaving a review.
For other wonderful stories, please visit our
on-line bookstore at *www.wilderroses.com*.

For questions or more
information contact us at
info@thewildrosepress.com.

The Wild Rose Press, Inc.
www.thewilderroses.com

Stay current with The Wild Rose Press, Inc.
Like us on Facebook
https://www.facebook.com/TheWildRosePress
And Follow us on Twitter
https://twitter.com/WildRosePress